THE PIGEON

DAVID GORDON holds an MA in English and
Comparative Literature and an MFA in Writing from
Columbia University. He is the author of *The Serialist*,
which won the VCU/Cabell First Novel Award and
was a finalist for an Edgar Award. His work has
appeared in the *Paris Review*, the *New York Times*
and the *Los Angeles Review of Books*. He was
born and lives in New York City.

Also by David Gordon

The Joe the Bouncer Novels

The Bouncer
The Hard Stuff
Against the Law
The Wild Life

Other Books

White Tiger on Snow Mountain: Stories
Mystery Girl
The Serialist

THE PIGEON

DAVID GORDON

HEAD
of ZEUS

An Aries Book

First published in the US in 2023 by Mysterious Press,
an imprint of Penzler Publishers

First published in the UK in 2023 by Head of Zeus,
part of Bloomsbury Publishing Plc

9 7 5 3 1 2 4 6 8

A catalogue record for this book is available from
the British Library.

ISBN (PB): 9781837932894
ISBN (E): 9781837932856

Printed and bound in Great Britain by
CPI Group (UK) Ltd, Croydon CR0 4YY

Head of Zeus Ltd
5–8 Hardwick Street
London EC1R 4RG

WWW.HEADOFZEUS.COM

To Duncan Hannah

In loving memory

PART I

1

"**A** pigeon?" Joe asked. Gio shrugged. The two men were sitting in the back booth at Club Rendezvous, a strip club located conveniently close to JFK, which Gio controlled (though the owner of record was one Yettie Greenblatt, eighty-two) and where Joe worked as the bouncer. Joe was drinking black coffee. Gio was sipping an expensive single-malt Scotch. Sprawled facedown between them was a paperback copy of *Swann's Way*, which Joe had been reading when Gio came in and said he had important business to discuss. "Important pigeon business? What's that, a new statue in the park?"

"What can I say?" Gio said. "Alonzo keeps pigeons. I don't get it myself. To me they're flying rats. But he likes them. It's a hobby. And somebody stole his best one. So he asked me to ask you to find it. As a favor."

In addition to escorting out drunks and customers who don't know
how to keep their hands to themselves, Joe occasionally did favors for
Gio and his associates. Childhood pals from equally unusual backgrounds, Gio had gone into the family business and was now a Mafia
boss, while Joe, from a clan of thieves and grifters, had wandered, first
to Harvard, where he was kicked out, and then to the Army and Special Forces, where he was also eventually kicked out, returning home,
literally, to his grandmother's apartment in Jackson Heights, Queens,
with PTSD and a substance-abuse problem along with a whole new
set of lethal skills. Gio gave him this easy, low-key job at the club at
first out of sympathy. Then, when he began to suspect that terrorists
had infiltrated the criminal underground of New York, he thought
of another job for his deadly friend: the bosses made Joe their sheriff,
a fixer they called on when they needed help with something they
couldn't handle themselves, be it a domestic terrorist with a dirty bomb,
a heroin smuggler funding jihadists overseas, or a serial killer preying
on sex workers. When regular folks called the law, the outlaws called
Joe. They even branded him with a star as a sign to the world, their
world anyway, that Joe was working for them. But a pigeon? This was
not on his resume. He frowned at Gio. "I don't do lost pets."

"It's not a pet," Gio explained. He leaned forward, smoothing his
tie. Gio was, as always, sharply and tastefully dressed, in a gray flannel
suit, white shirt, and a dark blue tie. Joe wore what he always wore:
black Converse high-tops, jeans, and a gray sweatshirt over his black
T-shirt. It was early spring and the late afternoon air carried a chill.
"Alonzo raises them for racing. This one is his champ. It's some kind
of fancy breed. A Maltese. And it's been stolen."

"The Maltese pigeon," Joe commented. "Sounds like a joke. Who am I, Sam Spade?"

Gio shrugged. "It's worth over a million. That's no joke."

"No shit?" Joe said, a little more curious.

"Anyway, that's what Alonzo says. And he's offering a five percent finder's fee. And . . ." Gio held a hand out as if offering a treat, "he says he knows who took it. Some rich pigeon fanatic in town from Hong Kong. You go, grab the bird, cash in, and, not for nothing, keep our friends happy. Sound good?"

"Not really," Joe said.

Gio laughed. "That was a rhetorical question." He finished his drink, letting the liquor drip down his throat. "What's the big deal anyway? It's a nice easy payday. Usually we come to you with something impossible. But this? This is a piece of cake."

Alonzo kept his coop in Bed-Stuy.

A neighborhood native, he'd come up in the Bedford-Stuyvesant area of Brooklyn when it was at its most perilous, when the name Bed-Stuy was almost a brand name representing the worst of inner-city life. Now it represented a millennial, Gen-Z hipster hot spot and a good place to buy a house, if you could afford it. Alonzo had fought his way to the top of the heap, a heap that contained quite a few dead enemies and nearly as many dead friends, and today ruled an extensive network that controlled much of the illegal activity in central Brooklyn as well as far-flung legitimate enterprises, including restaurants, clubs, a boxing/MMA gym, and a record label and entertainment management firm. He also owned real estate, including the old tenement building where he kept his birds on the roof. He himself lived with his family in New Jersey, in a wealthy suburban town, next door to a dentist.

"I started flying birds with my father," Alonzo said. He said it out of nowhere, as if in midthought. He'd been conferring with Teddy, the building's super, who lived on the ground floor and took care of the birds, when Gio led Joe up onto the roof. They'd driven over with Gio's guy, Nero, behind the wheel, and Little Eddie—the six-two, 240-pound son of Big Eddie—riding shotgun. Nero and Little Eddie were left to mind the car, double-parked behind Alonzo's driver in his Caddy SUV. Another of Alonzo's guys, big as Little Eddie but with a head shaved smooth, was waiting on the stoop. They both wore expensive tracksuits and nodded at each other in acknowledgment. Then he pushed back the door and told Gio, "Upstairs." Gio and Joe trooped up six flights and opened the door to another world.

The coop was big, covering much of the roof. It was constructed of wood and chicken wire, and freshly painted white, with a human-sized door and a side hatch that could be propped open. The inside was lined with shelving whose horizontals and verticals formed hundreds of cubes. A smaller shed beside it held supplies for feeding and cleaning as well as a sink and faucet and a power source for the hoses and lights that ran all over.

But none of that was what Joe noticed first, stepping onto the roof. The immediate and overwhelming impression was of light, space, and motion, of flickering wings and the constant burble of pigeons cooing and clucking like a stream running past. The sky was sharp blue and piled here and there with curdled white clouds. The city, dense and turbulent as ever at street level, both chaotic and humdrum, now resolved itself into a landscape in motion, a vast pattern that somehow all fit together. Men in orange vests and hard hats labored on a roof in the distance, like tiny dolls operating a toy crane. Kids played in a schoolyard, their happy shrieks carried by the wind. A fluid line of traffic moved through an intersection, then stopped for a light and, like an opened valve, the other side began to flow.

The roof itself was alive with birds. Teddy was checking them over, whistling uncannily as the creatures fluttered and throbbed around him. Others filled the coop, nestling in the cubbyholes or flying back and forth, while more strolled along the edges of the roof, or hopped into the air, cruising from ledge to ledge. Feathers drifted around like snowflakes, settling everywhere, then spiraling up again on the breeze, as if in a shaken snow globe. Joe felt a little uneasy, and a little dazzled, but he tried to focus on Alonzo, who was dressed down in a leather bomber jacket, chinos, and loafers, and on what he was saying. "My dad kept a coop on the roof and started taking me up when I was six. He kept roosters too, in the backyard. He fought them. And raised dogs. Cats he respected, but didn't have as much, because of the birds. He loved all animals. When he passed, I was twelve, I inherited his birds." He chuckled sardonically. "What the hell else was I going to inherit? He didn't have shit besides that and this broken watch I used to wear till I finally admitted that the fucking thing couldn't tell time."

Terry nodded. "He was a true pigeon man, your father." He addressed Joe and Gio, explaining. "He loved and cared for birds his whole life, and they loved him too. Whatever shit was kicking off down in the street, it was always peaceful up here. Like heaven and hell." He reached into the writhing mass of pigeons, grabbed one, and began to stroke it, Gio stepped back, careful to avoid getting any pigeon shit on his freshly polished shoes, and nodded politely, though it was not hard to read the distaste on his face as Terry massaged the cooing creature in his hands. Gio was not a true a pigeon man.

"Some of these birds are the descendants of your father's," Terry told Alonzo, who nodded along. He let the bird go. "We released birds at his funeral. My kids know, when I'm buried, they're going to fly birds."

Alonzo shrugged. "My kids ain't interested. They think it's dirty, smelly."

"You still know how to put them to sleep?" Terry asked.

Smiling now, Alonzo lifted a passing pigeon and seemed to fold it up in his hands, then wave it gently back and forth, as though he were rocking a baby or performing a ritual. Carefully he set in on a crate. It didn't move. It seemed round now, a soft feathered ball. "Don't worry," he assured Joe, who was just staring, not sure what to think. "I didn't hurt it." He woke the pigeon, who sprang back to life, hopping from the crate and strutting about. Terry was grinning.

"See? He's still got the touch. Come on, let's fly them." He opened the hatches, whistling, and the birds came pouring out. The sound of wings rushed and rustled, answering the call of Terry's trills, and the birds took to the air, like synchronized divers in an old musical, leaping into space, one after another, seeming to free fall and then, with a few beats of their wings, rising, one small miracle after another. Joe was not a true pigeon man either, but he had to admit: it was a beautiful sight.

For the most part these birds were more dovish in appearance than the usual street pigeon, white with streaks of gray and brown, many with longer necks and pointier heads. They were banded in purple and gold, Alonzo's colors.

"So there's no way the pigeon you're looking for just flew away?" Joe asked.

"Ramses?" Alonzo scoffed. "Never. Anyway there's a microchip in the band. It went dead same time he went missing." He shook his head. "Somebody cut it off."

Or a cat ate it, Joe thought, but he kept it to himself.

Terry explained that, while pigeon fanciers, as they were quaintly called, did "steal" each other's birds on occasion, it was done in a prescribed way, in a spirit of fun. "Like on a summer night, pigeon wars be raging for sure," Terry said. "All the coops will be rolling out, all over Brooklyn." Guys—it was always guys—would release pigeons, and the flocks would cruise the skies, crossing and merging. Sometimes somebody else's birds joined your flock and came home to your coop, sometimes your birds were seduced away. But the whole point was to count them up and brag and laugh about it the next day at the shops that sold bird supplies or the joints where pigeon men hung out. Almost all had inherited the love of birds from a relative, and most were from working-class backgrounds, but otherwise they cut across categories. There were pigeon lovers of every race and nationality, with many professions represented, including cops.

"Anybody sees that band, they know whose bird it is," Terry pointed out. "All over. In Queens. The Bronx. Nobody gonna take that bird by accident."

"Even if they cut the band," Alonzo said, "nobody in New York is dumb enough to keep Ramses and think I won't find out. Even Mike Tyson knows who Ramses is."

Technically, he was Ramses II, a Maltese bird that Terry had bred, the son of the legendary Ramses and one of his best hens, Queenie. "It takes years to breed and train a flock like this. I give them vitamins, minerals. Garlic powder to purify the blood. Vaccine for paratyphoid. I give them the same iron solution they give to horses at the track. These birds are champions." Terry gazed up at the flock that turned above them now, a cloud rushing over the rooftops. "They royalty."

In fact, pigeons did have a noble lineage, Alonzo told them, stretching back to the real Ramses III, who used them to carry news about the conditions of the Nile in ancient Egypt. At the original Greek Olympics, each team had a pigeon that would be released to announce victory. They were called the Kings of Angels in the medieval Arab world. In parts of Italy and Turkey, vast contests were held, much like the Brooklyn Pigeon War, but involving up to five hundred flocks. Immigrants brought the customs, skills, and maybe even the birds with them, and the tradition continued in the skies of New York.

"Tell me about the betting," Joe asked.

Races were held almost every weekend, weather allowing, organized by clubs in each borough. The pigeons were driven to starting points, sometimes hundreds of miles away, then released, with heavy betting on favorites like Ramses and a purse for the winner, clocked with the chip in its band. Ramses had an impressive record of wins and had earned Alonzo a small fortune, even setting some club records. But his value as a breeder was too great to risk injury or loss. After his last victory, Alonzo announced his retirement. Offers to buy him poured in from wealthy collectors all over.

"It's like anything," Alonzo said, "horses, dogs, koi fish. There's always a few guys who are obsessed and have the money to make it happen." One Chinese billionaire, named Wing Chow, was particularly insistent. "He kept raising his offer," Alonzo said. "And I kept saying no. Finally it got up to a million euros, over a million bucks." He shrugged. "I didn't care. Not for sale. Next day the door to the roof here was broken, and Ramses was gone."

"So what makes you think the bird isn't in China by now?"

"Because Wing Chow is here. He's got a place on the Upper West Side. If I know bird men, he's got him close, where he can see him, feed him, stroke him. Then he'll take him home himself on the private jet. Which is why you need to act now. I'll pay a five percent reward." Alonzo, who'd been facing Joe and Gio, shifted his gaze to the skies. "What that dude doesn't get is this isn't just about money. That's my legacy. That lineage. The flock. It's all I've got from my dad. And I'm going to pass it to my son. Whether he likes it or not." He turned to Joe. "Bring my bird home, Joe," he said, quietly.

"Yes, sir."

There was a moment of silence as they all stared at the birds, now mere dots on the horizon.

"It's a magnet in the earth that guides them," Terry commented. No one replied. Joe felt like he'd read something about this, but not exactly that. Terry went on: "Even in the bible, the pigeon is a bird of peace. Noah sends it out just like we do, and it comes back with some kind of plant in its mouth, a symbol of hope."

Alonzo looked at his watch. "Okay, Terry," he said. "Feeding time. Let's bring them home."

Terry grabbed a bamboo pole, about twelve feet long, with a couple rags, white and red, tied to the end. Facing the edge of the roof, he began to wave the pole, weaving it back and forth, signaling the birds. Like a vortex, they slowly began to gather, circling the building, formation tightening as they closed in, knowing that they were going to be fed. Silhouetted against the skyline, wind in his hair, Terry swirled the stick, as if flying a kite, or leading a dance, while hundreds upon hundreds of white wings turned in the air around him.

3

Joe took the subway uptown.

According to Alonzo, Wing Chow owned an apartment in the Eleonora, a legendary old building that sat like a castle on Central Park West in the Eighties. Mirroring the neighborhood's own cycles of boom and bust, the Eleonora was built as a luxury dwelling at the turn of the last century, housing wealthy families and their servants, and then in the postwar years, some high-profile fashion, music, and publishing types. It fell into disrepute in the '70s and '80s. The roof leaked and the facade blackened with city grime. More of the renters were bohemians—artists, dancers from Broadway or the ballet, soap opera actors. Then, in the '90s, prices began to rise, as a new wave of wealthy professionals—bankers, brokers, media princelings—moved in with their kids and nannies. And in the last decades, even those rich folk had to go to Brooklyn. Being a mere millionaire was no longer enough, as apartments routinely went for ten million or more. Much more.

Not that Joe cared. He was just there to steal back a pigeon. He emerged from the subway and approached the elaborate rococo facade, which looked like a very old wedding cake, its towers and layers and balconies covered in flowers and swirls of gray icing, with gargoyles squatting or glaring from under the windows. He pretended to be a messenger, with an empty envelope for Mr. Chow, and found that the target was out for the evening. Asking the concierge to sign a receipt, he learned that the apartment was 10E.

Joe took note of the generic uniforms the janitorial staff wore and the side entrance they used, then headed downtown to a uniform shop he knew and bought an identical outfit. They even, without request, added a name patch that said, in cursive, Joe. Then he went back uptown, bought a Coke and a pretzel from a vendor, and sat on a park bench, waiting for darkness to fall.

He smiled to himself in the gathering dusk, amused both at the job he was on, one of the oddest in a career of very odd jobs, and at his own indignation, his sense of being above mere pigeon retrieval. There was a time, still not that long ago, when he had been a young delinquent, happy to shoplift batteries, or crawl in a back window to swipe cases of disposable ladies' razor blades, aided and abetted, of course, by his best friend, Gio. He also had to admit that, when Gio had called the night before and said he needed him, he had been relieved, glad to have a mission, any mission, to distract him from himself. He'd been in a bad place. And Gio, Joe suspected, had sensed it, though he would never, could never, guess why.

◆

Joe was right. Gio had in fact been worried about his old friend. Joe was the person Gio trusted most, the person, after his wife, whose opinions and insights he most respected, the person who, even more than his wife, knew his secrets. Since they met on the streets as kids, when Joe stuck up for Gio in a fight, they'd been like brothers. When Gio, haunted by a hunger he couldn't shake, had finally surrendered to his secret desire, to dress as a girl and be whipped by a handsome young man, blond and blue-eyed, Joe was the one person who knew. And when that handsome young man, Paul, had betrayed Gio to the law, and Gio's own wife, Carol, had killed him, Joe was the person Gio called to help cover it up. To Gio, those experiences forged a bond closer than blood. He loved Joe. He also felt guilty toward him.

While Gio had risen through the crime world on his own talent and guts, along with plenty of good luck, Joe had taken another path. His time in the military had left him scarred, inside and out. And while Gio had been the one to help Joe find his way back from that darkness, he'd also used Joe to his own advantage, recruiting his old friend first to take out the terrorists and then to serve as "sheriff" for all his fellow bosses, which only added to Gio's own power and prestige. So while he couldn't slay his friend's demons any more than he could his own, Gio appointed himself as Joe's guardian angel, watching over him. After several months in which he seemed better, happier, calmer, healthier, and less inclined to seek out trouble of all sorts, Gio had noticed Joe brooding, lurking in the back booth of the club. When Alonzo had reached out for help with his bird problem, Gio thought, "Perfect. A nice, easy job with a nice, juicy paycheck to keep Joe busy, to take his mind off whatever shit he's gotten himself into." And he was right. He knew his friend well. But what he'd never guess was the nature of the trouble, which was, in their world, so scandalous, so forbidden, so unthinkably taboo and dangerous that it made Gio's secret erotic life and hidden bodies seem like no big deal.

Joe was in love with an FBI agent, and she'd just asked him for some space.

4

"I just think maybe we should take some space."

Special Agent Donna Zamora was lying in her bed with Joe beside her in stunned silence. Her young daughter was out at a movie with Donna's mom, Yolanda, who lived across the hall. Just an hour before, they'd been making passionate love, and now, apparently, she was dumping him. Sort of. The fact that they were naked under the covers, proof of their intimacy, their trust, now suddenly felt weird and awkward, a sign of vulnerability: he had been caught with his guard down, unaware and unarmed.

"But why?" Joe asked. "I thought we loved each other. I know I love you. I thought you loved me."

"We do," Donna said, a catch in her throat, as if about to cry. "I do. But I don't know if that's enough."

"Of course it is. What else is there?" He rolled onto his side to face her.

She shook her head, waved a hand at the ceiling. "The whole world outside this room. The future." She smiled sadly. "I mean look at us, hiding from our families, our friends. If my work finds out about us, my career is over. And you . . ." She shook a hand at him, as if trying to wake him up. "Your so-called colleagues would literally murder you if they knew you were here tonight."

"Okay fine," Joe allowed. "We've got issues. Who doesn't?"

"The point is . . . this right here, right now, it's beautiful, but it's all it can ever be. A secret hour or two, now and then." She looked into his eyes, deeply, sadly, mixing hopelessness with entreaty. "Don't you want more?"

◆

He did. But he didn't know what to do about it, so he respected her wishes and gave her some space. They weren't broken up, exactly. They had tentative plans to have dinner together soon, Indian food out in his neighborhood, Jackson Heights, the next time his grandmother Gladys took her regular jaunt to Atlantic City, which further complicated things, since she was often joined by Yolanda, who was now one of her best friends. Neither woman knew about Donna and Joe. In the meantime, Joe brooded, and tried to avoid brooding too much by pestering his friend Frank, an older painter who kept a studio in Harlem, and his new friend and part-time business partner Alexis, who owned a used bookshop in the West Village. On an impulse, Joe had used the proceeds of a job to buy into the enterprise, and now he killed time by stopping by to "help," which really meant browsing the shelves, petting the cat, and distracting Alexis.

"I must say," drawled Alexis, lighting a long thin cigarette with his long thin fingers and blowing out a thin stream of smoke, "I was somewhat trepidatious about taking you on as junior partner, but my misgivings about being in business with . . ." he hesitated, searching for the right term.

"A criminal."

"Exactly, thank you, my misgivings about being in business with a criminal had to do with, oh I don't know, finding a severed head in the safe, not that you'd be moping about here wanting to discuss love of all things. I mean really."

"Sorry." Joe scowled. "You'd rather have the severed head."

"In a way. There'd be a certain frisson. But this is so blah, so . . . if you'll forgive my saying so . . . straight. Do I look like Dear Abby? I recommend books, not love strategies to heartbroken heterosingles."

Joe shrugged. The cat yawned at him, seemingly also bored with his love life. "So then recommend a book."

"Well . . ." Alexis tapped ash. "How serious is this? I mean, are we talking Stendhal, Tolstoy? I mean, is this Austen trouble, that can still work out in the end, or are we in Brontë country?"

Joe waved a hand at the packed shelves around him. "I'm in uncharted territory. I need a guide."

Alexis nodded. "Then I suppose there is only one choice, my boy." He stood and went to a shelf. The cat rolled onto her back, stretching luxuriously, and stared upside down at Joe, as if teasing him or perhaps trying to cheer him up. He stroked her belly. How did it get so soft? Alexis came back with a fat book bound in black fabric.

"Here you go, Proust. *In Search of Lost Time*, Volume One. *Swann's Way*." He handed it to Joe, and then went around to sit back at his desk. "And if that doesn't help, there's six more volumes to go."

Joe would wonder, on different afternoons, as he sat reading and petting the cat, if that had been Alexis's plan all along. Even if Proust provided Joe no relief, suggesting a three-thousand-page novel would at least provide Alexis some peace and quiet.

◆

Frank was more direct.

"How in the hell would I know what you should do? I've been divorced four times." He was in his studio, sprawled in his leather armchair, which was patched and cracked and leaking stuffing. Joe sat, as always, in the straight-back chair. The large, raw space around them was caked in paint, as if it had been raining slowly down from the atmosphere for ages, gathering on every surface: tables, easels, walls, floors. There were art supplies, books, papers, and rags stacked around, on shelves and tables and tottering towers. And there were canvases in various states, large nudes, and views down onto 125th Street, which he'd been painting almost daily for decades.

"I mean, the first one didn't count really," he added thoughtfully. He wore an old cashmere sweater with paint on it, pajama pants, slippers. His gray hair was cropped close and mostly gone on top. His dark handsome face was deeply lined, and reading glasses hung on a string around his neck. He held a brush and seemed to be jotting something on the air as he spoke. "I was only twenty after all, and so fucked up from Vietnam that I didn't even tell the poor girl I'd been in the service. She just thought I was a hippie like her. Nice Jewish girl from Barnard. And the second one I was drunk and high the whole time, and so was she, this white actress I met in San Francisco, so that was like, no harm no foul. But the last two." He shrugged, sighing deeply. "Those I really fucked up."

"You seem to have a good thing going now, with Kiran." Dr. Kiran Acharya was an ob-gyn and an environmental activist whom Joe had gotten to know a little. He liked her very much.

"Sure. I learned my lesson. It's like I'm back in the Marine Corp. I agree with whatever she says, make sure she comes first, and keep my opinions to myself."

"First in, last out."

"Exactly. It's simple." He shrugged, oblivious to the splotch of paint that flicked onto the floor. "But then again, she ain't no cop."

5

"**B**ut we'll just be working security for some rich spoiled brat."

"We always are, kid." Donna was sitting across the desk from her boss, Senior Agent in Charge Tom Foster. He was in Mentor Mode, trying to share some wisdom. He gestured at the newspaper spread open in front of him, as if the evidence spoke for itself. "You haven't noticed who runs things?"

He stood up, glancing out his window at Foley Square. This expansive view was one of the sweetest perks of his position—Donna worked from a windowless basement cell—yet it rarely seemed to bring him joy. He scowled at the passing throngs below as if every one of them were a potential offender or victim, and as such, a pain in his ass. "Kozco is a foreign VIP, visiting our jurisdiction, against whom credible threats have been made."

Now Donna scowled. She wasn't allowed to stand and pace like Tom, so she just sat up even straighter. "He's a rich official who's been run out of his own country, so now he's coming to us."

"If by us you mean America, and you're not happy about it, go vote." He waved a finger between them. "But if by *us* you mean you and me, then the person we work for is the Director of the FBI, who has not asked for our opinion." He sat back down, sighing. "Look Zamora, you need to think more than one move ahead here. For years you bellyached about wanting to be in the field. Okay, you achieved that."

"By stopping a terror attack."

He nodded. "I remember. A commendable action for which you received a commendation. It was also reckless, dangerous, and undertaken with no authorization or backup of any kind. Zero leadership skills."

"But then I led the team that busted that human trafficking ring," she pointed out.

"Right. And almost triggered a huge scandal by deciding, all on your own, to arrest all the high-profile clients, including judges, which might have sunk the case."

Donna said nothing. He was right, so she just glared as he went on: "Unless I accidently came to the wrong office this morning, that door has my name on it, and says AIC. That means I'm the asshole in charge. And I think it would be a good idea to assign you to a nice, safe, quiet protection detail, because I think you're an ambitious young agent with potential who is badly in need of some seasoning."

"But . . ." Donna opened her mouth but stopped when Tom held up his hand.

"Before you speak, there are only two acceptable responses. One is, yes, sir, I'm on it. Thank you for the opportunity to be of service to my country and the bureau. The other is, fuck you, I quit. Sir." He sat back, hands folded. "Now, it's your turn to talk."

Donna gritted her teeth, took a breath, and then finally chuckled softly, as a series of warring emotions rushed through her in about a second. She stood up, back straight, and looked Tom in the eye. "Yes, sir, I'm on it."

"And?" he asked.

She sighed. "And I thank you for the opportunity to be of service to my country and the bureau."

"Well done." He opened a folder and spoke without looking up. "Now go babysit that spoiled brat. And bring wipes."

◆

Evon Kozco was indeed very rich. From one of the ruling families in a tiny nation that sprang up when the USSR collapsed, he'd been educated abroad—Swiss French boarding school, then Cambridge—then served in the military, fighting religious fundamentalists on one side and Russian-backed insurgents on the other, reaching the rank of Colonel, all the while continuing to heap up the riches, while the US continued its support. But now the ruling party had collapsed and Kozco was here, with a lot of goodwill among local elites if little at home. He was, rumor had it, thinking about settling down in New York, though he was a little concerned about the big city's criminal element.

So was Donna. Specifically, Joe. When Tom had made his comments about how, as FBI agents, they kissed the pampered butts of spoiled brats, he was being cynical, making a point. But Donna had immediately thought, *Joe doesn't.* That was the true irony—the one person she knew who was in no way beholden to anyone, who did not defer to the will of the social order or betray his personal convictions, was himself a criminal. Did he vote? Who for? Was he even registered? Did he pay taxes? She wondered suddenly if he even had a driver's license and decided not to ask. But of course there was a lot she couldn't ask—that was one of their problems—and driving without a license was the least of it. How about, "Whatever happened to the body of that terrorist I killed?" Or, "How did that serial killer end up hanging from a pipe, in a suicide that suited everybody, including the law?" Was the problem really that Joe was dishonest or was it that she didn't want to know the truth? And speaking of honest, did she honestly want him to be more like her, or did she wish, deep down, that she could be more like him? Did she really want to invite Joe to bureau barbecues or take him along to meet the boring parents of her kid's schoolmates? Or did she wish that, like Joe, she could opt out, and simply turn her back on everything she found distasteful?

But of course there was more to it than that. After all, it was the Constitution she had sworn to protect, not the FBI, and it was her fellow citizens, and the cause of justice, that she served. When you turned your back on that, stepping outside society's bounds, you were in the wilderness, you were alone, and it was precisely that loneliness that she knew Joe hoped to cure with her. So there they were, as close as only lovers could be, yet on two different sides of the line, law and outlaw, with neither one ready to cross.

Still, she missed him. She had to admit it. And what was wrong with that, really?

Reaching for her phone, she texted:

Just wanted to say I'm thinking of you.
What are you doing now?

The answer came back swiftly:

Believe it or not, I'm helping a friend find a lost pet.
Talk later?

She smiled, not sure she did believe it, yet knowing anything was possible with Joe, even coaxing cats from trees. Feeling a warmth she could not deny, she typed back:

Sure.

"Hello? Anybody home?"

Donna, lost in thought, looked up from her desk to see Special Agent Andrew Newton standing in her door. They met during training and had been pals ever since. As a young, black, openly gay agent, he'd had to fight just as hard as Donna to forge a career, and they'd had each other's backs the whole way. He was also fun, which could not be said of everyone at the FBI.

"So how'd it go with the old man upstairs?" he asked, sitting on the corner of her desk. "And I don't mean Jehovah."

She tossed him the Kozco file. "We have been awarded the noble task of shepherding this rich tourist around while he visits the Statue of Liberty and shops at Saks."

"Great," he said, flipping open the file. "My cousin works at Saks, and they really need the business."

"Now you just sound cynical," Donna said. "You're too young for that. You should still be in your idealist phase. No wonder Ari wants you to quit and go to law school." She laughed. "Because we all know that's the cure for cynicism."

"Maybe so," Andy allowed, eyes still on the file. "But you sound burned-out and bitter." He looked up, lips pursed. "And we all know the cure for that."

"My sex life is fine, thank you."

"I'm not prying. Just wondering if you even read this file."

"I glanced at the first page."

"Because according to pages two through five, this Kozco fellow is a bona fide hero. Foiled a terrorist attack in his hometown, then tracked down the entire cell. Also stopped the sale of an old Russian nuke and led the campaign to seal the border against jihadists. Even took a bullet for it."

"Oh yeah?" Donna asked. "I guess I am getting too cynical. Maybe he is one of the good guys."

Andy leaned back, stretching his legs. "I for one am looking forward to this assignment. Riding in a limo with a suave foreign gentleman and watching while he selects ties sure beats squatting in a filthy van spying on hookers while you-know-who smokes and burps."

"Fusco," Donna laughed. "You better hope that's all he does."

Andy wagged a finger. "Now there's an example of what happens if you get too cynical."

"Yup. Burned-out. Bitter. Sour."

"Bitter and sour." Andy laughed. "No wonder his digestion is catastrophic."

"Right." Donna was grinning now too. "It's not the crap food he eats, it's his soul repeating on him."

They both had a good laugh.

"I kind of miss him," Andy admitted.

"The guy does grow on you somehow," Donna added. "Like a fungus." She looked at her watch and stood. It was time to get going. "I wonder where that rotten bastard is right now."

◆

As it happened, at that precise moment, Detective Lieutenant Francis "Fartso" Fusco, of the NYPD's Major Case Squad, was actually feeling warm and sunny for once. He'd won big on college basketball last night. True, these were mere pebbles in the canyon-sized hole of debt he had dug himself into with Gio Caprisi, but it gave him the sense his luck was turning around. Also, despite the smoking, the drinking, and the fat-, grease-, and sugar-based diet and ongoing gastric issues that gave him his nickname, he'd just had his departmental checkup and had been cleared for continued service. Granted, this only meant that allowing him to drive a departmental car and carry a firearm was not an actual liability at the moment—it had no bearing on his likelihood of surviving to retirement. Still, Fusco felt vindicated, and he celebrated by having two jelly donuts for breakfast, the evidence of which was now on his tie as he sat across from his own boss, Captain Maureen O'Toole, listening to her actually praise him for once.

"This comes straight from the Commissioner's office, and they want you on it specifically. Apparently, these VIPs called him personally and asked for you by name."

"I'm not surprised," Fusco said.

"I was. But I had the call checked and it wasn't a gag. Seems it's some foreigners who requested you, so that might explain it. If their English is shaky, maybe they're more likely to believe what they read in the paper."

She was referring to the coverage of the terror attack, which Fusco had helped stop and for which he had also been commended. He'd also stood up and accepted a medal on behalf of his young partner Gerald Parks. Parks died during that operation, shot down by a lethal and sadistic professional assassin, who had escaped in the ensuing turmoil and disappeared. But Fusco had never stopped looking. Parks's photo was on his desk, with a black ribbon pinned to the frame.

"What can I say," Fusco said now, leaning back and smoothing his tie, then, realizing he'd gotten jelly on it, licking it off his finger. "Some job notices read, 'heroes only.'"

"Exactly," O'Toole said, frowning as she handed him a carton of wipes. "That's why you're going to clean your tie, grab your cape, and fly uptown pronto to report."

"What's the problem?" Fusco asked, trying to wipe out the stain. "Another terror plot? Kidnapping?"

"Broken windows," she said, holding up a folder.

"What?" Confused, he reached for it, but she pulled away.

"Wipe your fingers first." He did, as she continued. "It's those goddamn Upper East Side parking wars. They're escalating and it's gone international."

As everyone knows, or can easily imagine, the competition for parking spaces in Manhattan is fierce and known to occasionally degenerate from verbal abuse to fist fights. But in certain neighborhoods the situation takes on more peculiar dimensions. The Upper East Side is one such zone: the large number of embassies and consulates means numerous cars with diplomatic plates. Diplomatic cars, like their owners, have diplomatic immunity, and can park with impunity, ignoring the laws and enraging the citizenry. Now some vigilante, pushed beyond the breaking point, had taken the law into his own hands.

"Talk about a hero," the captain mused. "This guy's been going around, smashing windows and slashing tires on cars with diplomatic plates. And he's going after the loading zone colonizers too."

Multiple luxury buildings had begun placing cones, signs, and even nightclub style velvet ropes over the curbs fronting their entrances, in an attempt, essentially, to save convenient spots for their wealthy residents. It was a scam of course, they had no legal right to the space, but most drivers didn't know it, and those brave or stubborn enough to try pulling in would often be blocked by officious doormen and thuggish building security. Sometimes they even painted their own yellow line along the curb, knowing that, in the unlikely event it was reported, all they risked was a fine. That occasional expense was well worth it, in a neighborhood where renting a spot cost more than a mortgage elsewhere. But now the Parking Avenger, as some had dubbed him, was targeting high-end vehicles left in those coveted spots as well.

"Anyway, the UN called the mayor's office," the captain concluded. "It's a major shitstorm, and they need a major case hero to go clean it up. So keep the wipes. You'll be shaking a lot of manicured hands."

"Fine," Fusco muttered, no longer feeling quite so lucky. He stood, clutching the file but ignoring the wipes.

"And take Chang with you."

"What?" He turned back. "Why?"

"You need a new partner and she's new."

Mood rapidly deflating, Fusco now felt the day's first wave of heartburn rising in his chest. "Are these foreigners Asian or something? You think I need her help to handle them? Rich, spoiled whining sounds the same all over. I don't need a rookie to interpret."

"There you go," the captain pointed at him. "That must be the velvet touch the mayor was hoping for. As you well know, asshole, Chang is from Queens, she has the same accent I do, and she is no rookie. Her clearance rate last year was better than yours. Hand-to-hand combat, IQ . . . the only test you scored higher on was cholesterol. I'm sending her along to protect you, in case shit gets hairy." She stared him down as he angrily chewed a Tums. "Then again, who am I kidding? Everyone who has to share the office restroom knows that with you, shit always gets hairy."

6

Joe crossed the street.

It was dark now, the dinner hour, and no one answering to Chow's description had entered the Eleonora, nor had the lights in 10E gone on. And while there would be a night doorman on duty, a quiet residential building like this would be running a skeleton staff, with most cleaning, repairs, and deliveries during the day.

Plus, he now had an incentive to finish this up early. The text from Donna had brightened his day considerably, and he took it as a good omen. Despite his total incomprehension at how so-called normal people conducted supposedly healthy relationships, he did have some experience with the deeper drives that powered the human heart, and while much of what he'd learned had made him the sort of guy who liked smoking opium, it also, in a strange way, made him a romantic: if he and Donna loved each other, and that was their fate, then nothing could stop it, not their family and friends and work lives, and certainly not common sense or rational thought. What chance did logic stand against desire? Why else would a man steal a million-dollar pigeon?

He went to the side door used by staff and quickly loided the lock, which he'd examined before, tripping the latch with a thin piece of metal. That was what he expected. With so many people coming and going, it didn't make sense to throw the dead bolt all the time. He wandered the empty corridors, painted a dull institutional green, and passed an employee changing room, a boiler room, and a storage room filled with cleaning supplies before he found the elevator, which he took up to ten. This corridor was much nicer—marble-floored, painted an immaculate white with handsome moldings, tasteful wall sconces, and big potted plants—but the lock on 10E was nothing special. This, too, was as expected. In a building like this, in a neighborhood like this, the residents relied on their doormen and concierges, their maids and drivers, their friendly, respectable neighbors, clean, well-lit streets, and frequent police drive-bys to make them feel safe. Street crime was almost nonexistent, and Joe guessed there hadn't been a random burglary in this building in years. He knew plenty of people in old doorman buildings who didn't bother to lock their apartment doors. Some didn't even carry a key. That, Joe reflected, was true luxury, true privilege: freedom from mundane worry and minor hassle. Freedom from fear.

The door at 10E wasn't unlocked, that was too much to hope for, but Joe got in without much trouble. His skills were nowhere near those of his friend, comrade, and exlover Yelena—she was a master safe-cracker among other dangerous things—but he'd broken into enough apartments in his life to handle this. When the lock gave, he paused, then opened the door slowly, holding his breath, and stepped in, shutting it fast and silent behind him. Then he waited in the dark, listening carefully, letting his eyes adjust and making sure he was alone. He had a black cloth bag over his shoulder, a loose weave that would let air in for the bird. For now, it held a few tools, including a flashlight, which he turned on, having covered most of the lamp with tape already, so only a thin beam emerged.

He began to make his way, methodically, from room to room, letting the light play over the ornate antique furniture, the oil paintings, and the glass-front cabinets full of Asian ceramics, delicate and sublime. Joe was no fence, but every single item he saw seemed to be worth a fortune. He crossed an elaborate dining room and a huge living room, if that was the right word for a hall with a concert piano and a chandelier, nosed through a couple sumptuous bedrooms, ignoring closets and bathrooms for now, and finally found his way into a study with a balcony overlooking the park. Moonlight poured through the glass doors. There was a large leather-topped desk with a fancy penholder and letter opener, big wing-backed leather chairs, a fireplace, and bookshelves holding row upon row of leather spines. There were several paintings, one of which Joe couldn't help pausing at as the light picked over the room—Cubist chunks building a still life, guitar, bottle, glass. He fought the urge to stop and stare.

There was also a birdcage. It was not, as he'd imagined, an ornate old fashioned one, with gold bars and a domed roof—just a plain metal square of thin bars, but larger than he'd expected, too big to carry away. And it did indeed contain a bird who matched the description he'd been given, a white bird with a long neck and pointed beak. Ramses. The champ. The bird wasn't sleeping, Joe didn't think, but it was still, and when he passed the light over it, the little black bead of an eye gave nothing away. Then, as he moved toward it, it hopped and opened its wings, separating each feather as if stretching himself into a fan, and then folding back up, a small wonder of engineering and design. He was not impressive in the way that say, an eagle or a peacock would be, but he called attention to how fantastic all birds were. This creature could fly.

And then the thought came to Joe, unbidden, as it sometimes did: You know, life isn't really so bad. He'd seen a remarkable sight that day, all those birds circling the roof in a gorgeous clear sky, and he had good friends like Gio, and maybe things could still work out with Donna after all, and he was, don't forget, about to make the easiest fifty grand (rather, fifty thousand euros) of his life. Maybe he was wrong to scoff at this job. It was, as Gio had said, a piece of cake. A big fat slice all covered in frosting.

Joe smiled to himself as he opened the bag and went to the cage, and he was just reaching for the latch, maybe laying one light finger on it, when all hell broke loose.

◆

The lights came on. All at once, the room was illuminated, even the bird was shocked, fluttering and hopping in its cage, and Joe turned, reflexively aiming the now redundant flashlight, and saw two men—big men in black suits with white shirts and ties and wires running from their left ears, so professional muscle—coming through the only door.

Joe took in all that in an instant, and as the men came at him, he threw the flashlight—it was a Maglite with some weight to it—and hit one guy right on the forehead.

"Oof," he moaned, grabbing his head as the flashlight bounced off. "That hurt."

Then, as Joe saw the other guy reaching under his jacket for what Joe did not think was a flashlight, he bounded forward, crossing the carpet in a leap, and brought his foot up fast, like he was kicking a field goal, landing a good one right below the kneecap. That guy moaned even louder than the first, losing balance as his joint folded. Joe grabbed up an antique chair and threw it through the glass door, shattering the pane, then followed, leaping out onto the balcony. A shot popped through the other door panel beside him, leaving a small hole and a long diagonal crack in the glass. A second shot shattered it.

The balcony was filled with potted plants along with a table and chairs and lounges; Joe ducked out of firing range, pressing against the wall beside the door, and grabbed a terra-cotta pot. As the guy with the gun came through, Joe swung hard and smashed it on his head, showering him with soil and sending him stumbling back into his partner, who was trying to follow him out. Joe grabbed another pot, a ceramic bowl that held a large leafy green plant, and pivoted into the doorway. He faced the gunman, who was now clutching his head, and kicked him, hard, in the nuts. With a grunt, the man bent over double, grabbing his groin and exposing the guy behind him, who looked at

Joe in surprise, just as Joe brought the ceramic crashing down onto his face, cracking the pot in two.

Joe slipped back inside. He knew the gun had fallen somewhere, but there was no time to look. Or to grab Ramses, whom he glanced at wistfully as he dashed across the room and into the hallway, where two more guards, dressed in the same suits, were coming toward him with guns already drawn.

Joe turned and ran back into the study, slamming the door behind him, just as the first two guards were coming around.

"Hey!" one said, groggily, seeing Joe leap over him, just before a barrage of bullets came through the door.

"Hold fire," the guard called out, his partner shouting frantically in Chinese as they both hit the deck. As the door burst open, Joe ran back out onto the balcony and, without any other options left, jumped.

7

Joe did not jump ten stories to the ground. Things were not quite that hopeless yet. But they were bad enough that, quickly assessing the physics, he made a running start, planted one foot on the couch, followed that with a foot on the railing, and leaped onto the next unit's balcony, a distance of about six feet. Quite doable, really, in a track meet. Utterly terrifying when you glimpse a concrete sidewalk far below before landing with a thump and a groan and a crash onto a small metal table and chairs, covered with yet more plants, all of which collapsed beneath him.

Although his back didn't appreciate it, this was actually fortunate, because it put him out of range and safely on the floor of the new balcony by the time the guards opened fire, shooting across from next door. The pots around him exploded in quick bursts.

"He's going to 10D," he heard someone yelling as the shooting stopped and the men ran back inside. "Intruder in 10D!"

Realizing there was no point in entering 10D now, Joe scrambled across to the other end of the balcony where, along with the bullet-riddled planters, there were additional pots hanging from chains on hooks, spider plants and other long, viney specimens. He picked the planter with the longest chain, yanked it free, and tied it around the railing, then grabbed on for dear life and lowered himself over the side. Meanwhile, lights came on in the interior of the apartment above, and he heard more shouting, this time, he thought, in Russian.

The chain was about three feet long, but with his arms extended, that was enough to let his feet touch the railing of the balcony directly beneath. He swung for momentum and, pushing off with his toes, tumbled onto the floor of the balcony of what he assumed was 9D.

This balcony had fewer plants but more furniture: a round table and chairs with an umbrella, two lounges with a small glass table between them. On the table was a half-finished whiskey on the rocks and an ashtray with a stubbed-out cigar. And one of the doors was propped open. Staying on the floor, Joe crawled carefully to the threshold and peeked in.

This was another office, but as modern as the other was antique. The desk was a slab of glass over a marble pedestal. There were severe chairs of steel tubing and black leather. There was a carpet covered in geometric designs and a mirror over a fireplace. Set in one wall was an open safe, with the painting that must normally cover it, a black and white abstraction, set to one side. Standing over the desk was an older black man in some kind of uniform Joe did not recognize, but, considering the elaborate gold braiding and the stunning number of medals, he had to be some kind of general, at least.

Luckily for Joe, he was too preoccupied to notice him or hear the commotion upstairs. He was counting gold coins, Krugerrands, Joe thought, and adding them to a cloth bag that sat beside other full bags on his desk. Finished, he hefted a bag and carried it over to the safe. Joe sprang to his feet, darting across the carpet toward the door, quietly, he hoped. But the general caught a glimpse of his reflection in the mirror.

"Hey!" he yelled. "Who are you?" Joe ran into the hall. He moved quickly down a long corridor hung with black and white photos depicting the African savannah, hoping it led to a front door. But then, as he turned a corner, two tall men in tan uniforms crossed his path. They had sidearms.

"Excuse me, I'm a little lost." Joe spoke quickly, before they could react. He pointed to his name patch. "Maintenance. I'm supposed to check a leaky faucet in the kitchen?"

They pointed. "Thanks," Joe said and, as he hurried on, he heard the general's voice ring out. "Guards! Come quickly!"

He crossed a large living room, filled with sumptuous furniture and high-end electronics, the walls covered with large dramatic masks and the heads of animals. A long tusk lay in a glass display case. Next came an ornate wood-paneled dining room, where a uniformed maid was setting the table. A tall, elegant woman in a silk dress was supervising.

"Sorry ma'am," Joe muttered, touching his cap as he hustled past. They ignored him. Next, through a swinging door, was the kitchen.

It was a large and no doubt sunny room in the daytime. The table was heaped with food—vegetables, a case of wine, a raw chicken marinating in a dish. Hoping to find a rear exit, he opened a door that led to a tiny bathroom.

"He went that way!" He heard shouting from the interior. "To the kitchen, quick!"

With no more time to run, Joe snatched the plastic bottle of dish soap from the sink and squeezed a thick ooze of liquid onto the tile floor. Then he grabbed a heavy iron skillet from the stovetop and stepped behind the door as it burst open. The first guard tore in, slid immediately, his feet jerking out from under him, and fell, hitting the back of his head on the tiles. His companion stumbled over him, fighting to maintain balance. Joe sprang out with the skillet and gonged him across the back of the head. Carefully avoiding the slick, he tried the next door, a laundry room, and then finally found a service entrance, leading to a narrow back stairwell.

Now Joe moved fast, rushing down a flight and past stacks of recycling and cartons of bottled water, until he heard noises from below and paused. It was footsteps and the telltale squawk of walkie-talkies. "Six is clear, over. . . ." he heard a man's voice. He paused, thinking of going back up, but then he heard the African guards from above. "You go upstairs," a voice with a rich accent ordered. "I will check down here."

Joe hurried down the hall, knocking on the service doors, skipping one that had several days' copies of the *Wall Street Journal* stacked in front of it. Finally, one opened, and a small dark-haired woman in an apron and headscarf peeked out.

"Hello madam," he said, pushing gently in as he spoke. "Do you smell gas?"

"*No hablo inglés.*" She shook her head in confusion as Joe stepped into her kitchen, shutting the door behind him and locking it. This kitchen had bags of oranges and limes and bottles of mineral water on the counter and a large cutting board where she'd been peeling onions and chopping tomato.

"*Humos de gas!*" Joe said, holding his nose. "*Peligroso!*"

"*Ay sí,*" the woman said and promptly ran out of the kitchen. Joe listened at the service door and heard the men shouting to one another as they rattled the knobs outside. He couldn't go back that way. He went to the window and saw there was a wide ledge. He pushed it open and crawled out, shuffling to the side and pressing himself to the wall as the kitchen door opened. The woman came back, accompanied by a young man with a shaved head and a lot of gang tattoos. Joe held still. The gangster checked the stove, confirmed the door was locked, and, with a shrug, got a beer from the fridge. He sat down at the table while the woman went back to work, chattering away in Spanish. Joe was stuck.

He looked around, taking stock of his predicament. He was eight stories up, standing on a ledge over an interior courtyard. It was dark out here, and mostly quiet, though he could see what looked like security guards moving around with flashlights on the ground below. Some of the windows were lit, and though Joe knew the inhabitants could not see him on the dark side of the glass, it made him even more leery of moving too much, and the warmly lit scenes of people cooking, eating, talking, and watching TV together deepened his sense of precarious isolation.

But he was not actually alone, unfortunately, because he was, of course, completely surrounded by pigeons of the plain old city variety. Street birds. Cooing and clucking, hunting and pecking, they swarmed around the ledge, which was caked in ancient layers of their crap. Others flew around, settling on one sill then another, spiraling down into the courtyard and soaring up over the roofs, flapping free, away over the city and off into the twilit horizon, as if to mock both his failure to nab one of their kind and his own present predicament, cowering in the shadows, a prisoner of height and gravity. How had he ended up in this situation, when he should be home, too, warm and cozy, watching *Jeopardy* with his grandmother? And why, he wondered, now that he had the chance to think about more than how to survive a few seconds at a time, had the security response been so overwhelming? It seemed a bit over the top for a bird, even a Maltese pigeon named Ramses. Joe could see one that looked pretty much the same to him, right here, taking a crap on an air conditioner. He was tempted to just grab one of these birds, a near enough relative, stuff it into a pocket, and bring it to Alonzo, but of course he'd know the difference in a flash, seeing with the eyes of love.

But the first and, at the moment, only important question was, how was he getting off this ledge? And for that, Joe had a possible answer. He remembered the stacked newspapers by the apartment down the hall, and he figured, counting kitchens, that it had to be the window three over, at the corner of the courtyard, which would correspond to the spot on the corridor. It was a safe bet that no one was home there, at least safer than trying to fly. Taking a deep breath and trying to ignore the reek of bird and the distraction of feathers dancing around him, he began to edge slowly along the ledge, palms on the bricks, feet shuffling sideways, step by step. Only one of the windows he had to pass was lit. A white woman in jeans and a sweater, dark hair pulled back in a tight ponytail streaked with gray, was preparing dinner, which meant shifting slices of pizza from a cardboard box onto plates, while a kid, Joe assumed her daughter, added a side salad, scooping it from a container. Her own dark hair was loose, and she wore a Ramones T-shirt, jeans, and the same sneakers as him, Converse high-tops. The table was set for two. It was surreal to inch by them—fingers sliding along the top of the window frame, careful not to brush against the glass, as invisible as if passing behind a mirror—while they poured drinks, soda and a large goblet of red wine—and then sat to eat, a couple feet away.

He breathed a sigh of relief as he moved on, passing dark windows, and finally arrived at his goal: the kitchen with the newspapers stacked outside the service door. It was, as far he could see, dark and silent within. Before proceeding, he took a last look around, checking for peeping neighbors. And that's when he saw . . . something. Someone. At the roof of the building, each corner was topped with a narrow tower, like on a castle, with a tiled, pointy roof, a weathervane, and a small, cuplike balcony. Now, in the gathering gloom, Joe spotted the vague form of someone standing in the cup. The figure seemed to have long gray hair, wild and hanging past the shoulders and, as far as Joe could make out, was wearing a purple robe covered in glittery stars. A small glow provided another clue: the mysterious figure was smoking and, after a few more drags, tossed whatever it was, and watched the ember drop like a falling star into the dark courtyard. It struck ground with a tiny flash and was gone. Then, like the ghost of Hamlet's father, the figure vanished too, back into the tower. Joe waited, wondering if whoever that was had been watching him all along. But nothing happened, and anyway, there was no turning back, so he went on.

He took out his small metal strip, and slid it between the top and bottom windowpanes, pushing the lock open. That was the easy part. It was actually trickier, and far more dangerous, to squat and push the window up, trying to find the right leverage without stepping too far back and toppling into the courtyard below. Finally, with a slight moan, the window lifted a half inch. He got his fingers under it and pulled. As soon as it was open, he stepped in and shut it behind him, dropping to the floor.

He froze. He crouched there, listening to the silence, peering into the dark, waiting for his eyes to adjust and making sure the place still felt empty. Reassured, he got up and carefully began to look around.

It was even emptier than he'd hoped. A big place like the others, and also well-furnished, it nevertheless felt more like a hotel suite between guests than a home. The drawers and closets were mostly empty—except for linens and towels—there were few objects on the dressers and tabletops, and only the bare necessities in the bathrooms: soap, shampoo, toilet paper, but no cosmetics, no meds. These people weren't away on business or vacation, liable to walk in any second; whoever they were, they were gone, living elsewhere. Nevertheless, the large number of plants, all thriving, and the pile of junk mail on a console in the foyer addressed variously to Jon or Layla Dunwoody, suggested that they did maintain some sort of presence.

But not tonight, Joe concluded, finally letting himself relax a bit as he went back to the kitchen, drank from the tap, then used the bathroom, washing the grime from his hands—the building exterior had been filthy—and repeatedly rinsing his face in warm water, as if to gently wake himself from a bad dream. He selected a sharp knife from the kitchen, grabbed some throw pillows from the couch, and found a comfortable, quiet, hidden spot, on the thick carpet in the corner of the living room and settled down to wait. And rest. And think. His plan was to lie low until it got late and they all gave up the search, and then, after the building went to sleep, sneak out somehow, though that was as far as he'd got. Then his phone rang. It was Gio.

"Hey," he said, keeping his voice low, though he knew no one could hear. The walls and floors in these old places were thick.

"Please tell me you're on your way back with the goddamn pigeon," Gio said. "Alonzo keeps calling and breaking my balls. He interrupted family dinner twice so now Carol and my mom are both pissed at me too. The whole point was I was supposed to be home for meals more during this delicate stage for the kids, but apparently it doesn't count if I'm not present."

"Um, listen Gio—"

"And apparently present doesn't mean what you think, because obviously I am present, I mean I'm fucking here aren't I?"

"Gio," he spoke up. "I have bad news. The situation with the bird has gotten a bit complicated."

"Complicated?" Gio asked. "It's a fucking pigeon. What did it do, shit on your head?"

"I'll explain later. I can't really talk now. I'm in the middle of something and the signal kind of sucks. . . ."

"Wait. Joe. Don't hang up. I told Alonzo—"

Joe hung up. Then, reluctantly, he texted Donna.

Sorry but I don't think tonight will work.

Soon?

He switched off the ringer and lay back, sighing deeply, and shut his eyes. What he needed right now was peace and quiet, so he could rest. And wait. And think. And about twenty minutes later, he was just drifting off into a snooze when the front door opened and the lights came on.

8

olonel Evon Kozco was not what Donna had expected. For one thing, he was handsome: tall, strong, elegant, with thick gray hair swept back from a noble forehead, high cheekbones, a Roman nose, and unusually voluptuous red lips for a man, setting off his piercing blue eyes. Not that she was the sort of superficial person to be charmed by a handsome devil, but Andy was, and his obvious swooning, as well as the winks and gestures he made behind Kozco's back—fanning himself, miming a blow job, and egging Donna on to flirt with him—introduced a kind of adolescent tone to the proceedings that made it hard to retain her indignation at even being on this job.

And for another: when, after meeting him in the lobby of his hotel, where he waited with his private bodyguards, Donna asked him where he wanted to go, he did not mention Tiffany's or Prada, like she expected; he wanted to visit a museum. "Can we please go to the Met?"

he asked. "It's been years, and there is an exhibit of European marquetry that I am dying to see. Do you mind? Do you enjoy marquetry, Special Agent Zamora?"

Having no idea what that was, Donna shrugged and said, "Sure." But Andy gushed, "I love it. We both do. Especially European. It's so much better than the regular old marquetry you get over here." He elbowed her. "Right, Donna? Don't you think?"

She scowled at him. "I think you should tell them to bring the Colonel's car around, and I'll go check the museum."

But here Kozco interceded, charmingly. "Won't you be accompanying me? I confess, more than protection, what I really need is a true New Yorker as my tour guide. And you are a true New Yorker, are you not, Special Agent Zamora?"

"She sure is," Andy said. "Born and raised. And you don't have to keep saying Special. We know she is. Just call her Donna."

"I'd be delighted," he said, bowing a little to her. "But only if you call me Evon," he added, pronouncing it Ee-von, which she had to admit, she liked better than Ivan. More elegant.

Marquetry, it turned out, was elaborate inlaid wooden designs, and the exhibit did indeed contain some wonderful examples, about which Evon was quite knowledgeable, but that was just the beginning. As they wandered the museum, he discoursed freely on Medieval armor, Egyptian artifacts, classical sculpture, and European painting, always insightful and amusing and always being sure to ask her opinions and then listen thoughtfully while she spoke. The bodyguards hung back discreetly, and Andy forged ahead, checking out each room before they entered and communicating with their backup via his earpiece and mic.

It was, Donna had to admit, wonderful. She couldn't remember the last time she'd been to a museum other than on a school trip with Larissa, where the conversation mostly revolved around not touching things, not commenting too loudly on the statues and paintings of naked people, and complexly orchestrated visits to the restroom. Now, when they needed the restroom, Andy would speak into his mic and a team would sweep in, clearing the way, then step respectfully aside to wait. It was—and this Donna did not want to admit or even let herself think—like a great date. Why didn't she and Joe ever do things like this? This was one of the problems with their relationship, she told herself, why she needed to step back and rethink. But was it really Joe's fault? At least he was a serious reader; she barely got to the second page of a magazine before falling asleep. And could she really blame it all on their need for secrecy? What were the odds of bumping into either an FBI agent or a gangster in the Temple of Dendur?

Am I the one who's keeping her distance, Donna suddenly thought, stopping in her tracks, *and avoiding real intimacy, real commitment with him?* Just then Evon approached her, murmuring something, touching her just slightly on her elbow.

"Sorry," he said, when she looked up. "You were lost in thought."

"No . . ." She shook off the cobwebs. "Not at all. What is it?"

"The museum is about to close and I'm getting a bit peckish. I was wondering if you would mind if we stopped somewhere for a bite?"

"You must try some of this pâté," Evon said. "It's delicious." He scooped a healthy spoonful onto a cracker and handed it to her. "Please. As a favor to me."

She did him the favor. It was pure pleasure. Evon chose a wine and ordered all the most alluring items on the menu, while Andy sat with the bodyguards at the next table. The conversation had gotten around to what neighborhood he should live in if he moved here and brought his children.

"They've been in London with my sister, since my wife died last year."

"I'm so sorry to hear that," Donna said.

He nodded. "Thank you. She was the love of my life, but even without her, life goes on. You have children?"

"A daughter."

"And her father?"

Donna hesitated. Her toxic ex was a crooked CIA agent who'd redeemed himself, perhaps, only in death. "Also dead."

Evon smiled, though his eyes remained sad. "Then you understand." He sipped his wine. "To be honest, I'm really selfish. What I really want, even more than access to schools and stores, is to be near a good bookshop, a quiet café for reading, and a park where I can jog."

Donna was charmed. How could she not be? He was the most modest billionaire imaginable. "There are a lot of great buildings around Central Park," she offered.

"Yes, I suppose I should try to stay close to Central Park, it's so good for kids. But Riverside is actually my favorite. I love taking long walks along the river."

"Really?" Donna asked. "I grew up near the river, uptown."

"See?" he said, touching her hand, briefly, his fingers brushing hers far too quickly to be improper, yet just enough for a pulse of warmth, a tiny spark of electricity, to pass between them. "Another taste we share." Then, with a smile, he served her more pâté. "You know, I hate to keep you out working when you have a child, but I was planning on attending the ballet tonight. Do you think that would be possible? It's a private booth in the balcony, so if you get bored you can nap."

She laughed. "No problem. Duty comes first. I'll text my mother." She reached for her phone. That was when she saw the text from Joe, canceling for tonight. Apparently finding that lost pet was more complicated than he thought. If it was even true. She wrote back:

No problem. Something's come up at work anyway.

And maybe, she thought, as she texted her mom, it was for the best after all.

9

"**D**on't mind if we park here, do you?"

The doorman—dressed like a member of Her Majesty's royal household cavalry in a red uniform resplendent with gold braid, big brass buttons, white gloves, and what looked to Fusco like a baton-twirling majorette's hat, complete with chin strap—had come rushing over when they pulled into the wide-open space in front of the Excelsior, waving his hands and pointing at the sign that read, Resident Drop-Off Zone Only. Fusco, who was at the wheel, dismissed the man as he backed up.

"Hey, watch out for the . . . never mind," Detective Ellen Chang told him as he ran over the cones that had been set out to save the spot. "That's fine."

"Come on, Chang," Fusco said, opening his door and hoisting himself out. "Let's see what the admiral has to say."

"Oh sorry, officer, I didn't realize," was what the doorman in fact had to say, when Fusco flashed his badge and introduced himself, then jerked a thumb at his new partner. "That's Detective Chang."

"We're here to ask you about this series of attacks on vehicles parked in the area," she said, holding out her badge as well.

"Terrible, isn't it?" The doorman shook his head, oddly stiff, as if he had to stand very straight with that tall hat balanced on his head. "Doctor Boyd's car was attacked right out here."

"When was this, sir?" Chang asked. She had her tablet out and was rapidly tapping notes, while Fusco stared.

"Two nights ago. Around seven thirty. It wasn't even late. Is anybody safe these days?"

Fusco shrugged, declining to answer. "Were you on duty?" he asked instead.

"Well yes, it so happens I was, but I can't be out front guarding cars every second. I was helping Madam Von Forsthausen in with her dogs."

"Spell that please?" Chang asked, fingers flying as he unspooled the name.

"She's Austrian," he added. "Breeds Pomeranians."

"Got all that?" Fusco asked her. She nodded, then pointed at the camera above them.

"Can we see the footage from that night?" she asked.

"Of course," the doorman said, opening the door. "You'll have to ask the manager."

◆

The manager was a short round man in a three-piece suit, the vest ready to pop across his middle. The scent of his cologne completely filled the small office, where he led them and cued up the footage.

"Here it is detectives, though I'm afraid it's not going to be much help."

The recording showed a black-clad, hooded figure beside a large black Mercedes, slashing two tires and scratching the side of the car before pulling out a ball peen hammer and smashing the window. Then he ran off. The whole thing took less than a minute.

"Can you send me this footage?" Chang asked and gave him her departmental email. The manager did so and also handed them a still photo.

"We took these for the record as well." It showed the damaged car in better detail. Scratched across the side it said: PARKING PIG. The manager sighed. "He's insured of course. But once the finish is ruined it's never really the same. You can just tell."

"Right," Fusco said. "Deep down you know the truth."

On the way out, they thanked the doorman and Fusco pointed at the cones smooshed under his tires. "You're going to have to move those," he said. "Can't block the street."

"Oh," the doorman replied, a little flustered. "Well actually, officer, this is the Resident's Drop-Off Only Zone." He pointed at his sign.

"Actually," Fusco commented dryly, getting into the car, "we're detectives, and there's no such thing."

Chang chuckled as they shut their doors. "Good for you," she said. "That's telling them, sir."

Fusco grinned. "Just because he's got a Drum Major's outfit on, doesn't mean he actually outranks us."

"I hate that entitled stuff. Putting out a sign."

Fusco nodded. He was beginning to like this rookie after all. "They think the street belong to them."

"Exactly. They should ban all cars from the city. Just bikes and mass transit. Maybe moving sidewalks."

"Moving sidewalks?" Fusco was incredulous. "What are you, some kind of commie?"

She laughed, equally incredulous. "Because I care about the environment and traffic congestion? I mean, something has to change. We need fewer cars stinking up the place, more bike lanes and walking streets. Maybe charging stations for electric scooters."

"Scooters?" Fusco scoffed. "Those are the real menace. That's what they should ban. Driving a car, and parking it in public, is a basic right for any citizen, unless they're under the age of eighteen. Scooters, on the other hand, should be illegal for anyone *over* eighteen." He started the engine.

"Sixteen," Chang said, softly.

"What?" he barked, as he pulled out without signaling. Someone honked.

"The age to get a license in New York is sixteen," she explained. "Though you probably can't remember that far back." She glanced back at the truck he'd cut off. "Or maybe you never got one."

He hit the siren for a second, scooted through a yellow, and made a wide right turn into the avenue. "Whatever. The question is, what next? We've spoken to three doormen, two managers, a concierge, and a parking attendant. And we've got bupkes. You know what that means?"

She nodded. "We don't got squat."

"Exactly. So looks like we're stuck lurking around tonight, hoping to spot this guy."

"I agree," Chang said. "Except we don't quite have bupkes." She opened the video on a still frame and showed it to him when he stopped at a light. "I'd say he's male, about five-ten, one-eighty. He's athletic, between twenty-five and thirty-five. And he's white." She used her fingers to close in on the image. A thin strip of skin appeared between cuff and glove.

"Oh," Fusco said, sliding on his reading glasses and peering close. "Yeah, I see that. Though, let's face it," he went on, "an angry vigilante type in this neighborhood? He's white. We knew that already." Chang sighed and shook her head. The light changed and he drove. "If we're going to be out on the hunt, I've got to eat. And I don't know about you, but I'm going to pull into a place I know, right up here, makes the best double-cheeseburger and curly fries in town."

"I love that place," Chang said, grinning. "But the onion rings are way better than the fries."

Fusco smiled. "Point taken, Detective Chang."

10

Joe was wide awake, instantly. As the light filled the room, and the door clicked shut, he rolled onto his hands and knees, clutching the knife and crouching behind the sofa. He waited, holding his breath, tensing his muscles, and as the sound of footsteps passed the sofa, he sprang at the intruder, coming up from behind, knife high.

It was the kid from down the hall, the dark-haired girl who'd been eating pizza.

She gasped, eyes wide in fear. Joe immediately lowered the knife, concealing it behind his leg.

"Don't worry, I won't hurt you," he said, calmly. "You just startled me. What are you doing here?"

"Watering the plants," she said, plaintively, gesturing at the many plants as if that proved it. Then she gave him a puzzled look. "Are you friends with the Dunwoodys?"

"Yes," Joe said, realizing as he did how lame a lie it was. "I'm visiting but they didn't tell me about you, so I got worried when the door opened. I was asleep." Her quick, intelligent eyes took in his uniform, the piled cushions, the glint of the knife that Joe was now trying make seem harmless, something he just happened to be casually holding.

"Why don't you sleep in a bed?" she asked, reasonably, since Joe himself had counted five, including the king in the bare master bedroom and the twin beds in what looked like an equally bare kids' room.

"I was just taking a nap," he offered. "Sorry if I scared you. I guess we scared each other." This was patently ridiculous, he was a tough-looking man, twice her size and armed, and he felt a little embarrassed to even say it. Then again, she didn't really look that scared either. Her eyes narrowed in inquiry, then went wide.

"You're the burglar," she said, more with the air of someone guessing a riddle than someone fearing for her life. "Everyone is talking about you," she added, a little impressed.

"Oh yeah?" Joe smiled. He knew how to scare people if need be, but he didn't want to scare this girl, or sense he needed to. "What are they saying?"

She shrugged. "They think you're already gone. And they're pissed that security let you get away when they pay so much in maintenance. They're all sure you came to rob them."

Joe nodded. "Well don't worry. I'm not here to rob you. Or the Dunwoodys."

"I don't think the Dunwoodys have much here to steal," she noted. "I definitely don't." She rolled her eyes. "Not compared to some of the people here."

"But I am going to need to hang out here awhile," Joe said, watching her carefully. "Just to be sure it's safe for me to go. And I need you to keep that a secret. How do you feel about that?"

She shrugged. "Can I still water the plants?"

He smiled. "Go ahead."

So she did, filling a watering can in the bathroom and then moving through the apartment. Joe kept an eye on her, but she made no effort to run or hide.

"Do you know if the Dunwoodys are coming home soon?" Joe asked as she refilled the can at a bathroom sink.

"I doubt it," she said, focusing on the plants. "I've never seen them yet."

"You don't know them? But you water their plants."

She shook her head. "They bought the place a year ago and had a decorator come set it all up. Then they asked the manager to have someone water the plants. So they told the building staff, who suggested me."

"But they've never set foot in the place?" Joe asked. "Isn't that weird?"

"Not here. Rich people from all over buy apartments as investments. Some come like, visit for a while here and there. Some never even come at all. But hardly anyone really lives here anymore."

"No other kids?" Joe asked.

"Not really. And those who do come are mostly . . . like . . ." she hesitated.

"Rich spoiled brats?" Joe suggested.

"Pretty much."

"But not you?"

"Me?" She seemed genuinely surprised. "Ha! I wish! My Mom is a kindergarten teacher. We're renters, one of the last few."

"Your place is rent controlled?"

She nodded. In New York City, having a rent-controlled apartment was better than striking gold. It guaranteed the tenant's rights and set the very modest amount that the landlord was allowed to increase the rent and, like a precious inheritance, it could be passed down, sort of, as long as the family member also lived there. But once the lease holder gave it up, by moving out or moving on to the afterlife, the place returned to the open market, rising spectacularly in value. And with no laws in place to create new rent-controlled dwellings, the supply was constantly shrinking.

Now that she was relaxed, and warming to her topic, she was happy to answer Joe's questions and gossip about the neighbors, like grumpy General Mtume who walked around in his uniform, or the loud Russian, Mr. Volkov, who smoked cigars in the elevator, and whose young blonde wife would sneak out to visit the tough-looking Colombian downstairs, Mr. Lopez. She saw everything, but no one noticed her. She was like a ghost.

"My mom grew up in this building, when it was really cool and there was like a queer club in the basement." She smiled now, feeling proud, and the last of her wariness faded. "My grandpa was a reporter, and my grandma was a social worker. Back then there were whole swarms of kids. People didn't even lock their apartment doors because everyone on the floor knew each other. They went everywhere, up to the towers, down in the basement. They even rode the dumbwaiters, though that's super dangerous." She held up the empty can. "Anyway, I'm done watering. What should I do now?"

"Whatever you usually do."

Joe assumed she would want to go home and was pretty much ready to trust her discretion, as she was clearly no friend of the local authorities, but she pointed at the massive flat screen TV. "I usually play video games. If you don't mind."

Surprised, Joe held out a palm. "Be my guest."

She sat on the couch and reached for a remote. "I'm Sarah, by the way."

Joe settled in an overstuffed chair. "Nice to meet you, Sarah. I'm Joe."

"I know," she said, pointing to the patch on his uniform, and smiled. Then she picked up the game controller and began.

◆

Joe watched Sarah play. As far as he could see, it was a war game set in some kind of dystopian city, but mostly it was mayhem, with her sending her avatar—a cartoon-muscled woman in oddly tight-fitting body armor, boots, and gloves, but no helmet, hair flying free—as she sprinted and somersaulted through a wrecked city, blowing other fighters away.

"So how do you win this?" he asked.

"Last one standing," she said, eyes on the screen, as she shot off a big dude's arms, which, Joe noted, was not likely to happen so easily, though he admitted the animation was terrific. Having cleared the scene, her avatar pumped her fist, and a chorus of cheers went up along with a stream of emojis—thumbs-up, stars, a foot kicking an ass. Sarah pushed her hair, her real hair, back from her face and proceeded into another virtual building. "My mission right now," she went on, "is to find and steal this truck full of gold, but there are some great players on tonight, so who knows?"

"What do you mean?" Joe asked. "Aren't they on every time? They're cartoons."

She looked at him as if he were the one from another world. "These are real people."

"Define real."

"Actual humans playing the game with me, all over the world. Each one of those cartoons has a person controlling it like me."

"Wow." Joe was amazed. "And you don't know who these other kids are?"

"Some you do. Like they're from school. But it could be anybody, not just kids." As the action started up again, she nodded at an avatar of a hulk in torn fatigues and a helmet. "Like that guy is actually a forty-year-old banker from China. He plays at work."

She shot his foot off and his avatar screamed. "It's called *Call to Glory*. You really never heard of it? You never played a game?"

"Not really." He remembered seeing his pal Juno play one, and getting Joe to try it for a minute, but it seemed old-fashioned compared to this. "I watched a friend play once."

"We've got watchers too," Sarah told him. "Five hundred and twenty-two right now." Joe noticed the number in the corner, along with the stream of emojis and comments, like: *Kill 'em all Slaygirl!*

"So that's like an audience?"

"Yeah, there's this app that lets people watch you play, and they can sign up to be like your fans, send gifts and money and stuff. That's my account. I'm Slaygirl."

"So this is your job?" Joe asked, incredulous. She shot off the Chinese banker's right arm, which held his weapon, and he shook his left fist at her, till she blew his head off. "Does your Mom know?"

Sarah shrugged. "She's probably asleep by now."

"Right," Joe said, recalling the wine, as he watched Sarah, or Slaygirl, he supposed, work her way across the interior of a bombed-out warehouse, hiding behind debris. "You know," he commented, "it's impressive how you keep blowing limbs off, but it's more efficient to just take them down with a body shot, then finish them off with a head shot, or a second shot through the heart."

"Double-tap," she noted, solemnly. "True that." She glanced at him. "I thought you didn't play?"

Joe shrugged. "I read a lot."

She took his advice, wiping out, she told him, a married mom from New Jersey, a teenage boy from London, and numerous strangers, before she made it to the next chamber, where she found the truck. "Awesome!" she yelled, really seeming like a kid now, and hopped in the truck. Her avatar put it in gear and took off, plowing through the door. Joe watched in amazement as she navigated the streets, shooting out the window with one hand. He'd played driving games as a kid, in arcades, but they had actual steering wheels and pedals. This was entirely virtual yet uncannily realistic. Then again, he'd also stolen a real car at fourteen.

"Can I ask you something, or will it distract you from your driving?"

"Go ahead," she told him, eyes on the screen.

"Do you know an older guy, long gray hair, who lives here? Maybe up in one of those towers? Maybe smoking weed in a wizard robe?"

"Oh sure," she said. "Lucifer."

"Lucifer?"

"Lucifer Jones." She frowned at him. "Lead singer from the Wizards? The heavy-metal band?" She rolled her eyes. "They're from your era. So you never heard of Lucy Jones or played a game?"

"I guess I lead a quiet life. So he has a place here?"

"He never leaves. He owns three apartments, one's just got, like, instruments in it, you know, like a piano in the living room, a drum kit in the bedroom. Another one has his occult stuff, bones and altars and weird old books. A moon rock. He's a recluse." She shook her head. "I thought everybody knew that. Tourists come try to take his picture. I mean old ones, like you. No offense."

"None taken." He was actually relieved. Someone named Lucifer who smoked weed in his magical robe seemed unlikely to call the cops. "I was just wondering. Thought maybe the place was haunted."

"Oh it is," she answered, matter-of-factly. "There's all kinds of ghosts and spirits. The pipes bang and the wind gets in the hallways. But you hear voices and see things too. We're used to it."

"Oh yeah?" Joe asked, trying to be polite but unable to hide his doubt. She picked up on it and got serious, jaw set.

"Just tonight, for example, when we were eating dinner, we both felt a presence. Mom even said she saw a shadow pass outside the window. It's a spiritual emanation. Totally harmless. But real."

"I see," Joe said, chastened. "That does sound pretty real."

"My Mom told me about seeing them in the basement when she was a kid," Sarah went on, warming to her subject now, "and showed me secret passages where the servants used to bring in the coal and firewood and stuff. They're mostly sealed off now like the dumbwaiters, but you can still get to them if you know how."

"Oh yeah?" Joe perked up, looking from the screen to focus on the real person. "Tell me more about that."

◆

Joe got into the dumbwaiter.

He was leery, but after hearing her describe the building's security measures—cameras in the halls and elevators and guards around the clock—he decided it was the best way to at least get downstairs. The problem was where downstairs, exactly, he'd end up. The dumb-waiters went back to a time when the residents had servants who lived and partly worked in the basement, sending food and other items up via a miniature elevator. In some buildings they had been transformed into cupboards, but here, since they opened onto the service stair landing, they'd simply been sealed, disappearing from memory under a few dozen coats of paint. But the basement, too, had evolved. Once there were stables, coal bins, and sleeping servants. Then they built a *shvitz*, complete with saunas and a pool. Now there was also a gym, building facilities, offices, and storage. And security.

Sarah showed him the dumbwaiter access, just by the door where he'd seen the stacked papers. It was hidden under paint and behind a coat rack, and it would be a tight fit, but if he crawled in sideways it looked just wide enough to clear his shoulders. He rummaged in the kitchen. He'd been hoping to find tools but ended up using the sharp knife to scrape the paint away from the edges of the door, then a duller, flat knife and a meat tenderizer to pry off the nails that had sealed it. Once it was loose, he yanked hard, and it came free with a whine from the old hinges. He peeked inside. It was dark.

"I wish I had a flashlight," he commented.

"Use the one on your phone," Sarah suggested. Joe showed her his flip phone, ignoring the many missed calls and texts from Gio.

"God you really are like a time traveler from the past," she said.

"Maybe I'm a spiritual emanation," he suggested. She rolled her eyes.

"Hardy har har."

The narrow shaft contained a metal cable, which attached to a pulley up top. Joe yanked and the long-sleeping cable also complained at first, but eventually a box emerged from below. Except for being completely covered in dust, it all seemed to work, more or less.

"All aboard," Sarah said, urging him on.

"One second," Joe said. Noticing two expensive bikes parked down the hall, he ran over and got one of the helmets. He strapped it on, handing Sarah the cap he'd been wearing. "Here you go, a memento." He tucked the mallet and knives into his back pockets. Finally, he lowered the dumbwaiter until the roof of it met the bottom of the opening and climbed on. Squeezing and scraping, he managed to wriggle to his feet, standing on top of the box. He slowly lowered himself, until he could look out and see her. She was grinning.

"Wow this is awesome. I wish I could tell my mom."

"I'd appreciate it if you didn't," he said.

"Don't worry. I can keep a secret," Sarah said. "Take care, Joe."
She waved.

"So long, Slaygirl," he called back, as he lowered himself down the
shaft. He saw her above him, peering down into the shaft and watching.
Then she shut the door and he was sealed in darkness.

◆

The cable was tough on his hands. He was actually grateful for the
coating of grease that provided some small protection against the
blistering friction. And the dust was incredible. Each pull of the cords
triggered a little cloud fall of particles, but the entire shaft was also
caked with a thick layer of dust like the velvet lining of a jacket, and
whenever he brushed the sides, he was instantly covered. After about
fifteen very long, dark minutes, he was filthy, tired, sneezing, and
coughing, with aching hands, and, he thought, finally at the bottom,
as the box bumped ground beneath him and stopped.

Feeling around the shaft, he located the door and, by touch, found
where it had been nailed shut, ages ago. The box itself, on which he
stood, had come to rest about thirty inches beneath the bottom door,
which was now at about chest height for Joe. Crouching, he got out
the mallet and knife and pried open the door. The nails were rusty and
bent and after a few stubborn minutes, they broke away. Joe listened
for a moment and, hearing nothing, pushed the door back on its stiff
hinges and peeked out. He was in the basement, he surmised from the
concrete floor and ceiling, and the row of caged bulbs. This seemed to
be the building's waste management area, with several large, heaped

trash containers on wheels and piles of cardboard, plastic, and other recyclables against the wall. There were no cameras here—they weren't worried about anyone stealing the garbage. He closed the door to the dumbwaiter behind him, pushing a couple nailheads back in to hold it loosely shut.

The good news was that he was, for the moment, safe. But he was also stuck. The door to the stairs was alarmed, the metal rolling gate over the entrance, up a ramp, was locked. He had no cell signal. A wave of frustration passed through him, an urge to scream, curse, and turn a container over in a tantrum, but that was useless, possibly dangerous, and he had learned to control such impulses. He found a spot in the recycling corner, relatively hidden but as far as possible from the wafting reek of the garbage, sat with his back against the wall, and waited for something to happen.

11

Donna loved the ballet. She and Evon, as she now thought of him, sat in front, at the edge of the small private balcony that hung from the wall like fruit on a branch, poised over the orchestra below, with Andy and the bodyguards behind them and the other agents outside the door or taking tours of the hall and lobby. She'd always wanted to sit in seats like this, though in her fantasy she was wearing a backless gown.

"I feel a bit underdressed," she said as the usher showed them to their seats.

"Not at all," Evon answered gallantly. "You're in a black suit like me." In fact his was much nicer than hers, clearly custom-made of cashmere to fit him perfectly. He leaned in and whispered. "And it hides your weapon much better than those ladies' silly dresses." She laughed, dazzled by the lights and the height and the sumptuous decor.

"Although, perhaps . . ." he added, thoughtfully, then changed his mind. "No. Never mind."

"No," she touched him reflexively, playfully poking his arm. "What? Tell me?"

"Well . . ." he grinned mischievously. "I wouldn't want you to break any regulations, but I did think that you'd blend in better if perhaps, your hair . . ."

"Oh, right. . . ." she said, and reaching back, undid her ponytail. Her shining black tresses tumbled past her shoulders. She shook them out. "Better?" she asked.

He smiled. "Perfect."

She smiled too, as the lights dimmed.

◆

The first act was terrific, the premier of a new piece for the company. Then, during intermission, Andy checked the restroom before allowing Evon and his bodyguards to go in.

"Sure," he complained to Donna as they waited in the lobby, surrounded by patrons sipping drinks and chatting. "You're falling in love, and I'm turning into a men's room attendant."

"I'm not in love," she scoffed. "It's the job."

"Whatever, just let me know if you want me to call in a death threat. Then you'll have a reason to guard him all night."

She rolled her eyes as Evon returned, followed by his bodyguards, one of whom held a tray filled with sparkling flutes of Champagne. "Shall we toast to a magnificent evening, so far?" he asked.

"I shouldn't," Donna demurred.

"I will, thanks," Andy said and took a flute.

Evon chuckled. "Well done, Agent Newton." He held one out to Donna. "And you? Don't you need to check? What if it's poisoned?"

"Well," Donna said. "Maybe just a sip to make sure."

12

It took about an hour for something to happen. Joe was just beginning to accept that maybe nothing would happen till morning, when the day shift of building workers came in, and thinking about how to bed down, homeless style, on a nest of cardboard and newspaper, when a buzzer by the gate began to sound. While Joe crouched low and watched, the gate went up. Two guys in work clothes entered and began dragging the closest full container up the ramp. It was time for the garbage pickup and, seeing no other way out, Joe took a deep breath and crept over the side of the rearmost container, landing with a plop onto a pile of bags that were comfortably cushioning, until you inhaled, or thought about what was inside them that might be so soft. Trying not to think about that, he burrowed down, pulling a couple bags over his torso to hide himself better. One burst of course, and old bread, loose salad and pasta, coffee grounds, lemon peel, and, most notably, some diapers spilled out. He tried to focus on the lemon and hold still as he felt the container move, rubber wheels squealing on the concrete as the two men chatted and laughed, then huffed harder as they headed up the ramp.

"Here is good," he heard one guy say, panting slightly. "Let's get the next one." Joe heard them go and from the shift in sounds and temperature he knew he was outside. There was traffic, wind, and most significantly, the sound of a big truck idling. Carefully, he peeked over the edge of the container.

He was indeed on the sidewalk, near the corner of Central Park West, his container parked by another at the top of the ramp. On the corner, by the main entrance to the building, there stood a security guard, presumably watching while lazily checking his phone. And in the street was the truck into which the two men were unloading the trash. That was the problem.

There were, basically, two kinds of trucks it could be. One, the kind Joe hoped for, had a mechanism that would hoist the container, lift it over the high side of the truck, and tip it over, providing Joe with a stinky but safe and discreet ride to freedom. The second truck, the kind Joe feared, had a kind of maw in the back into which the container was emptied, which would grind up the trash as it fed into the belly of the beast. That's where Joe was headed if he didn't make a move. So he moved.

Joe knew there was zero chance of waltzing away unobserved, so he opted for surprise instead. Bracing himself, he climbed up onto the edge of the container, sneaker soles balanced for a moment on the lip, and then jumped, vaulting himself onto the sidewalk.

"Holy shit!" he heard one of the workers yell, seeing a man leap from the trash. Then the guard called, "Hey!" Dropping his phone—the screen cracked—and grabbing his radio, he shouted into it: "The intruder! He's here! In the garbage!" Then he pulled his gun.

As the uniformed doorman came out, also holding a pistol, Joe dashed madly across the street, ran across the sidewalk, jumped onto a bench and then over the concrete wall into the park, dropping down the other side just as a bullet clipped the top of the barrier.

Joe was surprised, and a little impressed, that they had taken a shot at him. It was most likely done out of panic, but it also reinforced his sense that there was something very strange about this building, a sense that grew as he glanced back to see the two men come over the wall in pursuit, as if Joe were a poacher in a private reserve. Meanwhile, two more guards came in through the park entrance at the end of the block, their flashlights scanning side to side. Joe broke into a run, heading for the nearest cover. Clearly, this was not your average co-op.

He ran full tilt, dodging trees and benches and lampposts, and before he had time to realize quite where he was, he came upon a fence, and a dazzling expanse of moonlit water spread before him like liquid glass, a window set in the greenery, mirroring the sky. This was the reservoir named for Jacqueline Kennedy Onassis, that great lover of the park. Joe turned right, following the path, and found himself in company, one of a line of late joggers strung along the edge of the water.

At first, he passed everybody. He had fear and adrenaline on his side. But as his energy flagged, he slowed his pace and fell into line.

Glancing back over his shoulder, he tried to fade into the scenery, jogging alongside two women in elaborate gear: spandex leggings and tops, belts with water bottles, iPhones strapped to their arms. At first they seemed not to notice him, staring straight ahead, ponytails bobbing, pods in their ears. Then one woman gave him a sidelong glance, frowning as she noticed his odd get up: a filthy janitor's uniform and Converse high-tops, ridiculous beside her own high-tech running shoes. She nudged her friend, who also looked Joe up and down. He smiled and gave a little wave. Like skittish deer scenting a muddy possum, both women immediately took off, bounding ahead of Joe and leaving him loping along in their dust. Suddenly exposed, he was caught in the beam of a flashlight.

"Hey you, hold it right there," a voice shouted. "Stop or we'll shoot."

Joe dropped to the ground and rolled into the bushes, too low to be seen by the lights, which now waved above him, like a spotlight on a stage, rippling out over the water. He crawled down the embankment, moving at a diagonal, then dashed over the path and crossed the Eighty-Sixth Street traverse, heading for the Great Lawn and, hopefully, an exit.

He would have made it too, except for the dog. It was a hound of some sort, big boned and rust-colored, with floppy ears and, Joe had no doubt, friendly intentions, but as he ran past the absent-minded owner, an older lady with a purse and a cane, the dog bolted, breaking loose and dragging her leash. She took off after Joe like he was the world's biggest rabbit, barking joyously.

"Go away! Sit! Heel!" Joe muttered, trying every command he could remember, as the dog happily nipped his heels. "Fuck off!"

The light swung their way. "There he is," a voice yelled. "Get him."

Then the old lady's voice joined in, as she waved her stick: "Ruby, come here. Good girl. Ruby!"

Joe had no choice. He broke into a cross-country sprint, with the dog at his heels and armed men in pursuit, like an old chain-gang movie. The moon rose above the open field and the flashlights came bobbing up behind him, casting their lights over the land. Unfortunately for him, it was a beautiful, clear night. With the dog yapping gleefully, now running beside him, a companion more than a hunter, he streaked across a softball field and, chest ready to explode, stumbled over the path that bordered the meadow and into the brush around the Turtle Pond, where he was soon knee-deep in murky water and mercifully hidden. He waded along the edge of the pond, sticking to the cover of the dense foliage, the dog eagerly following along the shore, and finally sloshed out on the south side, scuttling up a hill to the shelter of Belvedere Castle.

A Gothic-Romanesque folly, the castle was sealed for the night, but in its crannies and steps and the weird shadows thrown by the lights that beamed up at its towers, Joe found a safe place to hide and at least catch his breath. He sat on the ground, back against the stone wall, and the dog licked his face, then plopped down, panting beside him.

"Good girl," he whispered, stroking her back, hoping to keep her quiet. He was exhausted, filthy, and soaking wet from the knees down. His socks felt like sponges. He could hear the guards now too, stomping through the bushes, talking to each other over their radios. And then, faintly, he heard the old lady, calling "Ruby." Ruby, with her sharper hearing, jumped up immediately and, tail wagging, ran off. The sound of her rustling drew the attention of his pursuers, and Joe realized this was his chance to move.

Crouching low, he scurried along in the shadows, heading south. He still had the knife and held it point down as he ran, but he did not want to use it unless absolutely necessary. Hearing an approaching sound, he ducked behind a tree, only to recognize the distinctive clip-clop of one of those horse-drawn carriages making its way through the park. Seeing an opportunity, Joe squatted beside the tree, until the carriage came into view. It was black and open-roofed, with high spoked wheels and the driver in an old-fashioned top hat sitting behind a white horse. The carriage rolled slowly, at walking pace, along a lamplit path; as it passed, Joe ran swiftly and quietly alongside it and then, pulling the door back, hopped on board. Before the young blond couple holding hands on the back seat could react, he was sitting in the seat across from them, pointing the knife with casual menace.

"Good evening," Joe said. "And welcome to New York City."

They stared. "Thank you," the boy finally said.

"We are from Berlin, Germany," the girl added. She wore a denim jumpsuit under a ski jacket. Her hair was long and loose, under a wild hat that looked kind of like a WWI pilot's cap made of pink felt. The boy had hair that flopped over one eye, stylish glasses, and a bulky wool jacket that hung down over his jeans.

"Hey what the hell you doing back there, asshole," the driver called over his shoulder. Despite the Victorian getup, he was clearly from New York.

"Take it easy," Joe said, showing his knife. "Just hitching a ride. No one will get hurt as long as everybody stays calm." He smiled at the couple. "You don't mind, do you? You're going to have a real New York story to tell."

The driver grumbled but carried on as Joe spotted his pursuers, passing in the other direction. The couple chatted excitedly to each other in German but did not seem too afraid.

"Can we take your picture?" the boy asked, pulling out his phone. "I am a food blogger doing a story on the pizza."

"And I design hats," the girl added.

"Sorry no pictures," Joe said. "I'm a bandit after all. But for pizza, I recommend Joe's on Sixth and Bleecker. It's not fancy but it's a great regular slice."

The boy nodded and tapped at his phone.

"Did you make that hat?" Joe asked the girl. "It's really cool."

She blushed. "Yes. Thank you very much."

Things were going so well that Joe considered just riding with them all the way down to Central Park South, where the carriages parked, but then he saw one of the guards, standing down the road, talking to another carriage, and no doubt asking if they'd seen him.

"Don't worry," the boy said, seeing Joe's concern. "We won't tell the police."

The girl agreed, shaking her head.

"You know what? That's a very good idea," Joe said, thoughtfully. He smiled at the couple. "This is where I get off, I'm afraid," he told them, then reached into his pocket and pulled out a few crumpled twenties. He tucked them into the driver's hatband. "For your trouble, and your silence," he said, and then bowed to the couple. "Nice to meet you and thank you for your kindness." He waved as he hopped off. "Have a safe trip!" And they waved back as he darted into the Ramble.

◆

The police, Joe thought as he hid in the trees. *Why didn't they call the police?* He'd been so focused on escaping and surviving that he hadn't stopped to wonder where the cops were. That was what the average citizen would do after discovering a burglar at home, and the rich were especially prone to see, and to use, the police as an extension of their private security force. But there was one class that never called the law, no matter what: Joe's own kind, the criminals. Or perhaps, to broaden it a bit, the outlaws, those who, whether they pursued crime as a profession or not, lived beyond the boundaries of the social code and avoided the code's keepers. Like here, in the Ramble. This overgrown patch of wilderness within the manicured park was once a notorious cruising site, hosting generations of gay hookups. Times had changed of course, and fewer men had need of recourse to such haunts, but it still drew some—married men perhaps, or those craving anonymous encounters. Joe could detect a few now, shadowy figures like him, flitting along the dark paths. He knew he was safe; no way would they call 911. But the millionaires back at the Eleonora, and their servants and guards. What were they afraid of?

Joe leaned against a tree and, making sure he was out of sight and hearing, got out his own phone, and finally returned one of Gio's missed calls. He picked up on the first ring.

"Please tell me you're on the way to Alonzo's with that fucking pigeon."

"Sorry," Joe said, voice low. "But I don't have time to explain. I'm actually calling for help. I've got a situation here."

"Okay," Gio said, calm now. "What do you need?"

"That cop. The detective you own. Any chance of reaching him quickly?"

13

Fusco and Chang were sitting contentedly in the warm car, listening to the crackle of the police radio, and digesting their burgers and the double portion of curly fries and onion rings they'd decided to add. Mellow after feasting, and with the easy intimacy that grows during long hours spent sitting in dark cars, staring straight ahead at illegally parked luxury vehicles, Fusco had grown loquacious.

"It's not that I'm not open to it," he said, sipping thoughtfully on the remains of a large Diet Coke and drawing deep on his cigarette. Smoking was forbidden in department cars of course, but Chang said she didn't mind, something else that won Fusco's admiration. This kid was all right. "But with three ex-wives and four kids, I can't afford any more mistakes."

Detective Chang nodded. "I know exactly what you mean," she said, thinking he meant emotionally, when in fact he was referring to his crippling child-support and alimony. She mused on the passing traffic. "That's why I'm poly."

"Who?" Fusco asked. "I thought you said you were Ellen?"

"No, I mean polyamorous, where you maintain relationships with multiple partners. I don't believe in monogamy."

"Really?" Fusco asked, intrigued, belching softly. "Is that what that means? I thought it was a type of gay."

She laughed. "It can be. I mean, I'm bi too, but it doesn't need to be."

"Fascinating," Fusco said. "I should write that down." He wanted to be able to say it himself, in case a future girlfriend brought up marriage, but didn't want to misspeak and accidentally call himself the wrong one.

"Committed exclusive long-term things never really work out, do they?"

"Exactly!" He tapped his chest with his straw. "Look at me."

"People change, evolve. They have different needs that no one person can really supply."

"That is so true," Fusco said. His third wife had definitely fulfilled needs that his second couldn't, which was the reason for the overlap, but then as it happened, neither understood his need to disappear to Atlantic City for days at a time.

"And more and more," Chang went on, "I think I really identify as demisexual, maybe even with some asexual tendencies."

"Huh?"

"You know, I prefer the emotional connection sometimes, without the physical part."

Now he turned to look at her seriously. "So you mean you want to be free to *not* have sex with a number of different people?"

She smiled. "I guess so."

"Well Chang, isn't that what they call friends? Isn't that what we're doing now?"

Laughing, she punched him lightly on the arm. "And it's pretty good, too, am I right?"

He grinned. "Best I've had in ages." Then his phone rang, the private one, the burner and, knowing who it was, he frowned and sat up straight as he answered.

"Yes?"

He listened, glancing over at Chang and shifting uncomfortably. Already his secrets were affecting his new relationship.

"But I'm on a stakeout. . . ."

He turned away from Chang's curious stare, and she began to wonder if this was one of the ex-wives or traumatized kids.

"Okay," he said, softly. "I get it. I understand."

◆

"I don't get it," Chang was saying. "I don't understand."

"What's not to understand? I've got a lead on our case."

"So why don't we just drive over there together, if it's so urgent?"

"Because I told you, this informant is very deep inside, very squirrely, and won't talk to anyone but me."

"Deep inside the car-vandalizing scene?" Chang asked, doubtfully. "Look, we're partners. I know you're the senior partner, but still there is a basic trust and commitment there."

Fusco took a last deep drag off his smoke and tossed it out the window. "You're right. We are partners, Chang," he told her. "But just think of this as a poly thing."

◆

Finally, Fusco managed to talk Chang into taking a walk around the sector targeted in the attacks while he took the car to meet his supposedly secret source. He waited a couple blocks before he hit the siren. There were not many things Fusco was truly scared of, but Gio Caprisi was one. He'd said this was an emergency, and it made Fusco nervous about what would happen if he didn't get there in time. He was even more nervous about what would happen when he did.

He pushed through traffic, cutting lights, and entered the park on Seventy-Ninth Street, then proceeded as instructed to the route that took him along the Ramble, cruising slow with his siren whining and his lights flashing. After a few minutes, a figure stepped from the shadows, hands raised in surrender. It was Joe.

Fusco didn't know Joe Brody, but he knew who he was. He knew he was a bouncer at a club Gio controlled, that the two were friends, and that once or twice he'd been asked to help divert police attention away from him. He also knew Joe had an extremely unusual set of talents that he used to carry out highly secret missions for the underworld's top bosses. And that was all he wanted to know.

And now, this major criminal whom he, as a major crimes detective, had avoided knowing, was standing in his headlights, hands up, apparently surrendering himself to his custody. It made him very nervous. In fact, he wanted to light a cigarette, but he knew how Gio felt about smoking in the car and worried Joe might feel the same. So he silenced the siren, rolled the window down, and said, "Hi."

◆

Detective Ellen Chang was annoyed. She'd heard all about Fusco and knew that most of the younger detectives considered him a dinosaur. But she liked dinosaurs, as long as they weren't raptors, trying to dig their filthy claws into younger females. Fusco was definitely more of a brontosaurus, chewing his slop and burping, or maybe even a woolly mammoth. The truth was, despite sharing many of her generation's deeply progressive views on law enforcement policy, she also knew, as a member of an immigrant, minority, working-class community, how much they needed the police. To her, that was the problem: not only were they subject to mistreatment by the authorities, they were also deprived of the protection of the law. That was, in large part, why she'd become a cop.

On the other hand, she also knew, growing up on the city streets, that reality was often more complex than theory. During her rookie year, her first partner had been a hulking older white guy, much like Fusco, with a buzzed haircut and a roll of pink flesh over his collar, and during their first week, they were called to a domestic disturbance in the projects. Neighbors had heard screaming and crashing, and they'd entered the filthy apartment to see a young man choking the life out of an old lady. Chang's partner had grabbed the guy from behind and slammed him to the floor. Later it came out that he was mentally ill and the elderly woman was his grandmother. His shoulder was injured, and he sued.

Now, should it have been social workers, medics, and a psychiatrist who went through the door, rather than a big Irish goon who barely made it through high school? Perhaps. But then again, would they have had the necessary muscle? In a better world, Chang believed, the situation would never have happened: the young man would have had the proper mental health care, the old lady would have been in an assisted-living facility, and nobody would be living in that rathole in the projects. But it wasn't a better world, and when her partner fudged the report a little, to make it seem like the crazy grandson had fought back harder, posed more of a threat to their own safety, she went along with it. She understood.

That's why she was fine working with Fusco, who'd put away more actual bad guys than anyone she'd personally worked with ever, and why, if he had some personal errand to run, if he needed to meet his ex-wife or his kid, or smoke a cigarette, or if he needed to take a crap, she was fine with that too. But she wasn't fine with being left out in the chilly air to wander the streets alone like a dumbass rookie back on the beat. "Goddamn you, Fartso," she was muttering to herself, for the first time calling him what everyone else called him behind his back, when she heard something that snapped her back to reality: she heard shattering glass and then a car alarm.

14

When Joe heard the approaching siren, he began to make his way out of the Ramble. He felt confident that his pursuers did not want to tangle with the police, but not totally confident that they wouldn't try a shot, so he stayed hidden, watching as their flashlights cut through the trees. When he saw the unmarked police car, a black Impala with lights playing on its grill and in its rear window, he moved quickly, tossing his knife into the darkness, and stepped right out into the glare of the headlights, hands up. The car pulled up and Fusco rolled down the window and said "Hi."

"Hey," Joe said. "Thanks for coming, Detective."

"What seems to be the trouble?" Fusco asked, stepping out now, a little reluctantly it seemed, and tucking in his shirt as he looked around. A small crowd had gathered—a couple dog walkers, a late jogger, and a couple holding hands—though past that were two men in security guard uniforms, holding flashlights.

"I was in fear for my safety," Joe explained. "So I called the police."

"I see," Fusco said, not sure what that meant exactly. He certainly looked like something had happened to him: he was filthy, in wet sneakers, mud covering him from the waist down and wearing a torn janitorial shirt with a name tag that read, absurdly, "Joe." Fusco turned to the guards, who were now edging back, trying to fade. "And what about you two? Can you tell me what's going on?"

One shook his head and the other shrugged. Then the one who shook his head, seeing that his partner had shrugged, tried to explain. "Sorry, sir. We were looking for a lost pet."

Fusco could see that both men wore sidearms. "What is it, a pet tiger?" he asked, while Joe looked on with interest.

"We had a break-in," the shrugger explained. "Perp took off into the park. We pursued on foot but lost him."

Interest aroused, Fusco looked this guy over: hair high and tight, trimmed stash, chunky watch. "You on the job?" he asked.

"Used to be," he said. "Nassau County."

"I see," Fusco said, checking out his partner. This guy was seriously yoked, with the kind of muscle that took hours a day to keep, a goatee, and homemade tattoos peeking from under his cuffs and collar. Definitely not a cop—he avoided eye contact with Fusco, out of habit—so, probably, a con. An odd couple indeed. "A robbery and a runaway pet," Fusco mused aloud. "Busy night. Funny that no one called it in."

The ex-cop shrugged. "We didn't want to bug you guys."

"Any suspects?" Fusco asked.

Now neither man could resist glancing at Joe, who looked back, curiously. This time they both shook their heads. Just then they heard barking, and a dog appeared in the distance. A woman trailed after it, yelling "Ruby!"

Fusco smiled. "Looks like you've got a lead on this lost pet at least."

The guards nodded, sheepishly, and gave Joe a last look. He smiled and waved. "Goodnight," he said. They didn't answer.

◆

Joe got in the back of the Impala. He knew the routine, although this time he was uncuffed. Fusco also knew the routine, and while he was relieved to have his dangerous, mysterious, and totally foul passenger at a distance, he felt more like a chauffeur than a cop. "Where to?" he asked, pulling away.

"E train at Fifty-Third would be great actually," Joe said, as if accepting a lift from a pal.

And that was what Fusco did. They drove in silence until Fusco pulled up by the subway entrance, and Joe said, "Thanks," as he got out, and Fusco called back, "Good night." Then, finally, he answered his own partner, who'd been frantically hitting his phone and radio the whole time.

◆

When Chang heard the glass shatter, she jumped, and when she heard the alarm, she ran toward it, coming around the corner just as a figure in black, hood up with a black ski mask and black gloves, ran around the far corner, clutching a ball-peen hammer. She broke into a flat-out sprint, and she was fast, probably faster than him in a fair race. Even though she gained on him, he had too much of a head start, and after a mad dash across a couple long avenue blocks he hopped the wall into the park and vanished. She called it in, alerting patrol as well as her damned partner, and scouted along the edge of the park, but she knew it was hopeless and headed back to the scene to write it up. Another high-end car, this time a huge BMW 700 series with diplomatic plates. Both right-hand tires were slashed, the passenger side window was shattered, and scratched into the paint, again, was the mark of the vigilante: PARKING PIG. The car was in a bus stop too, blocking access, she noted. While she caught her breath and waited for backup, a bus came by, and had to stop in the roadway, blocking all the cars behind it. The truth was, though she fully intended to put the cuffs on this guy, part of her wanted to shake his hand too.

◆

Donna got in the limo.

"Do you mind if we circle through the park?" Evon asked, when they were settled in the back, with his bodyguard and driver in front and Andy with the others in another car that went on ahead. His hotel was on Central Park South.

"You're the boss," Donna said. "Your wish is our command."

"If only that were true, Agent Zamora," he said wistfully, as they headed across town and entered the park. "Take your time, please," he told the driver.

"Yes, sir," the driver said, slowing as they floated past the dark trees and sleeping hills.

He turned to her. "Did you like the ballet, Donna?"

"I loved it."

"The second half moved me especially. The new piece was great, but for me, the New York City Ballet will always mean Balanchine."

She smiled. "Well, I don't know much about it, but it was beautiful."

"Good. It was kind of you to join me." Then they fell silent and gazed out at the park, which displayed its mix of romance and reality. Lovers strolled, trees shook in the wind, a horse drawn carriage clopped by, lit by the old-fashioned lamps. But then, beyond that a car alarm blared, a siren drew closer.

"No matter what anyone says, there is still no place like New York," Evon commented thoughtfully, as if talking to himself. "I think I'm going to love living here," he added, turning to her in the dark. She smiled back, eyes on his, as an unmarked cop car rolled by, lights flashing.

◆

Joe went down into the subway.

It was late, he was exhausted, and now that his adrenaline was wearing off, he realized how very sore his body was going to be tomorrow, not to mention his pride. *What the hell*, he wondered, limping down the steps in his still soggy sneakers, *was the deal with that building?* Sure there were rich people living in it, even superrich, but even so, in a neighborhood with almost zero crime, unless you counted embezzling and private weed dealers, it just didn't make sense to have a more extreme security system than most banks and more guards than City Hall, armed guards who would actually pursue him off the property. And then, in total contradiction to that, to give up and walk away when the cops showed. It was all very confusing, but two things were clear: they were up to something, and they did not want the law to know.

But for now, Joe had other, more urgent things to worry about, namely Alonzo and Gio and that goddamn pigeon, which he knew he would have to answer for tomorrow. So he swiped in with his MetroCard and got on the train, fully aware of how terrible he looked, covered in mud, smelling like sewage, with his clothes torn and dirt on his face, even twigs and leaves in his hair. He looked and smelled like a homeless bum. No one said anything, of course. This was New York and people minded their own business. They did, however, give Joe a whole half of a subway car to himself, which was fine with him.

PART II

15

lake's day was off to a rough start. There were times when he
thought that perhaps living and working in the same building
was a bad idea, but when that building was the legendary Eleonora, a
magnificent prewar luxury fortress overlooking Central Park, the point
was moot: where else would the CEO of the building's management
company live? He was a king and this was his castle, though he often
felt more like its slave.

For instance, there was his wife, who, he supposed, was the queen,
or at least thought she was. Domenica had been a model, from an
Italian-Polish family living in Brazil when Blake met her in Miami. He
was running a nightclub there, fleeing the cold gray weather and cold
gray people of his own homeland, England, more specifically North
London, since he had hardly seen the rest of it. Fifteen years and two
children later, she was, he had to admit, as svelte and beautiful as ever,

maybe even more so, actually weighing less, and powerlifting more, than before she had the kids. A wonder of nature, people said, though Blake knew all too well that nature had nothing to do with it. It was science, hard labor, and money. There was plastic surgery, of course, fillers and implants and liposuctions and abrasions, a fortune in additions and removals. Then there was the dermatologist, who was almost like a therapist or spiritual advisor combined with a witch doctor, all those burnings and freezings. The nutritionists. The hair people, cutting and coloring, more expensive than a paint job on his Mercedes. (But the Mercedes was fine with being gray.) The body hair people—a crew of Russians—plus an Indian lady just for eyebrows. Exercise was a whole team too: trainer, yoga and Pilates instructors. And that didn't even figure in the clothes and makeup and the stylists and estheticians and cosmetologists, whose titles sounded like the faculty of a university's advanced physics and philosophy departments. But no one would make the mistake of thinking Domenica had a PhD. She was as dumb as a stump, though Blake admitted he had liked that about her when they first met. It didn't even bother him, back then, that she'd never really managed her adopted language. After all, he could barely order a beer in her native language.

It wasn't a sexist thing, either. He placed a low value on brains in general, at least of the bookish sort. He himself had never learned anything useful from a book, which perhaps explained why he had never finished one. Maybe the useful bits were at the end. In his own career, Blake had met some quite sharp characters along the way, and he had indeed studied very hard to get where he was, but none of it had come from reading or any school other than A-level Hard Knocks.

No, the problem was not that neither one of them was good at Scrabble. The problem was that now that Domenica had "retired" from the grueling job of standing around in some designer's fancy clothes and looking good and had devoted herself instead to buying some designer's fancy clothes and spending his money on looking good, she had grown from a bubbly, fun, silly girl, into a mean, demanding, but still rather silly woman.

"The chauffeur, he is sick," was how she greeted him that morning, as soon as he came stumbling out of his room, pulling his dressing gown on and trying to make his way to the kitchen for his morning cuppa.

"Of course he is," Blake mumbled, while waiting for Maria the housekeeper to pour his tea. "Milk first," he muttered as she smiled blankly and poured the milk in after. Another genius. Now he had to go out on the terrace for his morning puff. He was forbidden from smoking in his own house.

His wife followed him, stalking like a panther in her sleek black workout suit, a warrior from the future. "So now someone needs to take the kids to school, and my Pilates instructor is here." She shook her hair haughtily. "So I cannot."

"Of course not," he answered. "Unthinkable."

Then his son came in, holding his school blazer. "Look at this!" he blurted.

Blake looked. "What am I looking at?"

"This!" He pointed to a vague line that ran down the back of a sleeve. "Maria ironed it wrong! I can't wear this! How can I go to school like this?" He started hyperventilating and his eyes filled with tears. Jesus Christ. A twelve-year-old boy. By the time he was that age,

Blake could take a head-butting without a whimper. Okay, maybe a bit of whimper. But he had a bit of bottle—running errands and placing bets for the local faces. Not that he was ever a hard man, never physical aside from the standard pub brawl. He saw early that the real players weren't the thieves in the sharkskin suits, they were the sharks in the pinstriped business suits. Meanwhile, his own son was still scared to take the subway.

And his daughter! She already had a shrink, at the age of ten. She had issues. "What kind of issues could a ten-year-old have, besides the new issue of a Barbie comic?" he demanded when the counselor at the private school the kids both went to first recommended it. Blake was careful to pronounce it, *isss-you*, sounding the sibilant *s*.

"I'll take them in a cab," he said. "Just let me get dressed."

"Cab?" His wife looked disgusted. "They are so filthy!"

"Okay. Order an Uber while I get ready."

Now her eyes narrowed in fury. "I just told you my coach is here! We are already behind schedule!"

"Right." He looked at his son. "Fine. You call the Uber and fetch your sister. I'll put my trousers on. Maria will fix your jacket." He took a long, fortifying sip of tea. "Let's go."

◆

But that was just the beginning. A gentle warm-up to his nightmare of a day, as it happened. Ten minutes later, they were just stepping out of the elevator when he was assaulted by a collection of the building's residents.

"Mr. Blake, I must speak with you immediately." That was Antoine, head staffer and general bumboy of General Mtume who lived in 10D. He was over six feet, thin, and elegant. "The general wants to see you in his office."

"Not till you talk to me first," barked Fernando Alberto Lopez from 8C. He was half Antoine's height and twice his width, but ten times as intimidating. "That *ratero* almost attacked my *tia*. He was in the kitchen with her. That is unacceptable."

"Yes. Quite. I understand, Señor Lopez. Quite unacceptable."

"It's our apartment he was spotted in first." This was Li, who worked for Wing Chow, the Chinese billionaire in 10E. "We think he was after the Picasso."

"Gentlemen, I assure you, the matter is well in hand," Blake said. "Now if you'll just excuse me while I drop my children at school . . ."

"School?" Lopez, who had amassed several hundred million dollars without a grade school diploma, stared at him in amazement. "This is important!"

"I agree," Antoine put in from above. "This matter is of the highest priority."

"Dad," his son whined, "we're gonna be late."

"And I have the Jungian play analyst at nine," his daughter added, clutching her security blanket. Just then the voice of deliverance broke in.

"Good morning, sir." It was Blythe Bronstein, his executive assistant.

"Oh, Blythe, good morning . . ." Blake said, relieved to see a friendly face. Her curvy form, encased in a suit and set on sturdy calves in stylish but sensible shoes, appeared on the edge of the crowd. She bustled in.

"The conference room is ready as you directed," she reported, chirping as if predicting sunny weather. "And the Director of Security is ready to report on the situation."

"Ah, right," Blake said. This was all news to him. "Well done, Blythe, now—"

But she was already a step ahead. She snapped her fingers. "Jerry!" And the doorman trotted over.

"Yes, Ms. Bronstein?"

"There's a car waiting outside. Please escort Mr. Blake's children to school."

"Yes, Ms. Bronstein."

"And come right back."

"Yes, Ms. Bronstein."

"Now hurry along children," Blythe said, smiling warmly. "Franklin don't forget you have the orthodontist after school today. And Thalia, it's cognitive therapy for you this afternoon."

"Okay Blythe," they both burbled, beaming up at her. They loved her, everybody did. As the children followed the doorman obediently out, the other men, raging just a moment ago, happily obeyed as well and trooped toward the conference room at her command: "This way gentlemen, please."

"Thanks for stepping in there," Blake whispered to her now as they crossed the lobby. "I was in a bit of a muddle."

"Not at all," she cooed, patting his arm. "You were unflappable and charming as always. Like James Bond or one of those dukes on *The Crown*. Lord Mountbatten." She smiled. "Cool under pressure. It's in your breeding."

He smiled and chuckled, escorting her by the elbow, then straightened his tie. In reality, his old man had been a bookie, and he descended from a line of pub owners and barmaids. But when he'd first washed up on these shores, choosing Los Angeles for its weather and distance, he'd been amazed to learn that one of his few assets was his accent.

"Pure class," said the woman at the employment agency, which would have surprised the folks back home in Maida Vale. His accent was lower-middle class at best. But to Americans, apparently, they all sounded like bloody Shakespeareans. So he added a bit of fake posh and landed a job as a butler of all things. "You sound like Jeeves," said his boss, a big shot movie producer, who liked having a handsome Englishman in a black suit answer the door and didn't seem to know that the whole joke about Jeeves was that his employer was a simpleton.

But it gave Blake a chance to polish up his manners, and soon he was maître d' at a fancy restaurant in Las Vegas. Then, utilizing his other inherited skill, a fast head for numbers, he got work at the casinos coddling the high rollers. That led to managing an illegal casino in Miami, which led to the nightclub, which was a front, laundering money for his bosses. That's where Blake met Mrs. Blake, of course, and where he discovered his true calling: helping the very wealthy grow even wealthier by sanitizing their ill-gotten gains.

As he watched Blythe's ample bottom move with a businesslike swish into the conference room, he felt a wave of well-being. She was, it goes without saying, his mistress as well as his indispensable assistant. One might think that, if living and working in the same building was a bad idea, then sleeping with your assistant, who also lives and works in the building, is the worst idea ever, but Blythe was a wonder.

His employees feared and respected her. His wife admired and even deferred to her. His spoiled brat kids loved her. And his even brattier, more spoiled clients absolutely adored her. And as for Blake himself, her plush plus-sized body, with its voluptuous curves, thick ankles, and round belly, somehow inflamed his desire in a way that his wife's hard, glittering form never had.

In some ways she was a lot like Blake himself. She was from Forest Hills, Queens, and her dad was a big *macher* in the *shmata* business, which Blake now understood to mean a success in the garment industry. Her father had consorted both with preening, high-strung European designers and kneecap busting gangsters, all the while driving his sweatshop workers to sweat harder, bellowing with a cigar in his mouth, until his heart exploded at sixty-five. Her mother now lived mainly in Florida, which is where Blythe, too, met Blake when she was there on a visit. Like him, she craved the posh life, the world of luxury and power hidden behind the walls of the Eleonora, and had polished her own gleaming exterior to blend in. But underneath it, she was just like him, a plebian shark swimming in warm waters.

◆

"We gave chase and pursued the, um, perpetrator into the park." This was Mickey Person, Blake's Director of Security Operations, on whom nothing was polished but his black shoes. He was in a flashy suit that seemed ready to pop open across his wide chest. He'd said "poip-ah-tray-tah" but that was okay because he was good at his job. He was a thug, street-smart and tough enough to manage a team of thugs. Now he stood beside a monitor that displayed a grainy CCTV image of a guy in a cap with his back to the camera, and reported on last night's break in.

"My team were closing in, and we would have had him too, but the suspect was picked up by a cop. As far as we know, no charges were filed."

"Thank you," Blake said, turning in his swivel chair at the head of table. "Well gentlemen, there you have it. Unfortunately, through no fault of his own, I'm sure you'll agree, Mr. Person's team was unable to capture the intruder. But, otherwise, our system worked. The breach was detected and security was alerted. Building security coordinated with your private staff, the culprit was flushed out, and in the end nothing was taken and no one was hurt. A success."

"My men were hurt," Antoine said.

"And ours," Li added.

"Quite," Blake added. "Well, you know what I mean. Now, if you'll excuse us, I'd like very much to continue overseeing the investigation into this incident."

"Gentlemen?" Blythe asked, rising, and they rose. Hands were firmly shaken all around and, like a snake charmer, she guided them all smoothly out. As soon as the door closed, Blake turned to Person.

"Well Mickey?" He nodded at the screen. "Who the hell is this guy? Do you know him?"

"Sure," Mickey said, sounding like *shaw*, "everybody does. His name is Joe."

"Joe? And what does Joe do? Jewel thief? Art burglar? He's not political, is he? That's all we need."

"Nah," Mickey said. "He's a bouncer."

◆

Mickey Person was a thug from Staten Island and proud of it. He came from a long line of Staten Island thugs on both sides, and everyone he knew growing up was now either a wise guy or a cop, except for those who left to go into the military. When his turn came for a career, Mickey chose collections, strong-arming people into paying their debts. And when Blake needed someone to set up a security force for his very special building, Mickey, with his local knowledge and wide acquaintanceship on both sides of the law, was the perfect choice. It was his idea to exclusively hire ex-cons, ex-cops and ex-soldiers. The Ex-Men he called them, in a semiclever joke that only he still laughed at every time he said it, which was constantly.

"Did you say bouncer?" Blake was asking him now, as they sat chatting while Blythe watched attentively from a corner.

"Yeah, boss," Mickey answered. "At this place Club Rendezvous in Queens, out by the airport."

"So then, pray tell, why aren't you out there beating him senseless until he tells you why he broke in? Or, better yet, why isn't he out with your friends on Staten Island, being fed to the fish or whatever they do?"

Mickey shook his head, earnestly. "Sorry, boss. No can do. He's protected. Everybody knows that."

"Everybody knows what, Mickey? What the hell does everybody but me apparently know?"

So Mickey filled him in, explaining that the bosses of the New York underworld had made Joe their sheriff, a fixer who carried out secret missions on their behalf, giving him free reign and safe passage throughout all their territories, from Washington Heights and the Bronx all the way out to the far reaches of Brooklyn and Queens. Anyone who messed with Joe would have to answer to them. "Sorry, boss," Mickey said, looking genuinely aggrieved. "He's untouchable."

Frustrated, Blake sent him back to work, telling him to at least be on alert, doubling the guards and taking personal charge at night. As soon as they were alone, he turned to Blythe. "What do you think?"

"This is so much worse than I thought," she said, tapping her pen nervously. "A thousand times worse than an art thief. I mean, when you have great wealth, you expect the occasional burglar. That's what insurance is for. But he's no burglar. He does special missions. What if he was here to assassinate one of the residents?"

"You're right, that would be a nightmare."

"Or even worse, what if he's onto, you know, the business? Your business."

Blake didn't like that idea at all. His whole enterprise, the prosperity and safety of not just his residents but himself, was founded as much on secrecy as security. Now some kind of spy had penetrated their sanctum, like a rat in the walls. "Blythe, you know as well I do, that would be the end of everything." He took a deep breath, resolved. "At all costs, I shan't allow that."

She came and sat on his lap. "You're right of course. He has to be eliminated. Snipped in the bud, before he knows too much."

"Yes, but by whom?" Blake asked. "We can't use the Ex-Men. If only there were a way to take care of this that could never be connected to us."

"What we need are outside professionals."

"But you heard Mickey. No gangster in New York is going to touch it."

"Exactly what I was thinking, my love," she said and kissed him softly. "No gangster in New York."

16

Gio's day was off to a rough start.

He woke up to the sound of his wife arguing with his kids. Nora, his fourteen-year-old daughter, had posted a picture online that his wife, Carol, found unacceptable.

"It's a bra, Nora," she explained, loudly, in the hall outside his bedroom.

"It's a top."

"It barely covers your chest."

"So? What if it was a bikini top?"

"I wouldn't let you pose in a bikini either."

"I'm not posing. I'm wearing it."

"This isn't a debate about semantics."

"What's semantics?"

"It has to do with the meaning of words."

"Oh."

"But the point is, I don't want you objectifying yourself online. The world will do that enough. I want you to be a free, self-respecting subject with agency in your life, making mature choices."

"So why can't I choose to post a mature picture in a top?"

"That's not what I meant by mature."

Nora's voice rose to an operatic shriek. "I thought this wasn't about semantics!" And her door slammed, making Gio jump. Next, his own door opened.

"You up?" Carol asked, her face still red.

"I am now."

"Good," Carol said. "There's fresh coffee downstairs."

"Oh, thanks, honey."

"Then you'd better get dressed and take your kids to school because if I have to argue with her anymore, I might just crash the car."

"Right," Gio said, pulling on his robe. "I'm on it."

◆

Gio wasn't really that worried about his daughter. When he imagined the future, he worried more about his son, Jason, who was good-natured but a bit of a lump, more interested in video games than anything in real life, good or bad. Nora was "testing limits," as his wife, a child psychologist, might put it in a calmer moment. She was also smart and tougher than she looked, at least in the soccer and volleyball games that he faithfully attended. They were close. She'd even confided in him about an experience kissing another girl. He'd been flattered that she felt she could trust him and had tried to be nonjudgmental. But the honesty could never go both ways. His own secrets ran far too dark and deep. And how could his son's taste in violent video games possibly compare to the real-life violence Gio grew up around and soon learned to dish out? He lived in two worlds and had to keep secrets in both. However strained Carol was, he had to back her up. It was a truism: the shrink's kid was always screwed up. But what about the gangster's?

So, he showered, dressed, and got them to school, explaining to his son that he had to limit his screen time and play something, anything, in real life, even Dungeons and Dragons, and explaining to his daughter that her mother was just adjusting to her growing up and would unlock her account when she calmed down. Then he called his wife, catching her between clients, and placated her. And then, as if he hadn't already soothed enough anger and calmed enough complaints, he fought the traffic into Queens and then onto the BQE into Brooklyn to meet with Alonzo.

◆

"That looks great," Gio said, though he didn't really mean it. He was standing on the roof of a warehouse with Alonzo and Moishe "Rebbe" Stone. It was a lovely view, or rather it had been, right out over the river to the Chrysler building, like a gleaming sword on a sunny day, but now they just saw the skeleton of a rising, fairly ugly building that would eventually be twenty stories high, blocking the view entirely. All three men had used their influence to get the necessary waivers and variances for that, and the result would be profitable, a generic hulk of loft-style luxury apartments, but it wasn't exactly the Chrysler Building, was it? Rebbe owned the land it was on, and the warehouse from which they viewed it. He'd bought up real estate in Crown Heights, Bedford-Stuyvesant, and other parts of Brooklyn during the rough times, often from the city or from owners about to lose the property for taxes, then sat on it, using the properties as warehouses or parking lots for his trucking and bus companies, and waited, in some cases for decades, until he could cash in. That was Rebbe, always five moves ahead, and that was why Gio's father had respected and trusted him, and why Gio did too. Gio was handling the concrete and the electric on the new building and would have the carting once it was up. And Alonzo had the plumbing and the windows and would have the maintenance. But now he was unhappy.

"Cost of pipe these days," Alonzo was saying, "it's hardly worth it, is all I'm saying."

"So pipe costs a few cents a foot more than it did when we broke ground, is that what you're saying?" Gio asked him. "So does copper wire, so does concrete. Do you know what sand costs?"

Alonzo scoffed. "Sand? You go to the motherfucking beach and help yourself. Call your friend Yelena, she'll sell you a piece of Brighton Beach, by the truckload. I'm talking about pipe, motherfucker. You need to smelt that shit."

The two men were usually good friends, with a lot in common, including taste in clothes. Today both had expensive raincoats on. Underneath, Alonzo wore a blue pinstripe suit, and Gio a gray flannel, both beautifully cut by the same tailor. Rebbe was in black of course, a black suit and coat and the black hat pulled low in the wind.

"Smelt?" Gio muttered now. "All I smelt was bullshit. And what the fuck is going on with my lobsters?"

A couple of Gio's guys had a hookup for fresh seafood, which usually went to Alonzo's restaurants and clubs, among other places, but now a truck full of lobsters was sitting unclaimed and unpaid for. "You know seafood can't wait too long."

Alonzo shrugged. "The chef changed the menu. What can I say? Artistic temperament."

Gio nodded, sagely. "I'll send a couple of my restaurant supply sales reps around with a sample of our meat tenderizing mallets. They'll explain how hard it is to be an artist with two broken hands."

Alonzo snarled. "You send your meatheads to my place, they'll end up in the stew."

"Boys, boys," Rebbe said now, calmly, patting them both on the shoulders. "I've known you both your whole lives. You were always such good friends. Now you argue over silly little problems? For pipe you go to my cousin's nephew. He'll take care of you." He shrugged to Gio. "But I'm afraid he can't take your lobsters. Not kosher."

Alonzo laughed at that. "Sorry to drag you into this, Rebbe. You know how much I respect you. It's just upsetting for me, being on a roof like this. You know it triggers bad feelings."

"You're dizzy?" Rebbe asked. "Sit down."

"No, Rebbe," Gio said and turned to Alonzo. "This is all about your Chinese pigeon isn't it?"

"Maltese!" Alonzo told him. "The guy who stole him is Chinese. Maybe that's why your man fucked it up."

"Sure, now he's my man. When you were pushing me to let you use him, you kept saying he really works for us all."

"What's this *mishegas*?" Rebbe asked. "Did you say pigeon?"

"Look," Gio went on, "the place was like Fort Fucking Knox. Armed guards, cameras everywhere. They chased him through the park for fuck's sake. He barely got out alive. None of which you warned us about. But . . ." he held up a hand. "He did see the bird. He confirmed that it is there and in perfect health. And he will go back, with a better plan to account for these . . ." He waved his hand, searching for the word. "Contingencies."

"When?"

"I have a meeting with him later. I will let you know then."

"Fine," Alonzo said, buttoning up his coat. "I'll be eagerly awaiting your call." And he turned and went. Gio and Rebbe watched him go.

"Jesus Christ," Gio muttered.

"You said it, not me," Rebbe replied. "But go ahead and call him if he can help get this job going."

Gio laughed. "Sorry, Rebbe, all this bullshit is about this pigeon that . . ."

Rebbe waved it off. "Bulls, birds. I don't want to know." He pointed a bony finger. "But handle it. Business comes first, right boychick?" Then he winked. "And speaking of business, I'll call my friend Tariq who manages that place down by the shore." Rebbe patted his back. "He'll buy your lobsters."

Gio grinned. "But they're not kosher. Isn't that a sin?"

Rebbe shrugged. "So is letting them go to waste."

17

"I'm afraid today won't be as much fun as yesterday," Evon said as he sipped his cappuccino. "In fact, it will be rather dreary. I'm dreading it myself."

Donna shrugged. She had actually been looking forward to this assignment this morning, dressing with care, with a long leather coat over her best black suit and her hair down. But she hid her smile behind her latte. "I'm here to work, not have fun. Whatever you are doing today, we are happy to come along." She said *we* on purpose, to include Andy, who sat with the bodyguards at the next table in the café, all feasting on a big breakfast, charged to Evon of course.

Evon chuckled now, patting her hand, just for a second, not crossing the line, but still. "You are very gracious. And very well trained, of course. Pure professionals, the FBI." His eyes wandered over to where

Andy was dunking an almond chocolate croissant into his bowl of café au lait. "But this really is the worst."

Donna frowned at Andy, shaking her head swiftly, then smiled back at Evon. "Are you going to the DMV? The dentist's office?"

"Ha, no, I wish," Evon said, lifting his cup with a sigh. "Apartment hunting."

Donna laughed appreciatively, just as her phone rang. She glanced at it; her daughter, Larissa, was home with the sniffles and her mom was with her. But it was Joe. She clicked a button with a nail and sent him to voice mail. Then she took a deep breath and smiled. "I love looking at apartments," she told Evon. "As long as someone else is buying."

◆

"Sorry about last night. My errand got a little complicated. I have to work again tonight unfortunately. But it sounds like you're pretty busy too. So I guess just call me when you get a chance. Or text. Or whatever. Okay. Hope you're good. Bye." Joe sighed and hung up, then wondered if her phone had recorded his sigh. What did it matter, he asked himself as he dried his hair. He'd shampooed and scrubbed himself head to toe, as if to erase the disastrous night, his muddy uniform clothes tossed in the trash. Donna had talked about "taking space" and now he felt it there, a new space between them, like the cold, dark space between stars. He knew, in his heart, that their connection was real, but he also understood, perhaps not in his heart but somewhere in his gut, that it might not be enough. Feelings were just feelings after all, and in Joe's experience they didn't stand much chance against the brute power of reality. Especially when everything—work, family, society—the whole centrifugal force of life seemed to be hurling them further and further apart. How could the weak gravity of love, of two bodies clinging to each other in the dark, possibly hold them together?

Or maybe he'd just been reading too much Proust. Alexis was right—he did find it strangely soothing, those long sentences lulling him into a trance, transporting him to a kind of alternative reality, which ironically was no less bleak than his own, but somehow lit with beauty. His main complaint was that the book, even just volume one, was so big that he couldn't slip it in a pocket and take it on the train, as was his habit. He'd even considered joining the small discussion group that Alexis, a long-time Proust fanatic, led in the back of the shop. "Just a few Proustians, you know, going through the text together. I provide tea. The members take turns bringing cookies." They read it endlessly, in a cycle that repeated every couple years, though you were free to get on or off anytime. But Joe couldn't make it tonight. He was on at the club. Plus now he had this pigeon problem to deal with.

He sighed again as he finished dressing—clean jeans, a fresh T-shirt, a hoodie—and went into the kitchen, where his grandmother Gladys sat over the crossword.

"Girl troubles?" she asked as he poured himself coffee.

"No," Joe said. "Why are you asking?"

"Just all that sighing." She tapped her pencil. "Must be getting old then, like me. I sigh when I get up in the morning."

"You groan," he said, sitting across from her, taking a deep sip, and restraining the urge to sigh, this time in contentment. "That's different."

"Never mind," she said. "I'll mind my own business."

"Thanks," he said, glancing at the paper, seeing a headline: PARKING AVENGER STRIKES AGAIN.

"I've got better things to think about than your boring life," Gladys added, licking the tip of the pencil. "Like for instance, what's a six-letter word, often stirs the pot?"

"Gladys," Joe said. They both laughed and, as if on cue, Joe's phone rang and he jumped up and grabbed it, hoping it was Donna. It was Gio.

◆

"A pigeon? You got into all that hassle over a pigeon?" Juno stared at him in disbelief. "Say it ain't so, Joe."

"Hey, pigeons weird me out too," Cash offered. He was sprawled on the couch while Juno sat in his desk chair and Joe leaned against a wall. "Did it bite you?"

"They don't bite, Cash," Juno said. "They peck."

"And molt," Cash pointed out. "And shit everywhere. I wouldn't want to touch one of those nasty things either."

"I never even touched the pigeon," Joe said calmly, leaning with arms crossed. He knew he'd be in for some ball-breaking over all this and was prepared to take it with equanimity. But Joe had come to Juno's headquarters in his mom's basement—a personal Batcave jammed with technology, much of it purchased with proceeds from jobs with Joe, where he ran his highly profitable hacking business as well as his totally unprofitable music recording studio—with actual questions he needed answered. Juno and Joe had been close ever since Joe saved his ass during a job gone wrong. Cash was Joe's all-purpose wheelman—and a prolific high-end car thief for Uncle Chen, head of the Chinese mob in Flushing. "Forget the bird," Joe told them. "It isn't the bird that I need to know about. It's that building."

Juno spun to his keyboard and tapped. A photo of the Eleonora appeared, shot from a dramatic low angle. "All I know is what everybody knows," he said. "It's where Lucifer Jones lives."

"Yeah," Joe said, remembering the weird figure lurking in the tower. "Who is he?"

"Lucifer Jones? From the Wizards? Heavy-metal band? Bit a snake in half on stage and had to take antivenom?" Juno was incredulous. "I thought every older white guy from Queens knew him."

"Seriously, Joe," Cash nodded in agreement. "He's a famous rock star. I mean, his band broke up before we were born, and we still know him. That song, 'Soul Snatcher' is still on the radio. People sample it all the time." He turned to Juno. "But to me he's more prog rock than metal. I mean, look at *Mists of Infinity*. That's their best album."

"Guess I missed it," Joe said. "And he lives in the Eleonora?"

"He never leaves," Juno said. "He's a recluse." As Juno's fingers worked, more images popped open: a young Lucifer on stage, waist-length hair flying and eyeliner running as he screamed, plus hasty snaps of the older, gray figure Joe recognized, caught in a window or on a balcony. The song—"Soul Snatcher"—played as well, Juno and Cash nodding along.

"People say they see him in the park sometimes," Cash said.

"Right." Juno agreed. "Wandering alone late at night. Anyway, he owns three apartments there. They say one is like all his occult stuff, like a Satanic altar and the skeleton of a werewolf."

"I heard he had an alien baby in a jar."

"No, it's two different things: a two-headed baby in a jar and a dead alien that got shot down. Also a giant ballroom with nothing in it but candles and a black piano. This famous ballerina got hired to go dance blindfolded while he played."

"Yeah but later it turned out she was lying. Or it was a prank. I forget."

"Okay, fine, but . . ." Joe yelled over the music: "Hey turn this down!"

"Sorry, Joe." Juno paused it.

"Thanks," Joe said, speaking calmly again. "What I really want to know is who owns the building? Who lives there? Also blueprints, specs, anything you can tell me about security. Got it?"

"Got it, boss," Juno said, serious now.

Cash had turned back to the TV, where an image from a video game was frozen. It was a driving game, and Cash now grabbed the controller, steering a Formula 1 racer over what looked like an Alpine landscape while he spoke: "You going back in there, huh Joe?"

Joe, who had been distracted by the screen, remembering Sarah, the champion gamer, sighed yet again. "Somebody still has to go get Alonzo's bird, right?"

◆

"I found out about something interesting today," Blythe told Blake. "On the dark web." They were in bed in her studio apartment, relaxing after a "working lunch," which they often took naked and together, first making love and then eating hero sandwiches in bed, which was something Blake's wife would never abide.

Her place, like all the rooms at the Eleanora, was beautiful, with high ceilings, moldings, a (nonworking) fireplace with a marble mantle and big antique mirror, white drapes closed over a big courtyard window. But it was chaos, like a college dorm room, with clothes heaped everywhere, piles of magazines, empty water bottles rolling around. Amazingly, when collecting his shoes one time, Blake discovered a plate under the bed holding some half-eaten toast, a fork, and pair of used panties. It was so taboo that he was actually turned on. Domenica ran their home like a military encampment, overseeing the maids with such vigilance that it made him nervous. He'd wipe up crumbs after the kids himself just to avoid the yelling.

"Interesting how?" He asked now, reaching for his cigar case. Not only was he allowed to smoke here, Blythe even lit it for him and fetched a cut glass ashtray. She liked the smell. "Creepy interesting or profitable interesting?"

As someone who moved, managed, and hid money for villains, Blake was familiar with the anonymous and illegal underside of the internet but only ever dipped his virtual toes in the shallows, where people swapped Bitcoin and transferred secret funds to offshore accounts. The dark depths gave him the willies.

"Both, I suppose," Blythe said. "But it might also be extremely useful. There's a new site someone just launched overseas that brokers hits. The assassins are international. And totally anonymous."

"Seriously? How do you know it's real? Sounds like a scam."

"You don't pay till the job is done. But it's not cheap. For someone like this Joe, it would be around fifty thousand."

"I haven't got that cash on hand."

"Not personally. But it's in an account, right?"

"The management company's account, but you know that's not mine. It's only held temporarily. It's the residents' money."

"Yes, but this is to protect the residents. It's a business expense. And they'd never even know."

"How do you even know about this? I mean even on the dark web, surely, it's not like Amazon. You can't just order up a murder."

"No, you need the link. And a password. But I've got that."

"From the internet?"

"Nope. From our own little home network." As part of the Eleonora's top-notch security system, there were cameras and microphones throughout the public spaces. For the most part they were monitored by the guards on duty, who were only scanning for trouble. But it was all archived, and Blake and Blythe made a habit of snooping here and there, picking up useful information on their residents. This time, it had been Mr. Lopez, relaxing in the spa after a sauna and massage, chatting with Mr. Volkov, a Russian energy tycoon, both in robes in recliners while golf played silently on a screen.

"I guess Volkov told him about it," Blythe said. "It's the latest thing in high-end assassinations. Lopez was bragging that he'd eliminated a rival who was actually in Switzerland at the time." Grabbing her laptop, Blythe tapped the keys, and showed Blake a small news item. A Colombian tourist had been killed by a hit-and-run driver. The car turned out to be stolen. Police were asking for witnesses. "See?" she asked, back under the covers with Blake, balancing the laptop on her lap. "It's real."

Blake was digesting this, along with his sub, when his phone rang with more bad news. It was security; someone had tripped the building's internet firewall. The intruder's own security was good enough, hidden behind multiple proxies, to make identification impossible, but it was clear that some hacker was nosing around in their business.

"Maybe it's just a coincidence. Nothing to do with that Joe guy," Blythe said, playing devil's advocate.

"You know it's not a coincidence."

"No, it's him," she agreed, then leaned in to whisper in his ear, while also pressing a finger teasingly to his navel. "All we need to do is push a button."

18

"Hey, look who's here," Pete cried out as Joe walked into Club Rendezvous. "It's Philip Marlowe!"

Joe stared blankly, and Little Eddie and Nero, who were sitting at the bar with Pete, both shrugged.

"You know," Pete said. "The Case of the Maltese Pigeon."

"That's Sam Spade," Joe told him, taking off his coat. "Wrong private eye."

"Naw," Pete insisted. "Bogie played him in the movie."

"Bogie played both of them," Nero explained. "You're thinking of *The Big Sleep*, not *The Maltese Falcon*."

"*The Big Sleep* has a pigeon in it?" Little Eddie asked.

"It's a friggin' joke for Chrissakes," Pete said.

"Before your time, kid," Nero said. "Black and white movies. Classics."

"Bogie was the best," Pete agreed. "They don't make them like that anymore."

"What would he even be in, nowadays?" Nero wondered. "The market is saturated with superheroes and franchises like *Star Wars*."

"He'd knock them all on their asses," Pete averred. "He was a real tough guy."

"I don't know," Nero said, shaking his head. "I can't see Bogie in a cape, can you?"

"He couldn't smoke anymore either," Joe said, going behind the bar to help himself to coffee.

"That's true," Nero said, wagging a finger. "Very astute observation. Nowadays, you can show all the sex you want, but an actor smoking? Forget it. No drinking either."

Pete shook his head in disgust, despite the fact that he was drinking a scotch on the rocks and watching a nude dancer. "But you can chop heads off," he noted, "or show gang rapes and disembowelments all day long, no problem. And let kids see it too."

"I never saw none of that," Little Eddie objected. "Was it in one of those darker *Batman* movies?"

"Yeah, I don't know what channel you're watching there, Pete," Nero mused, sipping his martini. "But I do think Pigeonman could have helped out Joe here. Too bad you didn't shine the Pigeon Signal."

They all laughed and Joe smiled good-naturedly, lifting his cup in salute. "Next time I'll bring my cape," he said. There was nothing to do but be a sport and take it, until some new topic came along to distract them. Joe was more focused on his next step. Juno was due later with a report. In the meantime, he was hoping to retreat to his back booth till the club got busy and to spend a little time in Proust's childhood home in Combray, but then Josh and Liam walked in, two members of Joe's ad hoc crew.

"Hey! It's the Birdman of Alcatraz!" Liam shouted and Nero, Pete, and Eddie all laughed appreciatively.

"Look who's here," Pete called out. "Bartender, bring us a Guinness and a Manischewitz."

"They don't drink Manischewitz in Israel," Nero corrected him. "It's the desert."

Pete shrugged. "Okay. Tequila."

"Just a Coke and a coffee, if you don't mind," Liam said in his lilting Irish accent. "We've got a long drive ahead."

Pete mused while the bartender served the drinks. "Now Clint, there's a guy you can count on in the clutch."

Nero shrugged. "So? What's Clint Eastwood got to do with anything?"

"Alcatraz. He escaped."

Nero shook his head. "Wrong movie. The Birdman was Burt Lancaster."

"What did he do?"

"Nothing. He liked birds."

Pete looked unimpressed.

"Truck all loaded?" Nero asked Liam, quietly. He nodded and discreetly handed Nero a fat envelope under the bar.

Josh sipped his Coke. "I can handle birds," he said in his Israeli accent. "I once smuggled these rare parrots into the EU. The hardest part was making sure they didn't talk going through customs."

"Did they speak Hebrew?" Pete asked. "Then the cops wouldn't understand anyway." He snickered at his own joke.

"No," Josh answered flatly. "They were from Australia."

"Sorry we can't help you tonight though, Joe," Liam said. "We've got a little errand to run for Rebbe, hauling some lobsters down to the Jersey shore."

Finally they left, and the other guys moved closer to the stage to see the entertainment. Joe was heading to his corner booth to read when Gio walked in. He did not look happy.

"Joe," he barked out, heading for the booth himself, where there was always a reserved card on the table. "In my office. Now."

Joe closed the book.

19

Blake's afternoon was shaping up pretty much like his morning. Mrs. Kim complained that the water in the cooler in the women's locker room in the gym and health spa was too cold, while Mrs. Evenly wondered why they did not have ice or sparkling options. On the men's side, Mr. Kropotnik felt the sauna did not get hot enough while Mr. Evenly didn't think it was proper that some of the older gentlemen, like Mr. Kropotnik or Mr. Kim, did naked exercises in there.

Then Ernesto, the head of maintenance operations, also known as the super, came to him with a list of repair requests: "7D says the AC isn't working."

"It's barely sixty degrees out today," Blake pointed out. "It's not a fridge. Okay, what else?"

"11C reports bad smells in the hall."

"Right, that's 11B. Aren't they the ones who pickle things? Make sure their cook has the exhaust fan on."

"And 5D says she saw a mouse."

"What? That's impossible."

Ernesto shrugged. "From what she tells me I think it's a squirrel. It was on the balcony."

"Just put a trap out to make her happy."

"And 8B says her toilet is blocked and it's backing up into the bathtub."

"8B?" Blake paused. "That's a renter."

"Yes, old Mrs. Fanshaw. She can't even take a shower until we snake it."

"Good. Maybe she'll finally cave in and go. I told you Ernesto, I can't have you wasting time on the renters and their petty complaints. They already cost us a fortune."

"Yes, sir." Ernesto gave a sort of salute and walked off. He would see to Mrs. Fanshaw first and not tell Blake, who had already forgotten about it. Ernesto had been working at the Eleonora for thirty years and knew all the rent-controlled tenants well. They tended to be older, nicer, and more likely to tip. However, Blake was conducting a low-level war of attrition, trying to push them out with minor harassment from his security goons and denial of services: their places went unpainted, their repairs undone, their guests were kept waiting unannounced and their deliveries forgotten. The maintenance and repair staff tried to look after them anyway. To Blake, they were a nuisance, stubborn pests he couldn't eradicate, worse than roaches.

"It's really selfish when you think about it," Blake was musing to Blythe, as he watched Ernesto go. "One tiny person living in that huge apartment. There's a housing crisis going on."

"A classic six with park view," Blythe said, as if they were magic words. "And there are so many others in need. Growing families who could put the space to good use."

That's when Mr. Van der Pots came in. A South African diamond merchant who had been moving around since Capetown became less hospitable, he was just the sort of family man Blythe had in mind. His third wife was pregnant with their second child.

"Good afternoon, Mr. Van der Pots," Blake said now, "I'm afraid I'm in the middle—"

"Blake, old man, when are you going to do something about these bloody pigeons?" Van der Pots marched in and loomed over the desk, he was tall and bald with a droopy white mustache and red face, as if permanently scorched by his homeland's sun.

"What seems to be the problem?"

"The problem? They're still shitting all over my damned terrace, that's the problem. They must be telling every bloody bird in the park to come use my house as a public loo. My wife's scared to even eat breakfast out there, isn't she? Fears for the unborn child."

"Yes, well, I'm certainly sorry to hear that but I did suggest putting spikes on the railing like some other residents have . . ."

"Spikes! Why have a damned railing if you can't lean on it and have a drop of Scotch of an evening?"

". . . and then we offered to set out those pinwheels and shining foil strips that seem to scare them. . . ."

"Scare them? Damned pinwheels scare me. This is supposed to be a luxury apartment building, not a third-rate funfair."

"Yes sir, but it's a luxury building in New York, which is full of pigeons."

"You know some European towns have introduced falcons."

"Perhaps we can write to the mayor. Meanwhile, I told you how some residents screen the terrace in."

"Really, mate, why pay for outdoor space if you can't even step outdoors without getting beshatted?"

"But Mr. Van der Pots, I really don't see what more I can do."

"Exterminate them, man! Exterminate every one of the brutes!" He turned and stormed out, and before Blake could think what more to say, his intercom went off. Blythe answered.

"All right then, sir," Blake called after, "have a good afternoon."

Blythe was holding his jacket. "Here, put this on."

"Why? What now?"

"The new clients are here to view 6C."

"Oh right," he smoothed his hair and tie and made a grimace at Blythe. "Anything in my teeth?"

"You're perfect," she said.

"Exterminators!" Blake muttered. "What does that Boer think, they're like big game hunters out there with nets?" He chuckled. "Too bad we can't put one of these dark web villains on it. Or on those renters."

Blythe shrugged. "If the Brody job works out, who knows?"

"Wait." Blake did a double take. "You hired someone?"

"No, I just posted the job and now we see who claims the reward. You okayed it."

"I guess it didn't feel real to me. It seems almost like a video game."

"We had to do something. The residents here do not play games, my love."

"Very true."

"The threat had to be eliminated. And this way, not even the contractor knows who placed the hit. It's absolutely safe."

"Yes, you're right," Blake said, regaining his confidence. "As always, my darling," he added, squeezing her hand, just as the new clients were shown in.

"Welcome to the Eleonora," he called, crossing the room, hand extended. "It's a pleasure to meet you, Mr. . . ."

The suave gentleman in the beautifully cut black suit, a fine stubble offsetting his blue eyes and salt and pepper hair, put out a handsome hand. "It's Colonel actually. Colonel Evon Kozco."

Blythe did her little curtsey. Blake gave a firm shake and a confident toothy smile. He turned to the beautiful black-haired woman beside him, wearing a long leather coat.

"Of course, Colonel, and is this your lovely wife?"

"Oh . . ." He chuckled. "How embarrassing, for her of course, and flattering for me. Let me introduce Special Agent Donna Zamora, of the FBI."

◆

"And, voilà, there is the park, as you can see." Blythe drew back the curtains, dramatically. She always showed the apartments like this, in through the foyer and the living room, but with the terrace curtains drawn, then on through dining room and kitchen on one side, bedrooms and study on the other, and then back to the living room and the big reveal, a large terrace with a stunning park view. It was a deliberate trick, like a curtain rising over a stage. Blythe slid the doors back and escorted the clients out onto the terrace. "Here at the Eleonora, we like to say that Central Park is our backyard."

"Or front lawn," Blake noted, considering that the facade of the building fronted onto Central Park West. Blythe chuckled. He could be so literal, lacking the romantic gene she'd inherited from her family of salespeople, who had to know how to move a line of dresses. You couldn't just say that they were made of wool and kept you from being naked, could you? There had to be some reason you needed it when you already had a closet full. Some reason you were willing, not only to choose it over the competition, but to gladly pay more. That's why, in Blythe's mind, their residents happily paid outrageous prices for a piece of the Eleonora. For the person who had everything, it was the one thing almost no one else had.

Now Colonel Kozco stepped onto the terrace as onto the deck of a yacht, gazing out over the horizon, sniffing the air, flanked by his lovely companion, who despite having flashed her credentials, still seemed more like a wife or (since there was no ring) a mistress—a partner, anyway, not a servant like the bodyguards, the matching slabs of beef in dark suits and dark glasses who waited by the door. Were they lovers? Not yet, Blythe decided, though he clearly wanted them to be. The way he immediately turned to her, deferentially, and asked what she thought, as though already seeing her out there, breakfasting with him, in a robe. This was another side of things that Blake didn't pick up on, the psychological subtleties. He was brilliant, the most deviously brilliant schemer she'd ever met, and she'd grown up among the best. This building and the whole operation behind it were a kind of grifter's masterpiece. That's what he was, in her eyes: an artist. A great one. But like so many talented men, he was clueless about people, his own wife and kids being perfect examples, and about practical realities, like using the dark web to eliminate this Joe Brody problem. Then again, that's what he had Blythe for, the reason they made such a perfect team. She added the human touch.

"There's enough room out here for a dinner party," Blythe told Donna, as if she were the lady of the house, and once again, Donna had to ask herself the same question she felt this other woman asking with her eyes: Was this a security detail or a date?

As for Blake himself, he was still recovering from the minor heart attack he'd suffered when he learned he was shaking hands with an FBI agent, and he instinctively blamed this Kozco character for bringing her into his building. But Blake knew, from their prior communications, that Kozco was just the sort of resident he liked to do business with, and as his blood pressure returned to normal, he had to admit, the guy was slick, he'd gotten the FBI to cover his ass.

"Do you have anything on a higher floor?" Kozco asked. "I'm concerned this will be noisy."

"Well . . ." Blythe said, thinking of Mrs. Fanshaw sitting on her rent-controlled treasure-chest. "We hope to have something soon."

"How much more would that be?" he asked.

Now Blake, back on track, intervened. "Blythe handles aesthetics, but I'm the numbers guy. I suggest we discuss that privately in my office." He smiled stiffly at Donna. "While Blythe shows you our gym and spa facilities," he said, and when she frowned at him: "And security, of course."

Blythe placed a guiding hand on Blake's upper arm, an intimate gesture which Donna noted. *Were* they lovers? She revised her guess to yes.

"Why don't we give you two a minute to discuss the security aspects alone?" Blythe asked now, her voice like warm syrup. "We'll be downstairs."

Smiling and nodding, they bowed out, and Donna was alone with Evon.

"So what do you think, really?" he asked her, as they both leaned on the railing. "Should I live here?"

"I'm an FBI agent, not a real estate agent," she said.

"You're a native New Yorker, that's more important," he said.

"Well, we natives live in a very different New York than . . ." she began, then stopped when she realized where her comment was going.

"Than invaders like me?" he said, finishing her thought.

She blushed. "I didn't say that."

He shrugged. "It's fair enough. I spent my life defending a small homeland from hostile takeover by superior forces." He looked back out over the park. "But now I want to retire and live in peace, put down roots in a new place, be part of the community." He shifted closer to her, so that their shoulders were almost touching. Looking out with him from this magical castle of a building, out over the rolling green meadows and bunched trees of the park at the far-off towers like silver and gray peaks, it really was like a moment from a dream, or some fairy tale from her daughter's books, one of the ones Donna discouraged but that her doting grandma bought and the little girl ate up: the poor princess discovered by the dashing prince and taken to live, happily ever after, in the palace. "I'm ready, Donna," her Prince Evon said, now so close she could smell his cologne. "I'm ready to settle down and find a home. And this feels like it could be it. Do you know what I mean?"

She did. And she was just turning her head to meet his eyes and say yes, she understood, both what he was saying and what he was not saying, when the sound of a gunshot cracked out.

❖

When Donna heard the shot, her training and instincts kicked in and she threw herself at Evon, not diving into the arms of a lover, but knocking him over and shielding him from bullets.

"Get down," she ordered, pushing him flat beside the wall while she drew her weapon and spoke into her mic. "Shots fired, shots fired. The origin seems to be next door."

"Copy that," Andy's voice came squawking back. "We are on the way."

By then Evon's bodyguards were swarming in, and as he rose to his feet they huddled around him. "I'm fine," he said, flustered, then began answering them in his own language.

"Keep him here," Donna told them and ran through the apartment, reaching the hall just as Andy and the other agents were taking up positions at the door of the neighboring apartment. Andy pounded.

"Open up, this is the FBI!"

The door was opened by a maid, a real old-fashioned maid in one of those black and white outfits, something Donna associated with Halloween.

"Step aside ma'am," Andy said, moving her into the hall and leading the charge. Inside, the place looked like some kind of country estate from another century and another continent: there were a lot of Tiffany lamps and leather chairs, lace everywhere and highly polished wood and silver that kept the maid busy, but also a tiger skin rug and an umbrella stand made from the leg of an elephant.

"Hold it," Andy called out now as a tall white man in a neatly pressed tan shirt and pants stepped in from his terrace, holding what appeared to be a rifle.

"Officers, please," he intoned in a South African accent, but the agents swarmed him, seizing the weapon and taking him into custody. Andy frowned as he examined the weapon.

"This is a pellet gun," he told Donna.

She turned to the man: "Why were you firing this . . . weapon, Mr. . . . ."

"Van der Pots," he said, removing himself from the agents holding him with the ease of one peeling off a jacket. He smoothed his creases. "And it's hardly a weapon. It's my son's toy."

"Out here," Andy called from the terrace, and Donna headed out, suddenly feeling silly with her gun in her hand, and holstering it. "You've got to see this." And there, next to a very tasteful outdoor lounge set, was a dead pigeon.

"They shit all over the place and ruin everything," Van der Pots said from the door. "We can't even use the terrace. And the constant cooing makes your skin crawl. I thought if I eliminated one or two, it might scare off the others."

Andy shook his head. "You're lucky you didn't get eliminated yourself, by us."

Van der Pots shrugged, unconcerned.

In the end, they wrote it up and gave him a warning.

"And what about this other stuff?" Andy muttered to Donna, casting an evil eye over the trophies. "Talk about shit that makes your skin crawl." He pointed at the umbrella stand. "That has to be illegal."

Donna shrugged. "To import maybe. But not to own, I don't think. We'll check on it." Then she turned to Van der Pots. "Remember, sir, there's no hunting allowed in New York City. Not even on private property." And when he nodded, formally, like an officer under inspection, she added, to herself: *not even if Central Park is your backyard.*

20

"I think the guy's a real life hero. He's doing what no one else can, taking the law into his own hands." This was Pete, still at the bar, still chewing the fat with Nero and Little Eddie while others came and went. Now he was reading the *Daily News*, whose headline declared: PARKING AVENGER STRIKES AGAIN! COPS STRIKE OUT.

"That's where you're wrong," Nero said, shaking his head. "The guy's a menace."

"What do you mean? These rich assholes park wherever they want, they think the law doesn't apply to them."

"It doesn't. Not if they've got immunity."

Little Eddie perked up at that. "Can you imagine, what if we had immunity? Like maybe if Gio was a diplomat or ambassador or something. He could pull some strings."

Nero listened patiently. "But then he'd be an American ambassador, so he still wouldn't have immunity here. That's for the foreign diplomats."

Eddie snapped his sausage fingers, loudly. "Damn. So close."

"But here's my point," Nero went on, leaning toward Pete. "I'm not crying for those rich assholes either. Fuck 'em. But don't sneak around and vandalize a man's ride behind his back. What if everyone did that? You're parked illegally right now, out by the hydrant. What if someone messed with your Caddy?"

Pete bristled at the thought and, although the music was blasting, his ears seemed to prick up, listening for broken glass.

"Point is," Nero went on, resting his case, "that way lies anarchy, my friend."

They all fell silent, not quite standing to attention, but looking up as Gio stalked by, still moody but no longer barking at Joe, who walked beside him, nodding.

"Night, boss," Nero called out.

"Night, Gio," Pete added.

"See you in the morning, boss," Little Eddie chimed in.

He merely grunted, but at the door, he gave Joe a goodbye hug, slapping his back firmly, then waved to the guys as he left. They grinned. No matter how much he might bitch and moan, they knew he'd never really stay mad at Joe, who now came to the bar for a coffee refill. He glanced at his watch while the bartender filled his mug.

"The night hasn't even begun and I'm already exhausted."

Nero nodded sympathetically. "Look on the bright side," Pete offered. "If you got to do a night shift, there are worse places to work." He gestured to the women gyrating on stage.

Joe lifted his cup. "Here's to a quiet night."

"Quiet night," they all agreed and drank, though of course there was no way it was going to be quiet, with the music loud, and the crowd growing louder by the minute, as more people packed in and got drunker and yelled more enthusiastically at the dancers, who performed greater and greater feats on the pole. In fact, it was so loud and so busy that no one, not even Joe, took notice of the two big burly guys, both with full bushy beards, hunting caps, and the kind of orange hoodies and camo pants that marked them as out-of-towners, who sat quietly at the bar and ordered beers. Plus, Joe had plenty else to think about when Juno came in to report. As for Nero, Pete, and Little Eddie, their eyes were on the stage, of course.

◆

Joe led Juno to the back booth to talk. A waitress wandered over, barely contained in the spangled outfit she wore, and asked Juno what he wanted to drink. He was a little stunned—in fact, he was still too young to be in this place, much less order booze. Then again, Joe was the bouncer.

"You don't got grape Snapple, do you?" he asked her.

She shook her head.

"It's a bar," Joe told him. "You think they've got Snapple on tap? Order a fountain soda."

"Grape soda?" he asked her now.

"Sorry," she said. "We got Coke, Diet Coke, ginger ale, Seven Up, tonic, and club."

"Um . . ."

"Bring him a Coke," Joe said, and when Juno objected, he added: "You're lucky I didn't order you a tonic water."

"I never had that, is it good?"

"It's bitter. There's quinine in it."

"Yuck. Why?"

"To prevent malaria."

"In Queens?"

His Coke came. "Thanks, miss," he said, then seeing there was a lemon wedge on the rim of the glass added, "Oh nice," and started squeezing.

"Okay," Joe said, leaning in to hear over the music. "Tell me what you've got."

"Right." Juno took out his phone and started scrolling. "The Eleonora. So construction began in 1900, completed in 1904. The owner was Rufus B. MacTeague, who named it after his mother, Eleonora, which is a name you don't come across much anymore, right?"

Joe shrugged. "Neither is Rufus."

"The building was first planned as a luxury residential hotel, with all kinds of conveniences, like Turkish baths in the basement and professional kitchens on each floor so people could order in gourmet food and eat it in their rooms. And check this out. There was a farm on the roof! The architect had this idea that it would be self-sufficient, so there was, like, eggs and milk and vegetables and stuff delivered to the rooms. They had cows, chickens, even a bear, though I'm not sure what that was for."

"What about the structure, like back stairs and tunnels . . ."

THE PIGEON

"Yeah, well like I said, there were all these services, food, laundry in the basement, shoe polishing and whatnot, plus wood and coal for heating, and all of this was transported via back hallways and service stairs and elevators, so residents didn't need to see the servants come and go. Some of that space was converted later and some was sealed off."

"Do you have blueprints? Specs?"

"Negative. They haven't been digitized."

"Okay. What else?"

"Um . . . the building is in the Beaux-Arts style, with a mansard roof and towers."

"I know that. I was there."

"Right. Lots of famous people lived there, like Harry Houdini and some opera singers and, oh yeah, Isaac Bashevis Singer, the Yiddish writer who won the Nobel Prize. Then, during the dark ages, also known as the sixties and seventies, the building fell into disrepair when the hood got sketchy. I mean, not Bed-Stuy sketchy, like no shooting galleries or squats or nothing but for middle-class white people you know, sketchy enough. The baths got turned into the legendary—supposedly, I never heard of it—Parkside Baths, which was a gay cruising joint where some famous singers performed. Then it became like a full-on swingers club called Athena's Den, which you won't believe the pictures, dude. Full-on orgies, with lots of old school hair, I mean crazy bushes and the 'stashes on the dudes too. And perms, like afros on the white people even. And a buffet! I mean, how can you stand around naked eating shrimp and pigs in a blanket and shit with someone's junk dangling over it? What about butts?"

"This is relevant how?"

"Okay, well, I have those pics if you want them. Even a commercial from public access TV. Man, the naked disco scene is hilarious. Anyway, all that is now part of the building's spa and gym." He swiped along on his screen. "Let's see, blah, blah. Okay, then in the early 2000s they tried to take the building co-op but ran into mucho problemos with like the landmark commission and the rent-controlled tenants. But then in 2008, during the credit crisis, the owners went bankrupt and the building was caught up in lawsuits. Then finally in 2015 it got converted to condos. Now here's something interesting: the management company, Blake Management International, is also the exclusive realtor. CEO is Jeremy Blake, this British guy."

"And who owns the condos?"

Juno grinned. "Now that is the million-dollar, or maybe billion-dollar question."

"And the answer?"

"Nobody."

"Nobody?"

"Well," Juno shrugged. "Some are owned by somebody. Like I already told you, Lucifer Jones bought up three apartments and put them all together. And there's Dr. and Mrs. Jonathan Feingold, a dentist with an office on Park Avenue, and Dr. Bauer, a gastroenterologist who practices at Columbia-Presbyterian. But these are all older residents who bought their places when it went condo or soon after. Every purchase in the last five years, and these are the big ones, at least ten million and up, these are all owned by holding companies and LLCs. Often both the buyer and the seller."

"So there's no name on the paperwork at all," Joe commented.

"Nope. And that is a big red flag."

Joe nodded. The chaos he had triggered by breaking into that apartment to steal back a bird was starting to make a bit of sense. "Yeah. It sure is. Thanks Juno. What do I owe you so far?"

He shrugged. "Let it ride. Just count me in on the caper."

"What caper? This was supposed to a simple errand."

"Joe, Joe, Joe," he repeated, grinning and sipping his drink. "How long have I known you?"

"Not that long, really. A year or so?"

"That's it? Seems so much longer. But still, long enough to learn that with you, no errand is simple. And there's always a caper."

21

After Juno left the club, Joe resumed his duties, and the night took on the hazy, dreamlike feeling of hours spent in a blur of noise, sweat, and skin. By midnight he was looking forward to closing, and, by one, things were finally winding down, so he took a short break to visit the men's room. The two big guys in the camo and hunting caps, seeing this, quietly got up and followed.

Joe was at the sink. Having already washed his hands, he was bent over, splashing cold water on his face to wake himself up for the homestretch, when he heard the door open and sensed the presence of other bodies in the room. Opening his eyes, he caught a glimpse of the two strangers behind him in the mirror, both in hunting gear, and the quick flash, really just a movement, of a hand emerging from inside a coat with a gun.

On reflex, Joe dove sideways, to the floor, as the mirror above him cracked, though the silencer on the pistol emitted only a sharp pop.

Usually, one's instinct is to get away from a gun as quickly as possible. But in close quarters, Joe knew, often rushing it is the best hope. That's why when he dove, he angled himself toward the shooter, grabbing his ankles and pulling him down before he could get off another shot. The shooter fell back on the tile, which was about as wet and gross and sticky as one would imagine a men's room floor in a strip club after midnight to be; his gun skittered to the side. As the second man, flummoxed, reached into his shoulder holster for his own gun, Joe rolled onto his side and came up fast, grabbing him by the balls. Hard.

The man howled, cursing as Joe twisted. Joe lifted himself onto his feet, brutally kicking and stomping the prone man beneath him, then seized the howler's gun hand with his left, while continuing to wrench the man's groin with his right. The man punched Joe frantically on the side of the head as they struggled. Joe fought to keep the muzzle of the pistol, another small caliber automatic, away from himself and buried in his attacker's torso. They were close now, almost intimate, and he could hear the man grunt and feel the prickles of his beard, smell the stale beer on his breath. Slowly, as he looked into the gunman's eyes, Joe worked his finger onto the man's finger that was now bent over the trigger. As the gunman's eyes widened, Joe exerted pressure, and the gun went off, firing a muffled shot into the gunman's own gut.

Joe let go as the man stumbled back, dropping the gun, astonished to see his own blood staining his clothes. Glancing down, Joe saw the first man, who had been crawling away, retrieving his gun from under a sink where it had landed. With no time to make it across to the door, or to grab the second gun himself, Joe dove again, to the other side, and rolled under the stall, while the crawling man sat up, firing wildly. Joe slid under the stall's closed door and then leaped up onto the toilet, frantically hiding from the bullets the man sprayed across the room: his first shot clipped a urinal, the second hit the wall, and the third, fourth, and fifth struck the stalls. One wedged in a door but two, hitting the hard metal frames, ricocheted, winging off. One hit the already cracked mirror, destroying it. The second ricocheted back at his already wounded partner, who was standing, dazed, still stunned to be shot, when another random bullet went into his chest. Amazed, he gawked at the new bullet hole, then he fell.

The remaining gunman regained his feet. Thinking he had Joe trapped, while also knowing he couldn't afford more misses, he came at the stall, gun extended, and pushed the door back with his free hand. Inside, Joe, standing balanced on the toilet rim with nowhere left to go, put his hands on the dividing walls beside him and raised himself, as though on the parallel bars in high school gym class, curling his legs up to avoid the swinging door and then kicking out high as the gunman entered. He came down on his shoulders, legs locking on the gunman's neck, and together they fell.

Joe knocked his head on the handle of the toilet going down—it was the old kind that pipes right into the wall—and his back, already sore from the prior night, took another hit as he bounced off the toilet. But the gunman was under him, breaking his fall, and got it worse, slamming his head and chest against the hard rim of the toilet bowl, with his gun hand crumpled beneath them both against the tile. Joe twisted onto the man's back, forcing his head into the bowl, and flushing to fill it with water. Joe pressed down, submerging his head, and worked a knee onto his back for leverage.

Dazed, the man struggled, first weakly, and then with the power of his mounting panic. But it was too late. Joe had his head lodged under the waterline, and his own weight set. Though he thrashed and splashed, it was no use, and finally, with a few last bubbles, he went limp. Joe checked his pulse. He was dead.

Breathing hard now himself, Joe grabbed the drowned man's gun off the floor, hoisted himself to his feet, and approached the other gunman, who lay moaning in a puddle of his own blood. Joe leaned over him and pointed the gun at his forehead. Suddenly awake, he opened his eyes wide.

"Who sent you?"

The guy shook his head.

"Nobody," he said.

But before Joe could press him further, the door to the men's room started to swing open. Joe jumped up and pushed it shut.

"Hey!" A voice yelled from outside. Concealing the gun, Joe opened the door slightly, positioning his body to hide the room, and sticking his head out into the hall. A guy in a leather coat with a goatee was waiting.

"Out of order," Joe told him. "Toilet's clogged."

"But I've really go to go. Can I use the women's?" the guy asked hopefully.

As the dissatisfied customer squirmed, Joe felt a clammy hand on his ankle. He glanced over his shoulder. The wounded gunman had crawled over and was reaching for Joe, while trying to grasp the pistol that had been trapped beneath his body. Joe kicked out, stomping his neck and shoulder.

"Hold it," Joe said. "Or go in the parking lot."

The guy stalked off, muttering, "What kind of strip club is this?" Joe turned back into the room, shutting the door behind him, just in time to see his remaining attacker, now on his knees, reaching up with the other pistol. Joe shot him twice through the chest. Pop. Pop.

He opened the door carefully and peeked out again, this time waiting till he saw one of the dancers come by on her way to the dressing room. It was Autumn, a tall redhead, who had pulled a light robe over her stage costume, the remains of which now consisted of red heels and glitter.

"Hey Autumn," he asked, keeping his voice level. "Do me a favor?"

"Sure."

"You know Nero and those guys, sitting up front?"

"Sure."

"Can you go get them and ask them to come here? I need a word."

She frowned curiously at that. "In the bathroom? You okay?" She leaned in, confidentially. "Belly trouble?"

"No, I'm fine. I just really need to talk to them about something privately."

She smiled consolingly. "I understand," she said, patting his hand, and hurried off.

22

"What about this one? Anyone recognize him?"

Bracing himself with a wide stance, Pete yanked the guy's head from the toilet, and held him up for display, water streaming from his beard.

Nero shook his head.

"I do," Little Eddie said.

"From where?" Nero asked him.

"From out front. Him and the other guy were sitting at the bar."

"No," Pete said. "We mean, do you know who they are?" With a soft grunt, he let the heavy body flop to the floor.

"Like, can you identify them," Nero explained.

"No. Sorry," Eddie said.

Pete shook his head. "Me neither. All these bushy beard dudes look alike."

"Check for wallets," Joe told them, and Nero and Eddie dug into their pockets.

"This guy's license says Daniel Tate," Eddie said, comparing the DMV photo to the drowned man. "He's from someplace in Pennsylvania."

"This one's Canadian," Nero said, emptying the other guy's pockets while careful not to get any blood on himself. "Jules Renard."

They looked inquiringly at Joe. He shook his head. "Never heard of them."

Pete shrugged. "Well they heard of you."

Nero straightened up and leaned against the wall. "Meanwhile, we've got a more pressing problem. How do we get rid of them?"

They checked in with Gio circumspectly on the phone and, with his permission, closed the bar early, sending Santa, the manager with the big round belly and long white beard, to make an announcement about a plumbing emergency. Without asking questions, he hustled the dancers out, then left himself, while the others reconvened in his office. Gio parked in back, came in through the rear door with his own key, and took a peek at the corpses in the men's room before joining them.

"Who the hell are those hairy mooks?"

Shrugs all around. Joe threw his hands up.

"I was thinking," Pete began, and Gio cocked an eyebrow. "Maybe we could get some cinder blocks and chain from the construction company and take them on the boat."

Gio shook his head. "My boat's in dry dock. They're painting and resealing it for the season." He pointed at Nero. "What about that spot upstate, in the woods? Ground should be thawed by now."

Now Nero shook his head. "Road construction. There's a detour, plus too many work crews and state troopers crawling all over."

"You know," Pete said, thoughtfully. "Sunday night, I was at Garden de Napoli, you know, old Louie's place on the wharf in Red Hook, with Marie and the kids and her parents."

"Good for you," Gio said.

"Well, boss," Pete persisted. "They got that old brick pizza oven in the garden. The wood burning one?"

"I love that square pie," Little Eddie, put in, patting his belly. "With cheese layered all through the crust."

"The best," Pete nodded. "But Louie owes us for clearing up that zoning problem and I was thinking, maybe . . ."

"A little old school, no?" Gio asked.

"Actually Gio," Nero was sitting forward. "That's not a bad idea. Those ovens get up around nine hundred to a thousand degrees."

"That's why the crust is so nice and crisp," Pete explained.

"I love that thin crust," Little Eddie put in.

"That temp won't incinerate bone," Nero went on. "But it will reduce everything else to ash and we have the river right there. Even a private pier."

Gio looked at Joe, who nodded. "Why not?"

"All right then," Gio said, standing, "let's roast those two pigs. Eddie, bring the dolly around. Pete, get the Caddy backed up to the door. We need that big trunk."

◆

It was, as it turned out, a nice night for a fire, as long as you sat upwind, away from the smoke and the disturbing scent of burning flesh and hair. But cold, fresh air wafted in from the river, and the empty garden, which was walled in with brick and plaster mosaics and normally packed with families at the now empty tables, was silent, except for the crackle of burning wood and the breeze through the trees and vine trestles. There were even a few stars out, here on the edge of the city.

"What about those white power gun nuts you pissed off last summer?" Gio asked. "I mean, these two look like hillbillies."

Joe considered it. He had been involved in a job that went wrong at a gun show, and Uncle Chen's nephew had been killed. Joe had been pressured into helping assault a survivalist compound where the killer was hiding out in Jersey. That was actually how he met Cash.

"Well the gun show was in Pennsylvania," Joe said. "But why would they come after me? That beef was between them and Uncle Chen."

"I still say they got to be guys you bounced from the club," Pete said. "You know how psychologically fucked-up some of these suckers get. Remember the one who got on stage and proposed to Caramello?"

"Oh yeah," Little Eddie said, loading more wood into the oven. "He bought a ring and everything. Whatever happened to her?"

"Her name was Carmel," Nero corrected, "like the town in California, where Clint Eastwood used to be mayor. She got her degree and she's a teacher now. Special Ed."

"I wish Clint was mayor here," Pete mused, sitting back down. "He'd clean up this town."

"Like the Parking Avenger," Eddie added, grinning. "He'd tell those foreigners where to park their damned cars."

"Talk about Special Ed," Gio said, shaking his head. "Meet Special Eddie."

They all laughed, including Eddie.

"What bothers me," Joe said, "is the weapons." He'd been leaning back, staring at the sparks that drifted up from the fire into the dark sky. "Gun nuts are going to bring out their toys: AKs, special mags, bazookas, whatever. A psycho is going to want power too, that's his trip. A nine at least. Or a .45, something that makes some noise. But these guys brought .22s with suppressors."

"You're right," Gio said, thoughtfully. "That's a pro's choice. Quiet. Neat."

Nero nodded. "Fine for close work. They weren't looking for the OK Corral."

Pete shrugged. "It's what I'd use to clip a guy in the toilet."

"So who'd want to put out a hit on you?" Gio asked Joe.

Joe just laughed.

"That's a long list, boss," Nero commented.

Pete nodded. "And it keeps getting longer all the time."

◆

Silence descended and soon the only sounds were the fire burning down and, in the background, the river slapping against the pier. Joe thought to check his phone. There was a text from Donna:

Want to meet up tonight? We should talk.

Joe did want to meet, though the phrase *We should talk* sent a shudder through him. But for better or worse, it would have to wait.

Sorry, he answered. Then, after a moment, added: *Problems at work*.

◆

When the last embers died out, Pete doused the ashes and cleaned the whole oven with a high-pressure hose and some high-powered soap. Little Eddie used a mallet to pound the remaining bits of bone into dust. Then they tossed it in the river, along with two belt buckles and a watch.

"I'm starved," Little Eddie announced, as they finished up. It was getting late, or early.

"Jeez, how can you think about food?" Pete asked.

"It's all he thinks about," Nero teased. "He's a growing boy."

"Sorry, but I haven't eaten since lunch," Eddie said, embarrassed.

Gio looked at his watch. "Yeah, what the hell. We got to eat." He looked at Joe. "What do you want?"

Joe shook his head. The thought of food was hardly appetizing, but his body disagreed. His stomach was empty. "Anything but pizza," he said.

"Yeah, right," Gio agreed. "Or barbeque."

PART III

PART III

23

Vicky cleared passport control with no problems. Her full name was Victoria Dahlia Amalia St. Smythe, though she went by Vick or Vicky. But in this case, that didn't matter. She wasn't traveling under her own name, which is why there were no problems. They waved her in with barely a glance and she was back in the USA. She was pleased. Vicky loved New York and was looking forward to having a ball, like last time, when she had made some new friends—and enemies.

On that visit, she had murdered numerous people, including a CIA agent who was also Agent Donna Zamora's ex-husband, and the NYPD detective who had been Fusco's last partner. She had also taken out their suspect before he could talk, thereby foiling Joe as well.

Then there was Yelena. Yelena Noylaskya—Russian master thief, equally skilled at cracking safes and skulls—had met Joe on a job. Their professional regard for each other led to a personal connection, just as volatile and dangerous, and they went from partners to lovers. But fate had led her to the upper reaches of the Russian mob in Brooklyn, and Joe's path had led to Donna.

Yelena did not like many people. But she did like Vova, an old man who forged immaculate documents. Vicky had killed him, torturing him horrifically first. And for that, Yelena was determined to kill her.

But despite the many potential dangers, when the opportunity arose to come back and have some fun while also making some money, Vicky just couldn't resist. Once the penniless descendent of decadent aristocrats, she was now one of the most highly paid assassins in the world. She was also a sociopath, or so she'd been told by shrinks in her childhood. An antisocial personality. A sadist. That is to say, she was one of those people whose motto was: love your job and you'll never work a day in your life. When they asked her, at customs, why she was visiting the US, she could only reply, for pleasure.

But for that she needed toys. So as soon as she dropped off her luggage and removed her makeup and prosthetics, she headed to the Meatpacking District to visit Adonis Torrentello.

◆

Adonis Torrentello was just 4' 11" and around 110 pounds, with a soft voice and shy smile to match. He had very long, very soft black hair that he generally wore loose, like a silk curtain framing his beautiful, gentle features and large dark eyes, and falling over his smooth back. But anyone who mistook this stature and demeanor for weakness would regret it, deeply and often loudly, as they died screaming. Doni was an arms dealer, a ruthless and dangerous one, who sold weapons to professional criminals. His cover, or "day job," ran from midnight to six, when he was the charming, elegant, but equally cruel owner of an exclusive, ridiculously expensive nightclub set atop a building on Gansevoort Street, in what was known as the Meatpacking District. The former center of the city's fresh meat supply, carcasses hanging from chains and butchers in bloody aprons were once a common sight. It was also once, punningly, a notorious center of the sex trade, featuring prostitutes of all types on display along the streets, and several infamous S&M clubs, where different sorts of prime bodies were hung and flayed. Nowadays, it was full of overpriced shops and restaurants, and attracted the sort of people willing to wait in line for the chance to buy champagne at five hundred dollars a pop: flashy tourists, overpaid finance bros, wannabe models, and minor celebs. And Doni ruled over them all, with a cold eye and a sweet smile that could easily curdle into a sneer. He slept in the mornings. And then, by appointment only, he met very special clients in the building's basement, far from prying eyes—and ears, since his customers liked to try their items out in his private shooting range.

But, despite the extreme discretion of Doni's arrangements, it was a small world that he moved in, or that moved around him, since he rarely left the building, and when Vicky climbed out of the black town car and headed down the basement steps, she passed a couple fellow

Londoners who had just come out, and who recognized her, though she had no idea who they were.

"Oi," said Rufus, the white one, who had a lumpy shaved head, tattoos on his neck and hands, many more tattoos covered by his Fred Perry top and bottoms, and a gold grill. "That's Vicky de Whoozit, innit?"

Milo, his partner, shrugged. He was slicker looking, a black guy in a black turtleneck under a black leather blazer, expensive jeans and sneakers, and a lot of gold chains and zirconium rings. "What if it was? Didn't come all the way to New York to fuck with some posh slag, did I?"

"Learn to listen, right? And listen to learn. I didn't say nothing about fucking her, did I?"

"I said fuck with, not fuck."

"Well I'm not saying fuck all about fucking in any form, am I?"

"All right," Milo paused and set down his bag. They'd just bought some gear from Doni, and it was getting heavy. They were on a picturesque street, near the river, with tourists now flowing around them like two rocks in a stream. "Then what the fuck are you saying?"

"Consider. We just saw a well-known London face, much like ourselves. And much like us, she shows up in New York, the same day as us, and stops by to see Doni, just like us. Now why do you think?"

Milo shrugged. "Job I suppose."

Rufus pointed a finger. "What job?"

Now the penny dropped. "Our job," Milo said, eyes narrowing.

"Exactly, old son. It's an open contract, innit? Like a bounty hunter. And she's here to claim it just like us."

Milo didn't like that idea. He showed his disdain by spitting through the gap in his two front teeth, which was his trademark gesture. The spittle hit a tourist in the cheek, but he wisely said nothing and hurried by. "So, we'll beat her to it. Get a head start like."

Rufus scoffed. "And have her sneak up on us from behind? No thank you. Plus, who's to say we get there first? Maybe she has inside information on his location and such."

"Strip club innit? He's the bouncer. We just look up the address."

"Maybe. What I heard, the last two who walked in there for that didn't walk out. Point is, this gig's militant enough, without competition."

Milo nodded. "So we clear the field like."

Rufus nodded back, tapping his own lumpy head. "Now you're finkin."

"Out here?" Milo raised the bag. "We got the mash."

"Nah," Rufus said. "Too many randoms. We go back to Doni's. Soundproof range, innit?" He grinned, showing his gold. "Strategy, my son."

Milo grinned back, rubbing Rufus's head. "Everyone says you got those lumps head-butting a statue when you was drunk. But I tell 'em, it's pure brain matter under there."

And they went back to Doni's basement.

◆

Meanwhile, down in Doni's, Vicky was trying to decide. She'd already made her biggest purchase, a top-of-the-line custom sniper's rifle, complete with scope and tripod. Now she needed a pistol and was trying to choose between the Beretta and the Glock. Doni gave her ammo and let her fire off shots from both while he watched and yawned. He was still in his silk bathrobe and doing his nails, lying on a plush couch. The shooting range was a long, narrow hallway that ran the length of the basement, connecting to the living room in front and the kitchen in back. The rest of his living quarters were quite elegant, windowless white boxes with fabric on the walls, thick carpets, sleek low furniture, and a lot of steel and glass and stone. He liked things simple, clean, very dark, and very quiet.

"Normally I'd just go with the Glock," she told him. "But this M9 just feels so . . . classic."

Doni shrugged. "It's what every Yankee soldier has, honey. If it's good enough for Uncle Sam . . ."

Then the door buzzed. Doni frowned. He wasn't expecting anyone. He looked at the little screen and saw Rufus grinning with that diamond and gold grill, Milo beside him. "Oi Doni," he called. "I forgot me fucking lighter I think."

"And I got to use the loo," Milo added, with a grin.

"What's that fool so happy about?" Doni wondered, then sighed. "Fine," he said into the intercom. "Come on down." And he buzzed the door.

◆

Milo and Rufus came in fast. Milo shoved the TEC-9 he had just bought from Doni into Doni's face, which he didn't like, and Rufus, who had the AK-47 with the modified pistol grip, moved toward the range. Vicky, meanwhile, had one of those feelings that people in her line of work must sometimes rely on if they are going to live very long. She'd clocked the two goons coming out of Doni's, thinking nothing of it. But when she heard them return, with thick London accents and, of course, heavily armed, she stepped gingerly into the corner of the shooting range, where the hall met the kitchen, which in turn led back into the living room, and she listened hard. When she heard a scuffle, she extended the Glock in her left hand, along the long wall of the range, and the Beretta in her right, along the other side, nestled a finger against each trigger, and waited. Just in case.

A moment later Rufus appeared, first the barrel of the AK, then his arm, and then his head and shoulders passing into the doorframe. Vicky fired, taking off the top of that lumpy head, just as Milo, dragging Doni along, backed into view from the kitchen side. She fired the Beretta, hitting him between the shoulder blades and stopping his heart. He fell. Doni, feeling Milo drop away behind him, and hearing the shot, just as he saw Rufus fall before his eyes, spun around to see Vicky, looking pleased as a cat with feathers in her grin, holding the two pistols.

"I suppose I'll just take them both," she commented. "Wrap them up."

Doni nodded, poking the corpse at his feet with a slippered toe. "The ammo is on me. Because of the inconvenience," he said, and then, considering how chic she looked, her red hair loose over her expensive motorcycle jacket, with tight black leggings and high black boots, added: "And if you want to stop by the club tonight, a reserved table just opened up."

24

The second attempt on Joe's life came when he was at dinner with his grandmother. They were at the same Indian place they'd been eating at for as long as Joe could remember, though Gladys recalled when it was a regular Greek diner back in the '70s. It still looked like a diner, with a long counter, rotating stools, and a row of booths, but the fake Doric columns of the old place were now overlaid with gold and red, and the servers wore saris or collarless silk shirts rather than old time waitress dresses. They'd eaten—way too much, as always—and Gladys was chatting with the wife of the owner, who was the son of the prior owner, while Joe went to the cash register to pay. He had to break a hundred. While Joe's habit of living mainly on cash made him a weird anomaly in many settings, immigrant business owners understood. They didn't trust banks either, nor did they want the government knowing what they were doing, though for somewhat different reasons than Joe. The owner, who stood behind the register at the end of the counter and greeted customers at the door, happily took Joe's hundred. Joe pocketed his change, peeling off a bill to leave as a tip, and was grabbing a handful of that anise seed and sweets mixture in the bowl on the counter before returning to the table when the three Chinese men entered. It was the look on the owner's face that probably saved his life.

"Good evening gentlemen, table for . . ." the owner was saying, glancing past Joe at the men in black suits who were coming through the door. Then he broke off, his face morphing, melting really, from professionally polished joy at new customers coming in late on a weeknight to stark terror. That look, the dropping away of a smooth, everyday mask to reveal naked horror, was deeply familiar to Joe, from war zones and barrooms all over the world. Something terrible was about to happen. Without knowing who or what was behind him, he ducked, crouching beside the counter, instinctively taking cover.

What the owner had seen was the first man, dressed like the others in a black suit, white shirt, and black tie, reach into his jacket and draw a handgun. Assuming this was a robbery, he immediately raised his hands, nodding at the still open register. "Please, take the money," the owner said, while Joe scrambled past his feet, "just don't shoot." The gunman, Black Suit Number One, scowled and pushed the owner aside, trying to get a shot at Joe, who had, by then, moved a few more feet down the counter, to where a glass kettle of chai tea boiled on a hotplate.

Meanwhile, the owner's wife and Gladys, seeing what was happening, had begun to react, though the only other customers, an Indian couple in a back booth, were still blissfully oblivious, eating their mango dessert. Seeing this seemingly harmless group of bystanders, the second intruder, Black Suit Two, made a fatal error: He waved his gun at them, eliciting a squeal of fear from the owner's wife, and then turned his back on Gladys, while his cohort, Black Suit Three, tried to help Number One by leaning over the counter and cutting off Joe. That's when Gladys, who had already grabbed a fork and concealed it in her lap under the table, came up behind Number Two and stabbed him in the side of the throat.

Number Two screamed. He clutched the sudden gusher of blood that spouted from his artery with one hand and, with the other, reflexively pulled the trigger on his pistol, hitting Number Three in the thigh. Three went down, and not knowing where the attack was coming from, began to scramble for cover. That's when Joe came up with the kettle of chai.

Hearing the tumult and catching a general glimpse of what was happening from around the counter, he saw his chance, as Black Suit Number One swiveled to see what was going on and tried to get a shot at Gladys. Joe sprang up and shattered the glass kettle across his face, scalding him, cutting his cheek, and blinding him with the boiling contents. Number One screamed even louder than Number Two and clutched his eyes with his left hand while Joe struggled to wrestle his gun away from his right. Meanwhile, Number Three, unable to stand on his wounded leg, tried to get a shot at someone, but Gladys was behind Number Two, who had collapsed onto her, and Joe was blocked by the counter.

Joe arm-wrestled with Number One, his right hand gripping the wrist that held the gun, while both men leaned across the counter. Then

Joe saw the cleaver lying on the cutting board beside him. Grabbing it with his left hand, which was a bit awkward, he nevertheless managed to raise it high and bring it down hard, right below the joint, severing the gun hand at the wrist. That was the loudest scream of all, but it was soon cut short, as Joe, wincing in distaste, picked the dead fingers from the pistol and used it to kill its owner, then leaned over the counter and shot Number Three twice in the chest. Number Two was dying, but he was still dangerous, vaguely waving his pistol, with Gladys clinging to him from behind. Joe tried to get a clear shot but was worried about hitting his grandmother.

"Gladys, get out of the way," he yelled finally. She dropped her arms immediately, and crouched beside the owner's wife, who was cowering under the table. Joe aimed carefully and shot him in the head. He collapsed like a rag doll.

As soon as the shooting stopped, the terrified couple ran out. Then the man doubled back, handing some cash to the owner's wife, who was locking the door behind them. Meanwhile, the owner rushed up to Joe, who had taken out his phone.

"No police, please," the owner beseeched him.

"Never crossed my mind," Joe said as he dialed. Like banks and the tax man, this was another idiosyncrasy they shared.

25

"This is getting to be a bad habit," Cash commented, staring at the corpses.

Joe's first call had been to Gio, who immediately sent Pete and Little Eddie, and Joe had them escort Gladys home. Then he called Cash, thinking that he might help identify the three Chinese assailants. It was Cash who, in turn, told him that Liam and Josh were in the area with an empty truck they'd borrowed from Cash's junkyard and auto repair business, Reliable Scrap, for a seafood delivery and were due to return. Now they were there as well, also regarding the dead men. The owners had left after giving Joe the keys.

"Lord knows, you've stepped on your share of toes," Liam observed. "But this can't just be a coincidence can it?"

From the three corpses, Joe had removed three Hong Kong passports, and three used boarding passes. "They're not local. They landed at Newark Airport today."

"Wearing matching black suits and shades," Josh noted.

"Like the Blues Brothers," Joe said.

Cash grinned. "I was going to say like a Tarentino flick, but that's a better reference."

Joe handed him the passports. "I want you to show these to Uncle Chen. See if you can find out who they are."

"Right," Cash said, and left immediately. Joe locked the door behind him.

"I've got the truck in the alley," Josh said, "backed up by the kitchen door. But where do we take them?"

"There's the pig farm upstate," Liam offered. "But that's a long way to drive with three dead passengers in an empty truck." He considered the bloody cleaver on the counter. "Unless we, you know, prep them here. Put them in some rice sacks or something."

"That will take too long," Josh protested. "Without saws or anything. We wouldn't make it to the farm before daylight."

"Fine," Liam said, lighting a cigarette. "Then what's your plan? Try being constructive instead of just criticizing."

"Well," Josh said, taking Liam's cigarette and drawing on it. "I hate to even mention this, but if you insist . . ." He sighed. "There is the meat plant."

"What's a meat plant?" Joe asked.

"You know," Josh nudged Liam and passed the cigarette back. "Rebbe's place out in Maspeth."

"Oh Jesus, not that place," Liam groaned. "The reek of it turns me stomach."

"Compared to a pig farm?" Josh scoffed. "You can smell that place for miles."

Liam shrugged. "It's a matter of cultural bias I suppose."

Josh turned to Joe. "It's close. We can use the rendering vats, turn these two to soup before anyone comes in."

"Can you get access?" Joe asked.

"I'll call Rebbe," he asked.

"Fine," Liam said. "We'll do it your way, since you dislike pigs so much. But I have to say . . ." He poked one of the bodies with his toe. "These three don't exactly look kosher."

◆

Rebbe wasn't pleased.

He disliked being disturbed after hours, especially with this sort of news. It was bad for his digestion. On his doctor's advice, he tried not to eat, drink caffeine, or deal with stressful business in the hours before bed. But seeing as it was an emergency, and that it concerned Joe, he agreed to see them. Reluctantly.

"What did he say?" Joe asked as he joined Josh and Liam in the front of the truck. They'd loaded the bodies, wrapped in plastic garbage bags, and cleaned and mopped thoroughly. Then Joe had done a careful inspection, first of the restaurant, then of the truck, to make sure that the brake and taillights worked and that the (stolen) plates were visible. It was one of the mottos he lived by—don't commit any misdemeanors when you're in the midst of committing a felony—and it went double when transporting the newly deceased. Or triple, in this case.

"He said to come by," Josh told him, putting away his phone. Liam put the truck in gear. "He wants to talk to you alone."

"I hope we didn't disturb his family."

Josh smiled at that. "It's Thursday. Tomorrow, for Shabbat, he'll be home with the family. Tonight he's with Esmerelda."

◆

Esmerelda was Rebbe's newest mistress, a short, plump Guatemalan girl whose waist-long raven-black hair was nearly as impressive as Rebbe's navel-brushing white beard. Her English, picked up mainly from Netflix and tourists, was spotty, but Rebbe's Spanish, learned from decades on New York streets, was surprisingly good, and she was now rapidly learning to speak both New York American and Brooklyn Yiddish at once. They made an odd duo, but the warmth between them was real and, Joe thought, surprisingly sweet.

"*Hace frío,*" she said, as Rebbe, dressed in his white shirt, black pants, skullcap, and slippers, let Joe into the small, tastefully decorated apartment. She wore a white terry-cloth robe over her pajamas, patterned with pink hearts, and fuzzy slippers. She fussed over Rebbe, helping him into his worn black robe, clucking, "*¿Por qué llevas este shmatah?*"

"We're fine, *mija,*" Rebbe said, patting her shoulder tenderly. "Go watch your show. *Solo un minuto.*"

Reluctantly, she tied his robe for him and then kissed his cheek.

"Gracias, Essie," he murmured as she retreated, shutting the bedroom door. Rebbe pointed at the couch and lowered himself into a chair. "Sit, Joey, sit."

Joe sat.

"Now," Rebbe said. "Is all this new tsuris still about that *fakaktah* pigeon? Those two redneck goys at the club and now these three?"

Joe shrugged. "Maybe. But I don't see how. Or why. I mean, killing me wouldn't stop Alonzo. And I didn't even get the pigeon."

Rebbe shrugged. "They're filthy birds anyway. *Trafe*. Which reminds me . . ." He pulled some keys from his pocket. "Here's the keys. Josh knows what to do. But for God's sake, please, make sure it's all cleaned up before the mashgiach gets there in the morning. He's a real hard-on. If that fanatic declares the whole place unkosher, oy will that cost a fortune."

◆

Chaim Kosher Meat Products was a food-processing plant where animals were prepared according to strict kosher rules, then distributed to kosher butcher shops, markets, and restaurants all over. Although scrupulously clean, there was something chilling about the empty plant, its rows of hooks and freezers, its tiled walls and drains. In one area, there were large steel tubs fitted with thermometers, pipes, and loading machinery, like supersized and superheated hydrotherapy equipment combined with an old-fashioned still. Joe and Liam, now dressed in white coats, rubber gloves, rubber boots, and hairnets borrowed from the employee changing room, wheeled over the large metal cart on which the three stripped corpses lay heaped, while Josh got the equipment going. The tubs filled and heated as they hoisted the bodies onto the conveyor belt.

"Okay," Liam called to Josh. "Hit it."

The bodies would be roasted, dissolved with acid, boiled, and finally pulverized into a powder that would normally be pressed and formed into sheets of gelatin but, in this case, would just be washed away during the superheated automatic sterilization process.

"Don't skip that cleanup step," Liam reminded Josh as they watched the bodies tumble into the machinery. "Sounds key."

"Yeah, that's a must," Josh agreed. He started to light a cigarette, then thought better of it. He didn't want to leave a smell of smoke.

"What do they normally make in here?" Joe asked, staring as the odd contraptions steamed and bubbled.

"*Ptcha,*" Josh said.

"What?" Joe asked.

"I know," Liam put in. "I can't even pronounce it."

Josh shrugged. "It's a delicacy made of jellied cow's feet. Very hard-core."

"I realize Irish cuisine is nothing to brag about," Liam said. "But my God that stuff is horrific. How can you folk eat it?"

"I've never even tasted it," Josh said. "Just seeing it in the jar gives me the shudders."

"Maybe your grandpa ate it?" Liam asked.

"Maybe Rebbe's grandpa," Josh said.

"It's peasant food," Joe offered, relieved there wasn't much of an odor, only a vague scent of broth overlaid with disinfectant and acids.

"You see it in every culture. Poor people need to use every scrap, and over time it becomes a delicacy."

"But it's got to be kosher right?" Liam asked. "Gelatin made from the bones of a cow, a kosher cow, and not a pig."

"I think gelatin is pareve," Josh said. "Anyway, Jell-O is allowed to call itself kosher, from some kind of loophole." He pushed the bubbling mixture around with a paddle and shut the lids. "Apparently," he went on, "some rabbis decided that due to all the processing, Jell-O was reduced to a level where it is no longer meat or dairy. It's a neutral substance. Like bread or water."

"Doesn't look neutral," Liam said, frowning at the vat. "What a bonkers religion."

"And what about Catholics?" Josh asked. "You magically turn bread and wine into the flesh and blood of Christ and then eat it. All we do is turn bones and fat into a vegetable." He shrugged. "Let's just agree they're both miracles."

"So then," Joe said, grinning for the first time since this whole evening's adventure began, "whatever other laws we've broken tonight, we can tell Rebbe that everything's kosher."

26

Joe left Liam and Josh to finish running the cleaning cycle and returned to his apartment, where Gladys was playing poker with Pete and Little Eddie. Half-full cups of coffee cooled at their elbows, beside half-eaten slices of Entenmann's coffee cake, and a small pile of cash and chips rested in the center of the kitchen table.

"Hey, Joe," Little Eddie said, staring at his cards and biting his lip hard. "I raise twenty," he decided, and tossed in the last of his chips.

Pete looked up. "Everything go all right?"

"Sure," Joe said, taking the other chair. "I'd hold off on the jellied cow feet for a while."

"Thanks for the tip," he said, then, to Gladys: "I fold."

"Let's see what you've got, big boy," she said, seeing Little Eddie's bet and peering at him through her spectacles. She turned over her cards. "Three kings."

Blushing, he showed a pair of sevens. "I was bluffing," he admitted.

"No kidding," she told him. "I would never have guessed."

"How did you know?" Eddie asked.

"You're sweating all over my cards for one thing," she noted.

"And you bite your damn lip every time you lie," Pete said. "You'd better hope the cops don't ever ask you nothing."

"I still do that?" he shook his head. "My mom told me the same thing."

Joe smiled. "If school's out, then I could use a ride."

"Sure. Where to?" Pete asked.

"If you don't mind waiting downstairs a few minutes, I'll let you know. I need a word with Gladys."

"She cleaned us out anyway," Pete said, standing. "You're still a shark, Gladys."

"You got cake and coffee, didn't you?" Gladys asked. "You don't get that at a casino."

"My grandma used to bake it," Eddie said. "You know, with the walnuts on top."

"I haven't had time lately," Gladys explained, gathering her winnings.

"You haven't had time in thirty years," Joe said. "Thanks again, guys. I'll be right down."

They left, and Joe cut a slice of cake while Gladys cleared the table, carrying cups into the kitchen.

"You okay?" he asked, as she came back and got the plates. "I'm sorry you had to see all that."

She smiled at him. "I've seen worse in my time, kiddo. You know that."

"I do." He kissed her cheek. "And never mind the baking, you're still handy with a fork."

She laughed as she headed into the kitchen. "Nobody fucks with my boy."

He followed as she turned on the faucet and began rinsing the dishes. "So I think you should find someplace else to stay," he said. "Just for a few nights, until I figure this out."

"Forget it. Too much trouble." She handed him a dish, and he began drying it. "And I've got a whole drawer full of forks."

"Well, I'd feel better," Joe said. "I'm going to lie low too for a bit. There must be someone you can call."

"Now?" Gladys dried her hands. "It's after ten. That's late for us old timers."

"Hit men don't clock in on union hours."

"Well. We were going to meet in the morning anyway. I suppose I could call her now."

"Who?" Joe asked.

"Yolanda," Gladys said. "You know, her daughter is that cute Fed, Agent Zamora."

"Right," Joe said. "Perfect."

◆

So Pete and Eddie took Joe and Gladys to Yolanda's. Carrying her suitcase and a small overnight bag of his own, containing a few clean T-shirts and underwear, his Proust, his toothbrush, and a Sig 9 mm with extra ammo wrapped in his socks, Joe sat in back beside his grandmother while Pete piloted them across what Joe still thought of as the Triborough Bridge, though it had been renamed for Robert F. Kennedy. Over Randall's Island and into Manhattan, then up the Harlem River Drive, the city flashed by the windows as it had on similar drives throughout his life, everything changing, yet here and there, something familiar appeared, like a flashback flickering by on the glass: the Keith Haring Crack is Wack mural on the handball court, Yankee Stadium, the eternal projects.

The whole way, Joe thought about Donna. Would she be there? Would it be awkward? Should he text her at least and tell her they were coming? The answer, which was contained in the very question, was no. Joe had other things to think about, like who was trying to kill him and what he was going to do about it. The fact that he could even be concerned at all with whether or not Donna was going to smile if she saw him walk into her mother's apartment was enough to let him know he was dangerously distracted. Like a fighter before a match or a soldier before battle, he had to focus and not waste any time or energy on this adolescent drama.

But then that was love. Passion, pleasure, laughter, admiration, respect, even longing: all were elements of it, sure, but nothing proved it, nothing locked in the diagnosis of love like a grown man thinking and acting like a blathering adolescent, a teenager obsessed with what *she* was doing, thinking, feeling, and wondering if it was about him. Typical enough, of course, whole industries, like pop music and rom-coms, depend on it, but not typical for Joe. He'd learned early on that feelings were a luxury, saved up for special occasions. If you got too angry, too scared, even too happy, if you wanted anything or anyone too much, it put you at risk. So you set it aside and didn't think about it or feel about it. Tricky to manage in the long run, of course, which is where first alcohol and then drugs came in. And even then they returned, those banished emotions, in bad dreams and panic attacks.

But for now all that was behind him. Joe was clear, he was focused, and he was reasonably content, except for Donna, who offered at first a new hope, a new possibility of a new joy, and now a new risk. And in Joe's world, where survival depended on absolute focus, and victory went to the one who acted immediately and ruthlessly, making the right move at the right time, without fear or anger or regret, Donna and the feelings she stirred up were a grave danger. Love was a risk Joe couldn't afford.

They cut across 155th Street to the West Side and went up Broadway for the last stretch, and by the time they pulled up in front of the building near the river, where Yolanda lived across the hall from her daughter and granddaughter, Joe had come to a decision. It didn't matter if Donna was there or not. He had other business.

"Wait here," he told Pete and Eddie. "I won't be long."

They buzzed in and rode up in the elevator. Yolanda was waiting in her doorway, arms opening for a hug as soon as they stepped into the hall.

"*Ay, Dios mío*," she called out. "Come on in. You must be so tired. A gas leak! How scary. I'd be terrified."

"It's no big deal," Gladys said, rubbing Yolanda's back, as if she were the one comforting her friend. "Just a precaution. And now we can get an early start tomorrow."

The two women had become pals and gambling cronies and had already planned a trip to Atlantic City in a van with some other gals. That suited Joe. As long as Gladys was offstage.

"Sit down, sit down," Yolanda said now, locking the door. They were in her large living room, comfortably furnished with a gold couch, two cushy armchairs aimed at the flat screen, family pictures on the wall, and soft blankets depicting tropical scenes draped here and there. "I'll make coffee. Unless you want decaf at this hour?"

"Nothing for me," Joe said, looking around, checking the dining room, the kitchen. "I have a car waiting."

"That's too bad," Yolanda said, turning to Gladys. "These kids. Always so busy. My daughter's the same. Again she's working late. Guarding some important VIP."

And just like that, Joe's cool was blown. His heart sank in disappointment. She wasn't there.

27

Donna was splitting a dessert with Evon. That was how she thought of him now, though Andy and the other agents called him Mr. Kozco and his own bodyguards still addressed him as Colonel. And while he had been scrupulously respectful, never making a pass or saying anything inappropriate, his interest was clear, in the attention he paid, the compliments he gave, the shine in his eyes. She knew that look. Every woman did. And while she would never cross the line herself, she couldn't deny she thought about it: what it might be like to make a life with someone like him.

Her father had been what the old-fashioned books called a bounder. Bound to let them down, that is. His nickname in the neighborhood was "*conejo*"—the rabbit. And he surely rabbited in more than one sense of the word. He'd gotten her mother pregnant, among who knows how many others, then lied, cheated, and failed to get a job, until he finally disappeared. No doubt that set the pattern for Donna herself: charming, handsome screwups, before she met her husband, who was the perfect match. Smart, loyal, hardworking, he was a clean-cut, ambitious CIA agent, who turned out to be an obsessive, jealous, controlling creep. And after that? She floated, or sank, really, dating here and there, letting her friends push her to meet this or that guy, set up this or that profile, but not really interested, not invested deep down in anything but her daughter and her career, both of which had grown, steadily and successfully. That fit the pattern too: Donna's mom raised her solo, got a job working in a token booth for the MTA, kept it for the benefits, and eventually retired. Donna had begun to think her path would be the same, except with a government job chasing criminals instead of selling rides.

Then there was Joe. At first he was like the punch line to the joke of her dating history. Forget the bounders and screwups and creeps, here was an actual criminal, the worst possible choice. But there was something about him that touched something in her the others had not. A place in her heart or soul that no one else had quite reached. An immense sexual attraction that was immediate and mutual, obvious to them both. But also something like empathy, understanding. And she'd been right. He was different than everyone else she'd known—so much better and so much worse. And now she was invested.

At the same time, it had all been unreal, dreamlike, and their need for secrecy, the fact that they only met alone, in a private world, allowed it to remain a dream, an unbroken spell. Perhaps that was the only reason she let herself go, fall into it like she did; if no one knew, no one could tell her she was crazy. It had the allure of danger, a moment that had to be seized in case it never came again, every night the last night. That darkness also gave them shelter, made it easy in the way fantasy always was. But could it survive reality, the hard light of day? The very idea of Joe with a mortgage, or at a school play or driving her and Larissa to one of her friends' birthday parties, seemed ludicrous. And that, she supposed, was where Evon came in. A different dream, one where they toured apartments together, then discussed them over elegant dinners in restaurants where she didn't have to worry about being seen. Was she going to run off or even hook up with this guy she just met a couple days ago, the subject of a VIP protection detail? No. She wasn't Julia Roberts. But if he really moved to New York, bought that amazing apartment, and was still looking for someone to help him furnish it . . .

"You know," he said now, finishing his espresso and leaving her the last bite of panna cotta, "at the risk of spoiling a lovely dinner, I'm going to say something I would never usually say on a normal, you know . . ." He nearly blushed, stumbling over the word, which delighted Donna. "Evening out," he finished.

"Oh really? Why is that?"

"Well, you know, it's foolish but we all want to seem perfect, don't we? In those situations? Meeting someone we like? No one wants to show their wounds or seem vulnerable. Men especially I guess."

"Some women appreciate vulnerability."

"Yes, that's what they say, but I'm not sure it's always true. A lot of people can't deal with the truth when they finally hear it. But that's what's different about you." He brushed his beard, a little sheepish. "I admit I checked you out a bit, when I heard you were going to lead my detail. Just due diligence. A few calls."

"And?"

"Exemplary, of course. That's why I agreed. A hero. But I also know, from your record, that you have been through a lot." He smiled, sadly. "Lost a lot. I have too. And now, getting to know you, I see it, that extra dimension behind the eyes. I know that if we ever did really talk, about the past, about the dark things, I know you'd understand."

Now Donna smiled sadly. "I'm not sure I understand darkness. But I definitely know it. Better than I'd like to."

"Exactly," he said. "That is exactly what I meant. You know. And it is only those like us, who know the darkness, who really appreciate the light. The warmth of family, friends, home."

Evon settled the bill—he'd sent dessert over to Andy and the body-guards' table as well—then held Donna's coat for her—despite the romantic vibe she was wearing a dark blue pinstriped suit with her pistol at her hip—and escorted her out, though in fact the doors were opened by Andy, who went out first to check the block, and held by one of his bodyguards. And it was Donna who guided him, holding his elbow while her eyes scanned expertly, right hand near her hip. This definitely was not a date. It was a fine night for romance though, crisp and cool with a faint hint of the coming spring in the air. Traffic flowed on Broadway like a two-way river of lights.

"Do you mind if we walk a little?" Evon asked, strolling in the general direction of the hotel. "I love this neighborhood."

"So do I," Donna said, smiling. Then, switching modes again, she muttered into her lapel mic. The guards moved with them, the waiting cars rolled.

"I'm glad," Evon said, as they sauntered, side by side, "because I have a small announcement."

"Oh really?"

He stopped and faced her. "Tomorrow I will put in an offer on that apartment. The one in the Eleonora with the park view. The one you liked best."

"That's wonderful," Donna said, smiling but keeping her voice neutral. "Congratulations."

"I'm hoping," he continued, standing in an oddly formal posture, with his hand on his chest, the slight wind rippling his cashmere scarf, his thick black hair, "that once I move in and am no longer a visiting foreign subject under FBI protection, that you will help me explore my new hometown . . ." He smiled warmly now, eyes sparkling. "As friends."

"Of course," Donna said, unable to keep the gush out of her voice, though she, too, remained in her professional stance, hands at her sides, feet apart, a decent distance between them. If this was a movie, they'd kiss, and the camera would swirl around them, like the spinning city lights. But it was real life, and the only thing that spun around them was trash in the wind. The mood was immediately shattered by a mad old lady, one of those typical street crones, wearing multiple coats, all hanging open, and men's boots, pushing a packed shopping cart, her long gray hair flapping.

"Remember me?" she howled at them. "Remember me?"

She came right over, a finger pointing. Despite all the security, this was still Broadway, and Broadway had crazies on parade. Nothing was going to stop that.

"Sorry, ma'am," Donna began but the old woman pushed by, pointing, Donna realized, at Evon.

"Remember me? I remember you!"

"No," he smiled sympathetically, "I don't. Sorry."

"No?" she asked, confused, then: "What about this? Remember this?" And she lifted her sweater. For a split second, Donna thought they might have to shoot her, and Andy was clearly ready to tackle her, but there was no weapon. All she revealed was her old-fashioned bra, one of those heavy-duty numbers with thick cup pads, wires, and lace, and then across her chest and stomach a series of terrible scars, purple lumps, healed but still vivid, painful just to see. "Remember this?"

She fixed Evon with a wild glare, more triumphant than pleading, more defiant than self-pitying or beseeching. She was furious. Evon met her eyes, and his own gaze seemed to flame up for a moment, filling with anger rather than pity or even horror. He was annoyed. Then the moment passed. Andy took her gently by the shoulders.

"Excuse me, ma'am," he said, calmly, steering her away. "Maybe I can help."

The bodyguards swarmed in, forming a moving wall. Donna took Evon by the arm and moved him toward the car, whose door was open. And as they climbed in, ready to be whisked off back to the hotel, she heard the mad old woman shout, "Remember me now, Colonel?"

28

Joe spent the night at Cash's place, which turned out to be a mistake. Not that he was a poor host. On the contrary, he was magnanimous, which was the problem for Joe.

After dropping Gladys at Yolanda's, Joe had asked Pete and Eddie to drop him there because he wanted to follow up on the passports and, when he called, Cash had invited him to stay. He lived in a brand-new complex on Main Street in Flushing, a glass and steel residential tower set over several floors of commercial space, parking, and a food court that had five kinds of noodles and four kinds of dumplings alone. But Joe skipped all that and rode up in the elevator to where Cash waited at the end of the hall.

His place was well-equipped, yet spare. There was a sumptuous three-sided modular couch plus two recliners and a screen bigger than most Manhattan movie theaters. There was a state-of-the-art sound system and a dining set for six. But the walls and shelves were bare. The kitchen was loaded with gleaming knives, a blender, a cappuccino machine, a juicer—but there was nothing in the fridge except condiments, beer, and soda, and nothing in the freezer but ice. The only thing stuck to the bulletin board were menus from the food court downstairs.

"Welcome, dude," Cash said when he walked in. "Put your bag in the guest room."

"Thanks," Joe said, popping his head into the room Cash had pointed to, which held a pristine bed, side table, and empty dresser, with nothing on the wall but a mirror. He dropped his bag.

"Want something to drink? I know you don't want beer, but I've got coffee, or um . . . we could order up. Sorry I haven't had time to shop." In fact he was flattered to have Joe as a guest.

"Water is fine," Joe said.

"Coming up." Cash got a glass and filled it with ice, then ran the faucet. "Sorry, I only have tap."

"Doesn't matter." Joe took the glass, had a small sip, and set it down on the counter. Feeling that the formalities were now over, he asked: "What happened with those passports? Does Chen know those hitters?"

Cash shook his head. "No. He's never seen them. But we sent pictures to friends overseas. Looks like they're pros out of Hong Kong. They usually work for the Tongs, there and on the mainland. But this was moonlighting. That's all I got so far. Sorry."

"Don't be. That still helps. Now we know for sure it's a contract. Them and the yokels both. Not some personal beef."

"Yeah, it's a job, for sure. But it could still be local."

"Go on."

"Well, the fact is, most folks would be too scared to try it here. Everyone knows you're off-limits. Even if someone wanted to put out some paper on you, no pro worth hiring would take the job."

"So they'd have to reach out," Joe said, nodding." Okay, that's smart. But who's going to hire a couple white thugs from the backwoods, and then a team of Tong hit men from Hong Kong?"

"Yeah," Cash agreed, opening a beer for himself. "That's the weird part."

"One of the weird parts anyway."

The door buzzed. "Oh shit," Cash said, "I forgot to mention, my friend is coming by to borrow a game controller."

Joe nodded. Cash opened the door, admitting Feather, a pal of Cash's whom Joe had met, who had a buzzed head and tattoos under his hoodie, along with another, younger guy with long hair in a ponytail, and three girls with braids or pigtails and cropped tops or hugely oversized hoodies and baggy jeans or sweats. All wore futuristic sneakers. Cash made introductions and Joe shook hands with Feather, while the others quickly swept into the living room, putting on music and the TV at once.

"You don't mind, do you Joe?" Cash was saying, "Ling Ling has a big match tonight and my TV is better." Joe said sure, but it hardly mattered because now Feather had pulled a bong from a cabinet and was loading hits for everyone, and Cash was opening beers. The party went on till four, with noodles and then ice cream coming up from the food court, a beer run, and at some point, another weed delivery, though by then Joe had retreated to the guest room, more to hide from the smoke and noise than because he expected to sleep. He read his Proust.

◆

For once, Donna was eager to talk things over with her mom. Living across the hall from your mother in the same Washington Heights building where you grew up had its minuses—like a total lack of privacy when your secret lover wanted to sneak over—but it had some pluses as well: on-call childcare, the support of what was essentially a small village, and one person who was even more fascinated with your life than you were, ready to parse the tiny ups and downs of work and love long after your friends got bored.

It was with this in mind that she hurried from the elevator down the hall and used her key to enter, already calling out, "Mami, wait till you hear what just happened with Prince Charming," which was what they'd taken to calling Kozco, whose name her mom always mispronounced as Costco. Then, locking the door behind her and stepping from the small foyer into the living room, she fell silent, freezing in panic, as if in a bad dream: Gladys Brody, Joe's grandmother, was sitting on the couch, wearing a bathrobe.

"Hi, hon," Gladys said, unfazed by Donna's posture of disbelief. "Late night at work? Catch anybody good?"

Before Donna had a chance to change gears, Yolanda came in, also wearing a robe and slippers and carrying two cups of tea. Was this some kind of slumber party?

"Mija," Yolanda swept over and kissed her. "How was work? Look who's visiting. Isn't that nice? Guess what happened? They smelled gas in her apartment. Isn't that scary? So I told her she could stay here of course."

"I see . . ." Donna said, sitting in an easy chair. "How is Larissa? She get to sleep okay?"

Yolanda sat on the couch. "She's sleeping like an angel in my room. So now tell us," Yolanda leaned forward, eager for gossip. "How did it go with Prince Charming tonight?"

"Who's that?" Gladys asked.

"Nobody. Nothing," Donna said.

"He's this big shot, General Costco, who Donna is protecting."

"Colonel, Mom. He's a colonel, and it's pronounced Kozco. Not like the store."

Yolanda shrugged. "Anyway, he's rich and he's after Donna. Wining and dining her, trying to sweep her off her feet. Like Cinderella."

Donna felt herself blushing. "It's not like that. And, anyway, it's classified."

Yolanda harrumphed, re-doing the belt on her robe. "Fine. But that's not what you said last night."

"You know who you should be catching?" Gladys put in. "The Parking Avenger. Now that's a mystery. And they say there's a reward."

"I think he should get the reward," Yolanda said, lifting her bottom to smooth the robe then settling back in. "Who do these big shots think they are, parking wherever they want? And they're mostly foreign!"

"Mom!" Donna scolded. "You're mostly foreign."

"You know what I mean."

"She's got a point," Gladys said. "Just because they're rich they think they own the streets. And half of them have immunity!" She laughed. "I wish I had that. Then I'd park anyplace I felt like too."

In fact she did not drive, nor did Joe keep a car, but because he often drove stolen vehicles or used fake plates and IDs, he actually did park wherever he wanted. No one would ever pay the fines.

"And how's Joe?" Donna asked Gladys. "Where is he staying during this gas scare?"

She shrugged. "You know Joe, he's got people to stay with all over. Not even I know where he is half the time. He's like a cat on the hunt."

"I see," Donna said. "Good for him. You should drink your tea before it gets cold."

"Yes," Yolanda said. "Do you want sugar for it? Or honey?"

"Actually . . ." Gladys reached into her robe's pocket and pulled out a pint of whiskey. "I was thinking we could sweeten it with a drop of this." Yolanda giggled as Gladys spiked their tea. "You should have some too, Donna," she added. "Then you can relax and tell us all about Colonel Charming."

◆

Joe woke up. At first, he had no idea where he was—in jail or a hotel, a jungle or a desert? And in that moment, before reality came flooding back, he experienced all the fear and anxiety he had not had time for earlier. He felt something close to panic, heart pounding, adrenaline coursing through his veins, as he rolled out of bed and reached into his bag for his gun. Then he remembered, he was at Cash's. He was safe. He was fine.

It was early, but he knew he wouldn't sleep again, so he took a shower, dressed, and then padded into the kitchen. Cash's guests lay sprawled and snoring on the couch. One girl, curled in a recliner, still clutched a game controller like it was her teddy bear. Their game was paused on the screen, displaying a Formula 1 racer on a city street with bad guys exploding around it. Joe quietly made a full pot of coffee, drank off one cup, black—there was no milk if he'd wanted it anyway—then left the rest warming as a token of thanks and went out, pulling the door softly shut. He took his bag with him.

It was too early to bug Juno, so he treated himself to a big Taiwanese breakfast: fried egg with brown sauce, a couple pork buns, and *youtaio*—the twisted cruller of fried dough—dipped in hot soy milk. Then he joined the morning commuters and took the train to Brooklyn.

29

Blake woke up before dawn, his heart thumping in his chest, like it had taken off running without him. His body was slick with sweat, his breath ragged in his own ears, as his wife snored peacefully beside him. Everything was silent, or as silent as the city ever got, a low hum of traffic and wind with a single siren far off. Everything was peaceful and dark, or as dark as the city ever got, with the ambient orange glow of the night sky, the lights in the buildings across the street, and the first glimmers of dawn coming from behind the line of towers across the park. Nothing out there had awakened him. The disturbance had come from within. But it was no nightmare. It was a premonition.

Blake pulled his robe on, slid into his slippers, and shuffled into the living room. Here the curtains were drawn, and he faced the rising sun as it backlit the wondrous skyline before him—some of the most valuable real estate on the planet. But the park remained in darkness, like a black pool he might fall into. The danger that lurked beneath his feet was only ever pushed back by the light, for a day at a time.

"Dad?"

He started. It was his son, rumpled in his sweats, rubbing his eyes. "Good morning. Why are you up so early?"

He shrugged. Yawned. "I'm hungry."

Blake smiled, shaking off his gloom. It was day. "Go wake the maid. Tell her to make you some toast."

◆

It was later, as he walked into his office, that the premonition of doom returned to haunt him. As usual, residents were surrounding him with their petty complaints: A toilet clogged because a child had flushed a Barbie doll headfirst, could they clear it and also not damage the Barbie? Someone's dog was disturbing their neighbor's cat, not by barking, but merely with its scent, which the triggered the cat's anxiety; she was already on Prozac, as was the dog, a prize-winning show poodle with its own management team. A car, a brand-new Tesla belonging to a resident, had been vandalized. The owner had been dining out, parked across town when it happened, but still wanted Blake's help, the way a spoiled child wants a parent to fix everything.

But then Blake saw Blythe, perched nervously on the threshold to his office, hands floating like underwater plants, resisting the urge to wave, vague smile attempting to cover the message in her eyes: *Hurry up! Get the hell inside here.*

"Sorry everyone," he announced, smiling as he brushed them away. "Something rather urgent has come up. A building safety matter. Please do put in work orders, and we will see to them promptly."

"But my car . . ." the Tesla owner, a Lebanese arms dealer, called after him in a wounded voice. Waving and smiling, as if the man were wishing him good day, Blake fled into his office. Blythe leaned in close, a hand on his arm, lips close to his ear.

There was a time, like maybe a week ago, when he'd hoped this was a sign she wanted a morning quickie. But now the knot of dread tightened in his stomach. *Please*, he muttered silently to himself, a gambler's prayer, *please let that bastard Brody be dead*.

"He's alive," she whispered.

He shut the door before answering. "Goddamn it. How? You said someone took the job yesterday."

She shrugged. "How do I know? They don't have a customer service number. The contract's still open. And the service provider who took the job is now listed as nonresponsive."

"That doesn't sound good." He rubbed his face hard as if waking up again, then shot his cuffs and smoothed his tie. "What about another provider? Any takers?"

"Not at that price. I think we're going to have to up the stake."

"How?" He waved an empty hand. "We're overextended as it is. Not that I have a problem with bullshitting, mind you, but I'm afraid it requires a thin veneer of reality. And we, my love, are skint."

And then, as if in answer to his grifter's prayer, the phone rang. "Ignore it," Blake said. "I have to think."

"But it's the direct line, baby," Blythe said, pointing.

"Fine, fine, okay," Blake said, waving her on as he sat behind his desk, as if taking his place in a play. She took a deep breath and answered the phone.

"The Eleonora, management and sales office, Blythe Bronstein speaking." Her eyes widened and she began to wriggle with glee, recovering some of her bubbly joie de vivre. "Good morning, Colonel. Hold just one second . . ." She turned to Blake. "It's him, baby. The Russian."

"He's not Russian. He fought the Russians . . ."

"Whatever. He's on the line."

"Right." Blake took a deep breath and answered.

"Good morning, Jeremy Blake speaking."

"Good morning, this is Colonel Evon Kozco."

"Colonel, how nice to hear from you. How can I help?"

"I wanted to let you know that I've made a decision . . ."

"Oh yes?" Blake asked casually, his throat tight and Blythe staring at him, bug-eyed.

"And I've decided I'd very much like to purchase that apartment, if it's still available."

"Well that's splendid, Colonel. I'm quite chuffed to hear it." He gave Blythe a thumbs-up and she literally jumped for joy, coming down on her heels. Her curves returned to earth one by one, with a soft bounce that gave Blake a quiver of desire, the first stirrings of an animal ready to live again. "And may I say, I am very much looking forward to our being neighbors."

"Excellent. I can stop by later to sign the papers and arrange a deposit. I will have it wired from my LLC."

"Yes," Blake said, relief flooding through him. "Just in time."

"Sorry?"

He sat up. "I mean, perfect timing. Another possible buyer was coming by today."

Kozco chuckled. "I see. Well don't let it go till I get there. See you soon."

"Till then. Goodbye."

He hung up. "Yes!" they both yelled and embraced, tightly. Blake grabbed a handful of bottom. "Maybe we should go up to yours and celebrate."

She slapped him away. "Not yet, naughty boy. Save it for lunch." She rushed over to her laptop. "Work comes first."

"What are you doing?" he asked, hands still grabbing air.

"I'm raising the price on Joe Brody's head, of course." She smiled at him. "Then we'll really have something to celebrate."

30

"**C**ash was wondering why you left," Juno told Joe. "He was planning on making French toast for breakfast." They were back in Juno's basement, and Juno was eating cereal while Joe sipped a black coffee he'd picked up on the corner.

"I woke up early and didn't want to disturb him," Joe said. "Anyway, he doesn't even have the ingredients for American toast."

Juno pointed his spoon at Joe's bag.

"That why you're only staying one night at his B&B? No toast?"

"Nope. Just don't want to overstay my welcome."

"You know, you'd be welcome to stay here, ordinarily." Juno cleared his throat. "But my mom's got her church committee meeting here tonight. Or maybe it's the neighborhood council. I forget. She's got so many."

"Don't worry. That's not why I came. I need you to work more of your magic."

"Right . . ." He pushed the bowl aside and rolled his chair in front of the keyboard. "The doctor is now in. What seems to be the problem?"

"Same problem, that building, the Eleonora. But a different angle. Now I want to know about the residents. Who owns these apartments?"

"I told you. They all LLCs. Which is how we know they shady."

"Yeah, but who's hiding behind them?"

"Could be anybody. Especially if they're based offshore."

"But what about when they're onshore? Like in the lobby. If you can hack into the security cameras, start capturing images. Then, I don't know, run some facial recognition software . . ."

Grinning, Juno snapped his fingers. "That I can do. Then we put some names to those faces. You're a smart man."

"I have my moments. But can you do it? Meanwhile I'll try and dig up those blueprints."

"Let's see." He scratched his chin. "Hack into their system without their knowledge. Then gain access to the necessary databases and maybe even match those up with the corporate filings." He grinned. "Of course I can do it. Easy as French toast."

◆

It was when Joe went home to pick up Gladys that the *sicarios* had first spotted him. They were a trio, the three musketeers, and had been working together for ten years, a century in their world, where fortune and death both came fast and often early, though never easily. They'd been born dirt-poor and got their start running errands for the local narcos. Then, as their boss's power grew, they began doing hits in their teens. They gunned down rivals, tortured and chopped traitors, even blew up the occasional cop or judge. They mastered their craft. Then, as their boss's rise was followed by his inevitable downfall, and most of the gang were arrested or killed, they went into exile, crossing the border and taking on a freelance life in the North. They worked mostly for La Eme, the Mexican mafia in California and Texas, but also did some hits for Black drug dealers in New Orleans and for Colombians and Cubans in Miami. They were in Atlanta when they saw the job listing, a huge paycheck for taking out only one guy, Joe. And just a straight hit too, no kidnapping, no torture on video to send the client. So they drove up, taking turns behind the wheel, stopping only for gas. The money they made here had set their families up with ranches and legit businesses back home. Killing Joe could put them over the top. The prospect of retiring, alive, at the ripe age of twenty-seven was almost too good to believe. Maybe someone would write a song about them someday.

For now, though, they were living in the car, pissing in bottles and eating take-out tacos, stalking Joe. When he came out the night before with an old lady, he had two bodyguards on high alert. So they followed, Uptown and back to Flushing. When he emerged early the next morning, they considered just gunning him down in broad daylight, but city traffic was too busy to escape in the car, and the sidewalks too crowded with witnesses to flee on foot. Instead, Flaco and Rico slipped out to follow him onto the subway, first to Bed-Stuy, and then into the city, taking turns to escape notice while Jaime drove the car. They'd follow, and watch, and wait. Then they'd blow away this gringo and go home in glory.

◆

Donna was at her desk early. Anxious to avoid another awkward chat with Yolanda and Gladys, she'd skipped her morning coffee, gotten her daughter to school with a pit stop for a croissant and blueberry smoothie on the way, and caught the express train downtown. It was a long ride from home in the Heights to her office in Foley Square. She spent it brooding. What was with this gas leak? Did she believe that? If not, then what the hell were Joe and or Gladys up to? What if Gladys reported back to Joe about Evon? And why did she care? She'd done nothing wrong. They certainly were not committed. Not to a future anyway. God only knew what he was doing while she did her job. Looking for a lost pet! Between that and this gas leak story, anything was possible. Why should she give a damn what he thought of her? And then there was Evon. What was the story with that mysterious figure, that ghost who had come out of the wilderness of Broadway to confront the colonel? How did she know him? And did he really know her?

With all that going on in her head, and without her dose of caffeine, the strong Café Bustelo she usually brewed up, she was already exhausted by the time she got off the train. Luckily, Sameer was on duty, manning his coffee station in the Plexiglas booth he set up on the corner in front of the Federal Building.

"Good morning, Agent Zamora," he called out brightly. "Latte?"

"Good morning, Sameer. Better put an extra shot in it today."

"Coming right up. Gonna catch some bad guys today?" he asked while he drew the espresso and added foam.

"I'm going to try," she said. "Got to tell the good ones from the bad ones first." They had always been friendly, but ever since Donna appeared in the news, receiving that medal for catching, and killing, a terrorist, Sameer had become her number one fan. He was especially pleased that this time the villain had turned out to be a white guy. He'd even asked for a signed photo to hang in his cart, along with the ones from Robert DeNiro, Audra McDonald, and Hugh Jackman, among others. She had to explain that the FBI doesn't issue PR photos of agents.

"You'll get your man," he said, confidently. "This will help." He handed over the coffee. "Maybe you need a donut too? Sugar is good for the brain."

"Good for the brain, bad for the booty. I'll stick with the coffee. Thanks," she said, handing over the cash and taking a big gulp as she started up the steps. And it did help. By the time she cleared security and got down to her little basement office, her brain was firing at full force. Which was perfect timing because she had a full inbox waiting.

Until recently, Donna's primary duty had been minding the hotline, the usually thankless task of shoveling through the endless flood of mostly useless tips and complaints that the office received or that were passed on from other federal agencies and local law enforcement. Finally, she'd been getting a shot at field assignments, but she still had to stay on top of what she essentially thought of as the bureau's spam folder.

But today one item, or series of linked items, caught her eye. For one thing, it was from the CIA, as well as Interpol, and even the NSA was cc'd. Despite all being on the same side, these agencies were not known for their mutual cooperation, with the CIA especially being full of what others called spooks and Donna called creeps, creep number one being her ex-husband. If the CIA was willingly sharing info, then it was worth a look.

The first item was ordinary enough: Three well-known hit men, employed by the Chinese Tongs, had left Hong Kong for New York. However, despite their deadly reputation, they were not wanted for any crimes, at home or abroad, and their papers were in order, so there was no reason to detain them. It was merely a heads-up. Still, it was notable that since landing they seemed to have gone off the grid, without even checking in to a hotel. Then there was the duo from England. Two London hard-cases, suspected in a string of underworld murders, they were being watched by Interpol and at large somewhere in New York, but no further trace had been found.

Still, this was hardly cause for alarm. In a city of eight million, how many villains were loose at any moment? What was a few more? But then, in the last twelve hours, multiple professional contract killers were reported on the move, worldwide, all heading to New York, throwing up red flags from Mexico to Italy to Russia. Something was going on. But what?

Donna sipped her coffee and mulled it over. Then, opening another window on her screen, she decided to check on the NYPD log of recent felony activity. Few, if any, of these crimes would fall under federal jurisdiction, but there were often matters "of interest" to the FBI. Now she was looking for murders, or attempted murders, something that might indicate whether these various assassins were here on business or pleasure. She scrolled through the listings, an average night of mayhem. Then she found it: two bodies had been pulled from the Hudson River in the early hours. Both male, one black, one white. Other details matched: a shaved head, gold teeth, tattoos, scars. It looked like she'd found the missing Londoners. That answered one question, but simply raised another. If killers were coming to New York, who was killing them?

Finishing her coffee, and already wishing she had another, she printed all this out, put it in a folder to make it look more professional, and hurried upstairs to her boss's office.

◆

"So what is it you're telling me exactly?" Tom glanced quickly over the file, which lay open on top a pile of others. "There's some kind of killer's convention going on?"

"Except two of them have been fished out of the Hudson," Donna said, pointing at the police report.

"So then it's more like a battle royale where they all knock each other off?" He smiled wistfully. "Now that's one event I'd be happy to see us hosting." Tasked with protecting the city from terrorism, he had developed a morbid hatred of all large public events and a bitter resentment of tourists, who made his life difficult by coming here to provide soft targets. All New Yorkers hated parades, unless they were marching in them, but for Tom they'd become a phobia.

"Well, I can't promise that, sir," Donna said. "But somebody killed these two. And there are more on the loose. It looks like something's up."

"What it looks like to me is these two London lowlifes came over here and got done in by our New York lowlifes. Aside from civic pride, sounds like business as usual. Kick it to someone at the NYPD, probably OC."

"Yes, I was going to liaise with them."

Tom laughed. "Oh, you were? That's nice of you. Except I seem to recall giving you an assignment."

"But this is different. This could be important."

"Fine. Then I'll have someone check it out."

"But that's not fair."

"Fair?" Tom stood, a sure sign he was going into lecture mode, so Donna sat down. She might as well rest her feet. "Fair? Fair is something your daughter—how is Larissa by the way?"

"Fine, thanks."

"Good to hear it." He took a breath and resumed. "Fair is what your daughter is hopefully learning about at school today. Here at the FBI, I expect my agents to learn all about unfair. Like people who commit federal crimes, for example."

"How about this?" Donna asked. "I'll save you the trouble of dealing with it. I'll alert the NYPD that we might have names for their bodies and let the spooks know that there's new info. Let them all do the footwork and meanwhile I'll focus on my assignment. Then, if it turns out to be something, I'll let you know. Meanwhile, forget I said anything."

He sat down, considering it, and considering his mountain of other files.

"Sound fair?" Donna asked, with a grin.

Tom laughed, shutting the file. "Get out of here, wise ass."

Donna complied, stopping at the kitchen to make herself another coffee—one of those automated pod things, not nearly as good or as strong as Sameer's—before returning to her own desk and calling her favorite NYPD liaison, Francis Fusco.

◆

"And that's why I think Major Crimes should take over," Fusco concluded, "with me and Chang on the case."

Captain O'Toole heard him out with a straight face. She was leaning back in her chair, feet up on an open drawer, a newspaper across her lap, paper cup of deli coffee, light and sweet, in her hand. She turned to Chang, who had been smiling somewhat sheepishly.

"You go along with this?"

"Um, yes, ma'am," she said. "I mean if you say so."

"And just out of curiosity, because I do happen to be in charge of this unit, when did you two wrap this up?" She held up the paper, front page facing them. TAKE THAT YOU SPACE HOGS. PARKING AVENGER STRIKES AGAIN!

"But surely this takes priority," Fusco argued. "This is a double homicide."

"Good point," O'Toole said, sipping her coffee. "That's why some very capable homicide detectives are conducting an investigation. But that's not what the mayor's office called me about this morning." She waved the paper at them. "They called about this. Which is why you're going to get your butts over to this building and bring me back a parking avenger, cape and all."

31

Joe began at the Department of Buildings. His regular clothes—hoodie and jeans—were good enough to blend in with the contractors filing permits or paying fines. But after a long wait on line, they couldn't help. They had many records of many renovations done over the decades, but as for the original plans of a building more than a century old, those were buried too deep in the department's own history. The clerk had no idea how to help. He would have to dig elsewhere.

"You're a contractor?" she asked.

Joe nodded vaguely. "You know how it is. My client is a nut for authenticity. Wants me to find out how it really was way back when."

"Well . . ." She chewed a pencil. "You could try the Avery."

Joe nodded vaguely again.

"Up at Columbia," she went on.

"Right," Joe said. "Good idea."

◆

For Columbia, Joe felt like he needed a bit more of an act, so he went to a place in Harlem he knew sold fake IDs. Nothing high-end, that would take time, but good enough for underage kids wanting to drink or illegals looking for menial work. He grabbed a pair of clear glasses at a makeup and hair supply shop too, with the nerdiest frames they had.

He entered the campus at 116th—it was open to the public—and found the Avery Library in the northeast part of the main campus. The girl at the counter perused his ID and looked for him on the computer and Joe made a very worried face when she didn't find him.

"But I came all the way from Boston this morning," he whimpered. He took his glasses off and rubbed his eyes. The clerk, herself a student doing her work-study job, clearly didn't want any hassle. Afraid he'd start crying, she contacted someone from the architecture school, and it was decided that as an earnest scholar from a fellow Ivy, he could come in and spend the afternoon reading, but couldn't take anything out. That was fine with Joe, or rather with Howard Simkin, which was the name on his card.

However, both Howard and Joe were disappointed. After two hours digging in the dusty archives, he was no closer to his goal. This time, he appealed to a professor who was down there poring over a huge book of bound architectural drawings, an older chap with a white beard and some very real, very thick glasses. Howard explained what Joe wanted. The professor sent them to the public library.

◆

Donna called the CIA. That was something she had not done, at least not willingly, since the split with her ex-husband, an agent who, at his worst, had used the resources of his agency against Donna, attempting first to dominate and control her, then, after the divorce, to undermine her career and take custody of their daughter. In the end, he'd been drawn into the dark side, a conspiracy of corruption, using drug money to fund terror and manipulate policy. Finally, he'd redeemed himself, partly at least. He'd taken a bullet in the field and died in Donna's arms, his last thoughts of their daughter.

But in death all sins were washed clean, and in the grave all secrets buried. Mike Powell was a hero now. And, despite the traditional antipathy between FBI and CIA, it was as a hero's widow that Donna called.

She got ahold of Carol Camden, her counterpart, more or less, an analyst across whose desk the same information passed. They'd never met, but she pictured her in a basement room of her own, buried somewhere beneath Langley, Virginia. "I just want to give you a heads-up," Donna told her, "I sent the details along, but two of those missing assassins, the Brits, have surfaced in New York."

"I see that," Carol said, no doubt looking at her own screen. "And surfaced is the word, all right. They popped up in the river?"

"Yup. Went in overnight, it seems. But killed elsewhere."

"Any idea who did the world this favor?"

"Not so far. But I will keep you in the loop."

"Sounds good. Anyway, the ball's in your court for now. You and the local LEOs."

In theory, of course, the CIA was strictly forbidden to operate on US soil. And crossing that line was one of the missteps that led to trouble for Mike. As if on cue, Carol added: "Listen, I didn't really know your husband, but I wanted to offer my condolences. He died preventing a terror attack and that's all anyone can ask of an agent. His star's on the wall."

Donna smiled, noting how Carol had, knowingly or not, elided the truth, smoothing over the touchy spots. But Donna understood—a fellow agent had died in the field, and the stars that hung on the wall of remembrance in Langley had nothing more to hide.

"Thanks, I appreciate it," Donna said. Then another thought occurred to her, "While I have you, maybe you can do me a quick favor. Just a little intel for another possible case."

"Sure. If I can."

"I'd love to know more about a Colonel Evon Kozco. Especially any dirt under his nails." Donna spelled it and filled in the basic info.

"No problem. I'll do some digging."

"Thanks."

◆

At the main branch on Forty-Second Street, the reference librarian was ready for the challenge. Whether due to boredom or dedication, she dove into the database, keyboard clicking while Joe hovered.

"Here's something," she said. "*Select Register of Fine Metropolitan Apartment Houses*, containing floor plans and detailed descriptions along with a map showing the location of said houses. 1919. And the Eleonora is on the list."

"Perfect," Joe said. "Can I take it out?"

"We're not a lending library, sir." She gave him a frown. "This is for research only. I will call it up and you can examine it here."

"Right. Sorry," Joe said, then had another idea. "How about a copy machine?"

"That will take a while. And get expensive. Why don't you just use your phone?"

"Phone?"

The librarian considered the look of confusion on Joe's face.

"You have a phone, right?"

He pulled out his phone and showed her.

"Flip phone, very retro-chic," she commented, examining it. "It has a camera though. Right there."

The book Joe had requested arrived, sent from the stacks, and she set him up at a table in a cordoned-off section of the vast, magnificent reading room, where, while other scholars pored over their own volumes in silence, she showed him how to photograph the large format pages with his phone, even gave him gloves to turn the pages on the heavy, leather-bound, and gilt-stamped tome.

"Sorry about all this," she said, before leaving him to his task. "I know it seems like a lot of trouble, but you'd be surprised how many people steal books."

He shook his head in disapproval. "I'd never even consider it," he said, which was not exactly true, he'd been considering it just before she suggested the phone camera, but in essence this was correct: To steal a book, especially a rare book, from a public library, was to him a grave sin and he was happy not to have it on his conscience.

◆

"All this *maricón* does is read."

Flaco was behind the wheel, across from library, trying to focus on the stone lions and not on his cousin, who was pissing into an empty Mountain Dew bottle—which, it just so happened, looked exactly the same as it had before he drank it. He wondered if it tasted the same too. Maybe they could return it to the deli, get their money back. Five dollars for a soda! Everything was crazy expensive here.

"He's supposed to be this big shot. This killer," Flaco went on. "He's more like a professor or some other kind of sissy. Going around in glasses with a book bag."

Finished refilling the bottle at last, Jaime peered at the library steps. "Maybe he's writing a book about all the bastards he killed. Maybe that's why they want him dead."

"You don't go to the library to write a book, *cabrón*," Flaco, who read the occasional comic, told his cousin. "You go to read them. For free. Like a damned loser." Their boss had had an elaborate library in his home, lined with real leather books, though no one read them—they went with the pool table and leather couches.

Jaime shrugged and tossed his repurposed Mountain Dew bottle out the window. "Who cares? I'm hungry. Where's Rico with the food?"

"Hey!" A face appeared in the window—a young white woman with blonde dreadlocks and a lot of piercings—ears, lip, eyebrow, and a big ring in her nose. Startled, Jaime jumped in his seat, rearing back. Flaco stared, bug-eyed. "Don't throw your trash in the street, assholes!" She threw the Mountain Dew bottle back into the car. It hit the dashboard, rolling as it spilled onto their laps.

"Bitch! *Puta!*" Jaime screamed, while Flaco frantically tried to catch the bottle. The girl gave them the finger and rode off on her bike.

"I should shoot her!" Jaime said, drawing his gun.

"Are you crazy? Put that away." Flaco threw the empty bottle in back and looked for some napkins. "You can't shoot her down in the street then sit here waiting for the maricón."

"We can't sit here like this. I'm soaked in piss."

"At least it's your own, *chulo*. Now I smell like you."

"We have to go change."

"We can't without Rico. And what if the professor comes out?"

Just then a loud, amplified voice barked from behind them, and they jumped again.

"Attention in the white Ford. Move this vehicle. You are in a no parking zone."

"It's the *policia*," Jaime exclaimed, reaching for his gun again. A blue and white patrol car had pulled in behind them, lights flashing.

Flaco pushed his hand down. "Be cool." He put the car in Drive.

"But what about Rico with the food?" Jaime asked.

"I guess we'll drive around the block," Flaco said.

"Move the vehicle immediately," the cop voice blared. "Or you will be towed."

Flaco waved obediently as he pulled out, muttering, "I fucking hate Nueva York."

◆

Meanwhile, after waiting on line forever, and paying a staggering amount for three hot dogs, two Cokes, and a Mountain Dew for Jaime, Rico was just about to head back to the car when he saw it pull away. *What the fuck?* He stood, confused, watching his ride float away into traffic. Then the phone in his pocket began to ring, but his hands were full, and he had to put the food down somewhere before he could answer. And that's when he saw him, the gringo Joe, come walking down the steps of the library, passing the big concrete lions, turning at the corner, and heading for the entrance to the subway.

What to do? He had to follow. Not losing the trail was the main thing. So with a pang of regret, he tossed the food in the trash and ran to catch up.

◆

Joe spotted the guy on the way out of the library. At first, mind on other matters, he just thought, *Do I know him from somewhere?* He was a young Latino, in jeans and a soccer warm-up jacket, with short hair, balancing several hot dogs and drinks, and he seemed to stare right at Joe in recognition as he passed. He looked vaguely familiar as well. But he said nothing, did nothing, and Joe went by. It was when, out of his peripheral vision, he saw the guy suddenly dump his uneaten food in the trash and follow that he knew something was up.

Moving with purpose now, but not rushing, Joe went down into the subway station, swiped in, and proceeded to the uptown platform. The guy followed, but kept his distance, and his hands were deep in his jeans pockets, which made an immediate attack unlikely.

The train came. Joe joined the crowd of people boarding, as did the guy, standing by the door, hands still in his pockets. Joe shifted slightly to the side, pretending to look at the map. Then, just as the doors were about to shut, he moved fast, shoving the guy hard to the side and yelling "Sorry," as he jumped out. The guy pitched forward and, unable to reach out with his hands trapped in his pockets, fell in the laps of several passengers, who reacted negatively, yelling, "Hey, watch it," and pushing him back up, while he struggled to regain his balance. The doors shut, and Joe watched the train slide away. Then he crossed over to the downtown side and went to see Josh and Liam.

32

Donna took Evon back to the Eleonora. It was, she had to admit, a beautiful apartment. Coming from where she came from, and growing up with the values Yolanda had instilled, she had never been jealous of those richer than her or lusted much over material things. As a child, having their own apartment, on a fairly high floor, in their building and neighborhood in Manhattan, with all their family and friends was already the best of all possible worlds. Why move? As for ambition, her mother wanted her to work for the MTA as well, get those benefits, that steady civil service job, but dreamed that, with her American accent, Donna could be a train conductor. The fact that she was a decorated FBI agent surpassed the imagination. But she had to admit, this brief interlude with Evon had awakened in her a new fascination with a life of luxury, of doormen and balconies overlooking the park, of fancy restaurants and chauffeurs and perhaps, someday, private schools. Was it because it all suddenly seemed possible that she wanted it? Was she suddenly entertaining that fantasy because, for the first time, it was real?

"Welcome back, Colonel Kozco," Blake was saying now, as he shook their hands, meeting them in the lobby with his trusty assistant, Blythe, by his side. "And Agent Zamora."

She smiled, noticing that she was automatically included now, while Andy and the guards were nameless figures, lurking in the background.

"I'm afraid I have a lot of boring papers to read over," Evon told her now with a warm grin. "But I'm sure it's very safe."

"Absolutely," Blake added with a chuckle, "safest room in the house."

"No killers lurking in the corners," Blythe added, laughing a bit shrilly at her own joke. Blake frowned.

"I'll just check quickly," Donna said, adding a "sir." Then, while Andy checked the lobby, she ducked into the office and took a glance around: windows shut and curtained, no other exit. Everything about the room—the fancy but still comfortable furniture, the soothing abstract art, the warm light and polished hardwood floors—was perfectly safe, reassuring. Nothing from the outside world would disturb this padded cell. Nothing would penetrate this bubble of a life. Except of course that moment when a crazy homeless woman might rear up, screaming *Remember me*, and show her scars. That was the speck of nightmare in the dream, the nagging thought that darkened Donna's romantic fantasy, and told her agent's mind that something was wrong with this perfect picture, something rude, troubling, foul.

"Fusco!" She spotted the inimitable sloping shape of her old pal, Lieutenant Francis "Fartso" Fusco, lumbering across the lobby like a bear in a wrinkled blue suit. To her surprise, she was genuinely glad to see him. "What are you doing here?"

He wheeled around, and though his smile showed true warmth, his dark eyes narrowed, and he let out a groan. "Ah jeez, the Feebs. Just when I thought this whole caper couldn't get any screwier. What happened? One of these zillionaires called the president?"

"As usual you are both nonsensical and rude," Donna told him, turning to the young woman beside him—clearly a detective, as much from her pants suit and comfortable black shoes as the badge and holster on her belt—who was listening to Fusco with a mixture of amusement and confusion. "I'm Donna Zamora, FBI."

"Detective Emily Chang," she said, shaking her hand.

"Detective Chang, maybe you can clear this up. What the hell is he talking about? For once his mouth's not full, but I still can't understand him."

Chang laughed. "That's only because I made him finish his jelly donut in the car."

She explained, while Fusco scowled and Donna and Andy listened with growing grins.

"The Parking Avenger!" Andy exclaimed. "Who else but our hero Fusco could save Gotham from this masked man? Did they send up the Fat Signal?"

"Good one, Newton, did you have that written down in your wallet all this time?" Fusco sneered. "Like you're not here for the same thing?"

"Absolutely not," Donna told him. "Only Major Case could handle something this . . . major."

"Then why are you here?" he asked. Donna and Andy stopped laughing.

"Security detail," she said.

"What sort of security?" He looked around. "Like doormen?"

"This foreign VIP is in town," Andy allowed. "And he's here buying an apartment."

"Ha!" Fusco shouted in genuine glee. "Babysitting some rich brat, huh? At least we're investigating a crime. A street crime."

"Hey," Donna asked, changing topics now that the ball-busting was done. "What do you hear about those bodies they fished out of the river?"

"Two dead limeys is all I know," Fusco said.

"Well keep me posted," Donna said. "I've got a feeling about this one."

"I've got the same feeling, Zamora," Fusco said. "It's the longing of a real detective for a real case."

The elevator opened and a broad man, dark-skinned and bearded, in an expensive tracksuit and a Rolex emerged. "Are you Detective Fusco?" he asked Chang, in a smooth accent.

"Here's my baby to sit," Fusco muttered from the side of his mouth. "Enjoy yours." He turned with a grin. "I wish she were sometimes, sir. But I'm afraid that's me."

◆

"The police are here, sir."

"What?" Blake sat up abruptly, sending his luxurious ergonomically correct executive desk chair rocking. He punched the intercom over which the doorman had spoken. "Why?"

Evon, who was sitting across from him, glasses on his nose as he read and signed a thick pile of papers, looked up with a concerned frown.

"I'll handle this," Blythe said, coolly, and picked up the phone. "Yes? Yes? All right then, thank you."

"It's about Mr. Khalil's car," she told Blake, who seemed to exhale. Blythe turned to Evon to explain.

"A bit of vandalism, I'm afraid. Someone damaged one of the resident's cars. Out in the street somewhere of course. Nothing to do with the building. Our security is top notch."

"I see," Evon said. "Well, it's still New York." Both Blake and Blythe chuckled loudly at this. He nodded at Blake. "But upsetting of course."

"Yes. Sorry. I just care so much about our residents, you see."

"Something you'll appreciate when you move in," Blythe added.

"Speaking of which," Evon said. "Be sure to give me your bank information."

"Of course," Blake said, a warm and genuine smile of relief brightening his countenance.

"When do you expect the transfer to go through?" Blythe asked, casually.

"Tomorrow," he said, then shrugged. "Anyway, it is already tomorrow in the Maldives."

33

"**A**re you sure he was after you? Maybe he just smelled those hot dogs and realized how disgusting they really are." Josh was pouring coffee while Liam and Joe sat at the kitchen table in their Chelsea apartment, looking out onto the backyard.

"What do you mean? Hot dogs are a New York classic," Liam said. "An American classic."

"I love hot dogs at Nathans, or when we grill them, but what's with those boiled ones sitting in that dishwater? Probably real dog in them."

"I've seen and smelled worse," Liam said, pouring cream in his coffee, and offering it to Joe, who declined. "Two words: Chaim Meats."

"True," Josh said. "Neither of us was really in the mood for meat today," he told Joe. "We had a salad for lunch. Speaking of which, are you hungry?"

"No. This is fine, thanks," Joe said, sipping coffee. "And you're right. I can't be sure that guy was after me. Maybe I'm getting paranoid."

"It's not paranoia when people keep trying to kill you," Josh said.

"So says the Israeli," Liam added.

"Unlike the Irish, who forgive and forget."

"And you reckon this one was Mexican?"

Joe shrugged. "He had a Mexican football jacket on."

"First two white hunter types from the boondocks at the club, then the Chinese hit team at the restaurant, and now a Mexican at the library . . ." Liam stirred sugar into his coffee. "Sounds like a very complicated politically incorrect joke."

"Or like you pissed off half the world," Josh added. "But what do people from these countries all have in common, except football?"

"I don't know, yet," Joe said. "But I definitely pissed somebody off. Or scared them."

"Well you're safe here," Josh said, sipping his own coffee. "But it may not be the most restful experience you've ever had."

"Aye," Liam agreed. "You're an honored guest in our warm and loving home. But it might be a wee bit too warm and loving for some right now."

◆

"You got robbed. That's all I can say."

"Mom it's a kettle, it boils water. It's no big deal."

Joe had been just about to ask Josh and Liam where he should put his bag when the front door burst open and a tough-looking man with a lined face, round gut, and full head of gray hair had entered, dragging two huge rolling suitcases secured with cords, followed by an even tougher-looking woman, tiny and svelte and with an even thicker head of dyed black hair. Josh's parents in from Tel Aviv. Apparently they'd checked out of their hotel after some sort of argument that involved complaints from other guests about Josh's dad going to the ice machine in his underwear. Of course they took immediate possession of Josh and Liam's guest room. Now his mom was making tea.

"Remember my cousin's son Rafi?" she went on, angrily waiting for the offending electric kettle to boil. "He has a discount appliance place in Riverdale. You should have gone there."

"Then I would have to go all the way to Riverdale and talk to Rafi," Josh explained, calmly. "Life is too short. I'd rather pay."

"Go ahead. Laugh at your own mother. But he would have had to give you wholesale. You're family so there's no choice. You know what that is? Half."

"But it only cost twenty-five dollars retail. And if it breaks, I can return it."

This whole time, Josh's dad sat impassively reading the paper, occasionally muttering, "Idiots!" though Joe assumed that referred to the news. He cracked a window and lit an acrid foreign cigarette from a duty-free carton.

"Where's that draft coming from?" Josh's mother asked, pouring the tea. "Shut the window!" she yelled at her husband. "Are you trying to make us all sick?"

"Sorry about this," Josh explained, drawing Joe into the living room. "Hopefully jet lag will kick in soon."

"Hey, it's your parents," Joe said. "What can you do?" He pulled his phone from his pocket. "Meanwhile, you guys have a printer, don't you? I was hoping you could help me get these pictures off my phone."

"Yeah," Josh said, examining the phone. "But the printer's in the bedroom. And we don't want to go in there yet."

"What do you mean?" Joe asked. Liam entered now, holding a steaming mug.

"You didn't tell him about Sean?" Josh asked.

Liam shrugged. "I was trying to block it out. I'm bringing him tea now, about half sugar."

Joe followed curiously, as Josh explained. Liam's middle brother, Sean, had come reeling in blind drunk in the early hours after a brutal argument with his girlfriend, no doubt over his being drunk.

"I thought he was clean," Joe asked.

"He's off dope, sure," Josh said. "But whiskey is another matter."

Liam threw open the bedroom door to reveal his brother, bare-assed and snoring in their bed. "Jesus, what a sight. Keep your mum away," he told Josh, then gave his brother a resounding slap on the bottom. "Hey! Eejit! We know you're alive because you're snoring like a pig. Wake up and get this in you."

Sean opened one eye. It blinked at them like a red traffic light. "Fuck!" he groaned, shutting it. "I was hoping this was a nightmare." He took the mug in both hands and gulped gratefully.

"When Josh's folks called to say they were coming, we hid this one in here," Liam explained. "Now we'll have to burn these sheets." Sean gave him two fingers, while continuing to drink tea with his other, slightly steadier hand. "But that means a fight for the couch tonight," Liam went on. "I'd bet heavily on you to win."

"Sorry, Joe," Sean croaked, clearing his throat and sitting up a bit more. "I know you're supposed to stay here. I didn't know that bitch would kick us out. But I'll find a place. Don't worry. Or better yet . . ." He suddenly sneered. "Take my keys. Use my apartment. And you can go ahead and sleep with that slag if you want. I'm done with her!"

"You know what," Joe said to Liam, "I'm thinking maybe I can find someplace else to crash."

"You sure?" Liam asked. " 'Cause you're more than welcome. This trash can flop on the floor. He's used to it."

"Very sure," Joe said. He was thinking of the couch in Santa's office at the club. Or maybe the back room at the bookstore. Meanwhile, a phone rang, and Liam picked it up, speaking quietly.

"This phone is dead," Josh came back from the desk, holding Joe's flip phone. "You have to charge it."

"Dead?" Joe asked. No wonder he hadn't had any calls or texts.

"I'd lend you our charger," Josh said. "But we don't have anything that archaic."

Liam put down the phone. "That was Juno, looking for you," he told Joe. "He says your phone is dead."

"I heard."

"He says he's got something for you. A result."

"You know what guys," Joe said, pocketing his phone. "I think I'm going to see Juno. He'll have a charger."

"I'll drive you," Liam offered.

"No, I will," Josh said.

"I thought of it first."

"Not necessary," Joe said. "It's kind to offer, but I don't need a bodyguard."

"Believe me," Liam said. "You'll be doing me the favor."

34

Adonis was afraid of Yelena. That was why he called her to begin with but also why he had the two enormous bouncers from his club, gym champions in the gay muscle world of Chelsea, lounging like great cats when she showed up. They were working out, one doing bench presses, stripped to his tiny briefs, his chest and arms rippling stone, while the other spotted him, in a tight T-shirt and sweats, gun in a shoulder holster. Dressed in a white silk robe, with his hair loose, Doni posed casually on the couch.

Yelena came alone and unguarded. She had a driver, a young Brighton Beach thug, behind the wheel of the black Mercedes, but he was merely there to avoid the hassle of parking in this neighborhood. This was a private matter, and she would deal with it alone.

"Yelena!" Doni yelled, squealing in fake delight as Yelena entered, pushing the heavy metal door back and striding in. She wore black—boots, leggings, a turtleneck, and her cropped bike jacket—and her own long hair was braided. She was dressed for work. Doni jumped up and kissed her on both cheeks.

"Come in, it's so good to see you. Love the jacket. You remember Pepe and Charles."

Yelena looked at the two giants who loomed over her, one dressed and armed, the other almost nude. "Get out," she told them.

"Yes ma'am," Pepe, the armed one, said, then added, "Hurry," to Charles who was grabbing his clothes.

"Yes, see you later, boys," Doni called after them. "Yelena and I want to have a private chat."

They hustled out through an inner door and shut it behind them.

"Have a seat," he said now, pointing to one of the armchairs and sitting back on the couch. Yelena stood over him.

"When did you see Vicky? Why was she here?"

◆

During Vicky's last visit to New York, she had killed, or intended to kill, several people, including, at one point, Yelena herself. That was just business, and Yelena would not take it personally, any more than she herself had any ill will toward the people she robbed. But Vova had been different. Yelena had grown close to the old man over her time in Brooklyn. She'd stop by, bringing caviar and vodka and other treats, he'd clear the table in his amazingly cluttered apartment and brew very strong tea. Not only had Vicky killed him, she'd tortured him first, hanging him from the balcony by his wrists, burning him with cigarettes. That was personal. And that was why everyone knew, if Vicky showed up, or you heard anything about her, you should contact Yelena, for the sake of your own well-being.

"Well, to be honest, come to think of it, she was here yesterday."

"Yesterday? Why didn't you call me then?"

"I wanted to . . . I mean I was going to, but then these two other guys came while she was here."

"But why didn't you call me before she came, Doni?"

He shrugged. His plan of course had been to do his business with Vicky first and then inform Yelena, thereby doing himself the most good. But things got out of hand. Now Yelena sat, but not on a chair. She sat next to Doni and stroked his long black hair, speaking in soothing tones.

"What did she buy from you Doni?"

He told her about the weapons, a slight quaver in his voice. "I meant to call but there was trouble."

Yelena drew a long combat knife from her boot, then pulled back his hair and looked deep into his dark eyes.

"Exactly what kind of trouble?" she asked. "Tell me everything, in detail, from the beginning."

PART IV

35

The sicarios were waiting for Joe at Juno's. When Rico lost him in the subway, he got off at the next station and called his brother and cousin, who were still circling the library. They worked out where Rico was, picked him up, and, with no other leads, headed back to the last place they'd seen him, the house in Bed-Stuy. And sure enough, a couple hours later, the target showed up, but in a car this time, driven by a white guy who behaved a lot like a bodyguard. He got out and scanned the block, which forced the three men to duck, with Rico hiding on the floor of the back seat, which he realized was full of discarded food, soiled napkins, and several plastic bottles of urine. The whole vehicle stank at this point, like bums had been camping in it, except they themselves were the bums.

"Maybe he wants to visit the Brooklyn library," Jaime suggested.

"If he does," Flaco muttered, "I will drive right up the steps and run him over."

Instead Joe got out and entered through the basement, disappearing down the steps. A moment later his driver pulled away, leaving them on the quiet block, filled with trees and well-kept brownstones.

"Finally," Jaime said. "This is perfect. We wait for him to come out and do it."

But about ten minutes later, there was a tapping on the driver's side window. A middle-aged black man was there, in a cloth cap and raincoat, holding a bulldog on a leash.

"Now what?" Flaco muttered and rolled it down. "Yes?"

"Excuse me, mind if I ask what you're doing here?"

"We are minding our own business," Flaco said. "Like you should be."

"I was. But you see, I live here, and you are parked illegally in front of my driveway."

"So?" Jaime asked, leaning over. In the back, Rico put his hand on his gun, seeing where this would lead. "You're not using it right now, are you? If you need it, we will leave, okay?"

"Otherwise you can call the cops and have us towed," Flaco added with a snicker.

That's when the dog walker showed them a badge. "Actually, I am a cop," he said. "But I really don't want to spend my day off on this bullshit. So why don't you just take whatever this is down the road?"

"Yes, sir," Flaco said. "No problem."

He started the car up and they pulled away, the guy still watching, his dog sprawled happily in the driveway.

"I fucking hate New York," Jaime muttered.

Flaco agreed, and, as they turned a corner to cruise pointlessly, burning more expensive gas, Rico had a sudden premonition.

"Let's forget it," he said. "It's awful here. It's cold and wet and the people are rude. Let's go home. We have enough. Let's go to Mexico."

But the others weren't paying attention.

36

"There's still a lot more to look at, but I thought you should see what I've got so far." Juno was manning his post, at the keyboard in front of the multiple screens, in his ergonomically designed executive rolling swivel chair, not quite like Kirk's chair on Star Trek, but serving the same purpose as he steered his own private enterprise through cyberspace.

"You found something interesting?" Joe asked, settled in a plain wooden chair beside him.

"That's one word for it, sure," Juno replied. "Another is sinister. Nefarious. Looks like you stumbled into some kind of clubhouse for archvillains."

"Show me," Joe said, pulling up closer. "Slowly."

"Right. Baby steps version." Juno brought up images on the screen while he talked. "Basically I spent the day scanning through security footage, especially around the time you were there, grabbing every face that looked like it belonged to somebody relevant. Then I ran the faces against a bunch of different databases."

"And you got matches."

"Did I ever." On the screen a row of faces appeared, all men, say thirty-five to sixty-five, but otherwise a mixed group: a bald black man with a goatee, an Asian man with gray hair and glasses, a clean-shaven white man with cropped blond hair, a Latino with a neatly trimmed beard. "What we've got here is what I'd call a rogues gallery, dude."

"I met him, briefly," Joe said, pointing at the bald man in the military uniform. "But we didn't have time to trade names."

"Probably for the best. That's Jean Mtume, former general and right-hand man to a corrupt African dictator. His specialty was wiping out villages and hiding the bodies in the mines they used to rape the country's resources. Supposedly he left with his luggage full of gold and diamonds and shit." Juno hit the keys and expanded the next photo: "Or perhaps bachelor number two is more your type. Meet Mikael Volkov, Russian oligarch. Or is it plutocrat? Oliplut? Plutoligarch?"

"Enough," Joe said.

"Sorry. Too many hours running on sugar and caffeine."

"Just finish explaining and we'll get some food. On me."

"Right. Anyway, he's suspected of everything from sex trafficking to brokering deals on nuclear rockets. But then he fell out of favor with Putin and apparently moved to the Upper West Side. Next up . . ." He scrolled. "Fernando Lopez, known as The Snake. He's just an old-fashioned cartel boss. Anyway, the local politicians he was supposedly backing lost, so the new regime blew up his house. But it seems he has a nice pad here as well. Should I go on? Or can we order the pizza?"

"Order. Then, while it's coming, tell me which apartments they own."

"No can do, boss," Juno said, tapping the keys again. Data flashed on the screen. "Like I said, they're all owned by LLCs, dummy corporations set up overseas."

"Okay, I have another idea. But order the food first, Juno," Joe said. "I don't want you spinning out on me."

"Already did." He pointed at another window that was open in a corner of a screen. "Large pepperoni and mushroom and a six-pack of grape Snapple should be here in twenty-three minutes. You said you were paying right?"

"Right. My bad. Let's carry on." Joe leaned forward and pointed at the faces. "What if I can remember a few of the apartment numbers?" Closing his eyes, he recalled the apartment he began in, the ill-fated 10E, then worked out the African general's, the Russian's, and the Colombian's. Juno pulled up the records. Meanwhile, on another screen, he restarted the security footage from the building lobby, which sped by, pausing when the program focused in on a face.

"So, as I said," Juno said, "those apartments are all owned by dummy corporations, but as you can see, looking at the ownership history, there is a lot of activity, with resales every couple years. All between LLCs, though, so there's no way to confirm if those guys are the real owners."

Joe looked at the generic corporate names—initials, streets, names of trees and animals. "What about the banks they use, and the lawyers who set up and administer the corporations?" he asked. "That's public record, right?"

"Sure. They're listed right here with the transactions." Juno tapped some keys. "Huh, that's interesting. It's the same. Seller and buyer both used the same lawyer and overseas bank."

"Right." Joe sat back, looking satisfied. "Now I know who's trying to kill me. And why. Well, more or less." He snapped his fingers. "Shit!" Then pulled his phone from a jacket pocket. "Here. Can you plug this in somewhere and print the photos off it? It's the plans I need to the Eleonora."

Juno dug through a box of chargers, then reached down to the power strip under his desk and plugged in Joe's phone. Joe leaned back, lost in thought, till his eyes lit on the screen, where the footage from the lobby of the Eleonora continued to play. Suddenly, he bolted forward, resisting the urge to press a random key.

"Juno, Juno, the tape . . ."

"What?" He sat up abruptly and hit his head on the desk. "Aw, fuck . . ." He rose again, more carefully, rubbing his head.

"Sorry, you okay?" Joe asked.

Juno nodded, climbing back into his seat. "How many times I got to tell you, man? There is no tape." He reached over and hit a key to pause it.

"Go back," Joe said. "I saw something."

Juno reversed the recording, people walked backward across the lobby, backed on and off the elevator.

"Hold it," Joe said. "There. Those two."

Juno froze the image. It appeared to be a couple, laughing, the man's hand casually resting on the small of the woman's back. "Want me to search for their names? See who these two are?"

"Just him," Joe said. "I already know who she is." It was Donna. No wonder she'd been out of touch lately. Distant. Busy. Another mystery solved. Under the desk, Joe's phone beeped as it came back to life. Juno checked it, as Joe stared at the frozen image of a happy Donna.

"Um, Joe, I think you better check this." He handed Joe the phone. There were multiple messages from Yelena.

◆

"So what's up with you and Prince Kozco? Am I going to get to be in the royal wedding?"

Donna rolled her eyes at Andy. They were sitting in the car while he met with a lawyer on a high floor of a Midtown tower.

"He's not a prince."

"But he is tall, dark, and handsome, and he just put a deposit down on a castle. So I repeat . . . does the shoe fit?"

"Since when am I Cinderella?"

Now it was Andy who rolled his eyes. "You've been waiting for a ticket to the ball since I met you. Now you gotta get out there and kiss the prince before you turn into a pumpkin."

"According to my kid's books that was her carriage."

"After thirty it's your waist."

"You're such a romantic."

"I am. I'm a believer in marriage and traditional values—including the value of that real estate. Look, it's obvious the man is falling for you. Just let him know it's mutual is all I'm saying." Andy narrowed his eyes at her. "Don't even try to tell me it's not mutual. Unless giggling and blushing are now part of standard agent behavior."

Donna scowled at him, especially as she felt herself blushing. "I won't deny there's an attraction, but my behavior has been nothing but professional."

"That's what I'm saying! Too professional. You've got to go for it. I would."

"You're married."

"And you're not. Anymore." He looked her in the eye. "You're single and free and you just met a dream man, so what's really holding you back? Because I know it's not that badge."

Donna's only answer was a deep breath and a slow shrug. But in her own mind she responded: *Good question.*

37

It was Jaime's turn to walk the block, trying to look unobtrusive, and he'd just bought a Mountain Dew at the corner store when he saw the target, Joe, come out. But there was nothing he could do. A black Mercedes had pulled up, right in front of the driveway where they had been parked themselves, and as soon as Joe emerged, a gigantic, tattooed man in a black suit got out of the passenger side and opened the door, holding it with his left hand. His right hand was inside his coat, no doubt on a gun. Nodding his thanks, Joe hopped in like it was a cab. Jaime had to run back around the block for his partners, and when he finally opened his soda, in the car, it was all shaken up and it sprayed all over his lap. He really hated New York. But he also really, really wanted to kill this gringo Joe.

◆

Aside from saying hi when he got in the car and thanks when he got out, Joe didn't bother talking to the Russians in the front seat. Most likely they knew nothing, and if they did know, they'd shut up about it; Yelena would have trained them well. So he sat back and took the ride over the Brooklyn Bridge and back into the city. It was then, slumped silently in the back seat, that he found himself returning to the image of Donna that was burned into his mind, turning it over like it was a photo in his hands. She was laughing, smiling, standing close, almost holding hands with the handsome stranger in the clearly expensive, beautifully tailored blue suit, his neat beard and wavy dark hair frosted with gray. She looked happy. She looked like she belonged with him. Had she ever looked that way with Joe? Pain surged up in his chest, a feeling of loss, not just of what he'd had but even more achingly, of the future he'd allowed himself to imagine. And then, as the car approached the Meatpacking District, he stuffed that feeling back down. He turned the photo over and put it away.

The car stopped in front of a flashy new building, all angled glass and bent steel, like ice cubes stacked in a cocktail glass, with a neon-lit nightclub sitting like the cherry on top. The big Russian in the front passenger seat hopped out and opened Joe's door, gesturing toward the basement entrance.

"Thanks," Joe said.

◆

When Joe came in, Yelena was holding a vicious-looking knife over Doni, who looked like he'd been crying, though not yet bleeding.

Fine black hair had fallen, like dark leaves or ink strokes, across the white couch and white carpet and white robe. He looked at Joe beseechingly.

"She's torturing me," he said.

Yelena laughed. "Please. You needed a trim. All I cut were the dead ends, for now. If you don't tell us everything, I start cutting off living things."

"I did tell you everything!"

"Tell it again," she said. "For him."

She leaned back against the wall, knife resting in her hand. Joe sat on the coffee table across from Doni.

"Take your time," Joe said, his voice calm and encouraging. "Just relax." Doni sat up and retied his robe.

"Well . . ." He cleared his throat. "These two mechanics from London. Rough trade you know, but pros. They came to buy supplies."

"Guns," Yelena put in.

"Yeah, guns and ammo," Doni said, and took a deep breath. "Anyway, they were bragging, going on about this big hit they were here to do, but on spec like. There was a bounty they could claim from this new, super-exclusive secret website. You know, like in the Old West, wanted dead or alive." He shrugged. "Except for the alive part."

"You ever see it?" he asked.

Doni shook his head. Joe glanced at Yelena, who raised her eyebrows.

"I heard a rumor a couple weeks ago," she said, "about a hit in Europe, but I thought it was salami."

"Baloney," Doni corrected.

"What?" Yelena asked, pointing the knife.

"Nothing. Nothing."

"Okay," Joe encouraged Doni, "go on. . . ."

"So they bought their stuff and went. And then Vicky came by, she'd called and said she was in town and needed some gear."

"Which you were supposed to tell me," Yelena said.

Doni flinched, as if feeling the knife. "There was no time, she called while they were here." He looked back at Joe. "And then while she was here, they came back."

"The two Brits?"

Doni nodded. "Yeah. And they tried to take her out, like to eliminate the competition."

"But they didn't, did they?" Joe asked.

"No." Doni smiled despite himself. "She swatted them like flies." Worried again, he looked at Yelena. "Then she made me get rid of the bodies and swear not to tell. I mean, I was accomplice to murder!"

Yelena scoffed. "As if that was something new. Accomplice to murder should be your job description."

"Doni," Joe kept his calm tone. "Did they tell you the name of their target?"

He nodded.

"And?"

Doni shrugged, looking away from Joe. "This guy they call Joe the Bouncer." He cleared his throat again, and seemed to shrivel, as if trying to crawl away without moving. "Who I guess maybe is you?"

"Good guess," Joe said, still calm and smiling, but leaning closer, eye to eye. "And now, tell us how to find Vicky."

Doni twitched a little. "Last night she was at the club upstairs, in the VIP lounge. But now who knows?"

"VIP lounge, huh?" Joe asked. He looked at Yelena, in her all-black, tight gear, and back at Doni, still lovely in his white robe, despite the slightly shorter hair. Then he glanced down at his jeans, old sneakers, and hoodie. "Think I look good enough to get in?"

38

Donna and Evon were just ordering dinner, at a quiet place near his new apartment, a sort of celebration. He'd chosen a special, rather expensive wine, and the waiter had hurried off, all aflutter, to fetch it.

"So I wonder," Evon said, as soon as he was out of earshot, "if you happened to notice what lawyer I was meeting with today?"

She had not. She'd assumed it had to do with the purchase of the apartment at the Eleonora. "Meetings with lawyers are confidential," she said. "As you very well know. We're not allowed to ask."

He smiled. "I commend your ethics," he said, as the wine arrived. They paused while the waiter uncorked it and poured a small taste into Evon's glass. He swirled it expertly, then took a deep sniff and a slow mouthful. "And I commend your wine, sir," he told the waiter, who smiled and nodded as he poured. Evon raised a glass, as did Donna: "To ethics!"

She smiled and drank, feeling the warmth and flavor of the wine flow through her. It really was a wonderful wine—even she could tell that. Its deep red seemed to spread a rosy glow over her and everything in the restaurant—flickering candles, polished silver, white tablecloths, dark wood—seemed to brighten and gleam, reflecting in the windows an image of happy prosperity set against the dark outside.

"Well," Evon continued. "Since I am not held to the same professional standards, I will reveal that I was meeting with an immigration lawyer. I plan to apply for permanent residency. A green card."

"Really?" Donna felt her pulse quicken, as if this concerned her.

"Yes. I figure if I'm buying a place, putting down roots, I might as well make it official."

"Permanent resident," Donna murmured, smiling. She raised her glass. "I'll drink to that."

Laughing, they touched glasses, and Evon's hand found hers on the table, covering it. Remembering what Andy had said, she did not take hers away. For a moment she felt as if she were transported to some magical future, where they were already a couple, happy, settled, blessed, out to dinner with perhaps a babysitter minding the kids at home, at the Eleonora. Then her phone beeped, breaking the mood.

"Excuse me," she said, and checked. It was her work email. The report she had requested from the CIA had come through, Evon's classified background. "It's work."

"Can it wait?" he asked, with a smile. The waiter was bringing the first course, oysters. After that they were sharing the aged and rubbed rib eye for two.

She smiled back. "Of course."

In the club it was too loud to hear, too crowded to move, and too dark to really see who was there. Not an ideal setting in which to hunt for an assassin who might be hunting you. But the door guys—Pepe and Charles, now dressed in black and on duty—assured Joe and Yelena that Vicky had not yet arrived, and once inside, accompanied by Yelena's men, they did as thorough a check as they could, walking the perimeter of the main room, a large space covering most of the penthouse floor, with glass walls, modular seating on several open levels, and a dance floor in the center. In the middle of the dance floor was a large glass water tank, like an aboveground pool, where a few women in mermaid-inspired swimsuits splashed around, their long hair streaming and floating around them like clouds. As the night progressed, customers would join in their own swimsuits, then their underwear, then nothing at all. Meanwhile, Yelena and Joe retreated to the VIP room to wait and see if their blind date showed.

This was essentially a smaller version of the main room. It featured dark red leather couches around low lacquered tables, a small bar, and huge windows looking out over the street. The special touch was several large tanks containing tropical fish, which were set in front of the windows, creating the illusion that they were swimming over the city, or that lower Manhattan had finally been lost in a deluge.

They took seats on a corner couch that gave them a view of the door. A long-limbed, short-skirted waitress with moody eye shadow plopped two ice buckets holding bottles of champagne and vodka on the table before them, along with glasses, more ice, and lemons.

"Compliments of Doni," she announced flatly and slouched off.

"Miss," Joe called after her, then louder: "Miss!"

She looked over her shoulder.

"Some club soda too?" he asked.

She shrugged and stalked away, like a model on the runway, which was no doubt what she had come to New York to become.

"I can't believe people are out there hoping to get in here," Joe observed, looking over the room.

Yelena shrugged. She'd been here before. She frequented such places on different hunts, dancing, drinking, and seeking company for the night. Though she had to admit the idea of Joe doing any of those things here was comical. The Very Important People lounging about that night were an assortment of Wall Street bros paying thousands of dollars for the same bottles they had, accompanied by lithe young women, of the same sort as their waitress, who perched and preened and posed, managing to be both over- and underdressed. There were some bodyguards—big bodies in black suits—and some celebrities to guard: a rapper and his entourage, a football player and his entourage, a young TV actor and a rising pop singer on a date. Joe had no idea who any of them were. Yelena recognized the faces but couldn't place their names.

Of course, everyone there was also scoping everyone there, so Yelena and Joe were carefully, casually checked out, if only because of their prime table and especially tough-looking bodyguards, the only ones, Yelena felt certain, who were actual murderers. Then there was her own glamour—even in a room full of professionally beautiful people she stuck out as someone remarkable. She was fair and fit, clad in designer black but with her pale skin covered in Russian prison tattoos and icy killer eyes—like an Assassin Barbie.

And then there was Joe. At first glance he seemed just the opposite, completely unremarkable, like someone who should be delivering something to the back door. And that was how most of the VIPs regarded him, as the boring, ordinary guy with the hot, fascinating woman. But not the rapper, who'd grown up hard on the bad side of Philly, or the bodyguards, who were mostly off-duty cops—they took in the body language, relaxed but coiled, the easy half-smile that contrasted with the sharp, penetrating gaze that scanned constantly but did not flinch when met—and they gave Joe his space. Whatever he was here to deliver, they did not want it addressed to them.

The waitress returned and slumped over them. "This okay?" She set a bottle of Perrier before Joe.

"Yes, good, thanks," Joe said and reached in his pocket for a tip, but she had already moved on to better prospects—the Wall Streeters waving for more champagne.

Yelena poured herself a shot of vodka and toasted Joe before downing it and immediately pouring another. "I can understand why you don't drink vodka with me, but can't you at least have champagne? It's like ginger ale."

"Too sweet," Joe said with a smile. "Like you." He poured himself some Perrier and took a sip.

Yelena laughed and took another shot. "Well as long as I'm here I might as well dance. Are you coming?" She rose and offered a hand. Now Joe laughed.

"Maybe after a few more Perriers."

With a wave, she snaked away. Her bodyguards followed at a discreet distance. Joe was alone. If only he had those building plans with him, he could get some work done at least. Unbidden, the image of Donna and her Handsome Stranger floated up again into his mind. A sudden pain pierced his heart. Joe was a well-defended person who moved through the world alert and ready to act against danger. But how did you defend against these attacks that came from within? Feelings, he supposed they were called. Even when you thought they were gone, they were merely lying in wait, ready to ambush you again. If only he could eliminate unwanted emotions with the same ruthless efficiency with which he took out his assassins. And dispose of their remains the same way, leaving not a trace.

Then a sudden motion to the side caught his eye. He snapped into action, already moving as he spotted a young guy in baggy clothes, pointing what turned out to be a phone, not a weapon. But by then Joe had taken it from him, and forced him onto the couch, his arm twisted up behind him.

"Ow, ow, hey man, you're breaking my arm. . . ." the guy shouted.

"Not yet, I'm not." Joe applied a little more pressure. "Why were you taking my picture?"

"Not you, man," the kid replied, unable to keep a little disdain out of his voice despite the circumstances. "I wanted a selfie with Tad and Veronica in it, okay?"

"Who?" He added a little more pressure. The kid squirmed.

"Over there," he squealed. "I'm an influencer!"

"Influencing what?" Joe asked.

"I'm heyitsjustjimmmy, with three *m*s on Instagram," he pleaded. "I've got over ten K followers."

Joe let him go, examining the phone, but by then the young couple—the TV and pop stars—had sent one of their handlers over.

"If I may, sir," the broad fellow in the black suit asked. Joe handed the phone over while its owner rubbed his arm, relieved that it was in fact, not broken.

"Password?" the bodyguard asked the influencer, who started to protest. Joe gave him a look. He mumbled numbers and the guard did some tapping and swiping. "Here." He showed Joe a blurry shot of the kid looming into the camera, thumb up, with the celebrity couple over his shoulder and Joe a smear in the corner. The guard deleted it. "All gone."

He returned the phone to the kid as he led him out of the VIP room, still ruefully cradling his hand.

"Thanks dude, you really did us a solid there." It was the young guy, Tad, Joe assumed. He was very handsome and, like many celebrities, rather small with a large head. He was dressed similarly to Joe—jeans, T-shirt, hoodie—but somehow looked much better, as if it had all been perfectly crafted just for him. "It's so hard to just get a little privacy, you know?"

The girl, Veronica, was even smaller, though quite curvy, in skin-tight jeans and a T-shirt that showed her belly off. "Yeah, thanks so much," she chimed in. "You're the kind of fan we love. The ones who really understand us as people."

"Sure, no problem," Joe said as Yelena returned, trailed by her men.

"What happened?" she asked.

"Nothing," Joe told her, nodding at the celebrity couple. "Just chatting with um . . ."

"I'm Tad and this is Veronica," Tad said.

"Hi," Veronica said.

"And you are?" Tad asked.

"Leaving," Yelena told him, turning back to Joe. "I don't think there is any point in remaining here."

"Right," Joe said, as Yelena grabbed the bottle of expensive vodka and marched out. "Have fun, kids," he told Tad and Veronica. "Watch out for bad influencers."

Outside, Yelena's car was waiting. She and Joe got in the back.

"You'll stay with me tonight. It's safer," she said, then uncapped the bottle and took a swig, explaining, "It's a crime to waste good vodka."

Joe took the bottle. "You're right. And I've seen too much crime lately," he said, and then he joined her in a long swig.

◆

Vicky, as it happened, was at another, lesser-known club in a warehouse space in Bushwick. She'd been tipped off by Pepe, whom she'd bribed when she was there last night. She wasn't afraid of trouble—after all, she'd come all the way to New York looking for it—but she preferred it on her own terms, when and where she was ready. So she took a cab to the club in Brooklyn. And she danced.

39

Fusco and Chang came up with a new plan: this time they'd cruise the streets, snaking block by block through the target zone, with Fusco behind the wheel, and Chang, as the junior team member, ready to pursue on foot. She wore loose trousers and sneakers. They would also stay in constant contact with the local patrols, reporting their location, so that, if they spotted the guy, backup could swoop in and box him up before he reached the park.

"I also suggest," Chang suggested, as they cruised across Seventy-First Street, "that when we get to the north end of the zone, we pick up chicken parm heroes at the place on Eighty-Sixth."

Fusco nodded sagely. "Now you're really thinking like a detective," he told her. "Though I prefer a meatball parm sub or maybe sausage. It's just, I don't know, meatier."

"Of course you do." Chang grinned at him. "You know, if you got a side salad with that hero, or added the broccoli rabe to the sausage, the fiber would do wonders for your digestive problems."

"What digestive problems?" Fusco asked as he lit a smoke.

"Window!" Chang barked.

"Okay, okay," Fusco said. "I'm lowering it. Don't get your panties in a twist."

She laughed good-naturedly as they made another turn, south on Fifth, then back across the small territory where they were hunting the Avenger, an area that also happened to coincide with the most expensive patch of real estate in the known universe. Chang announced their progress over the radio: "Be advised, area units, we are driving west on Seventy-Sixth, heading toward Madison."

"Copy that," one of the patrol cars responded.

"Roger that, detectives," added another.

Chang hung up the radio, then coolly informed Fusco: "Just for the record, I'm not wearing panties."

He did a double take and almost rear-ended a bus.

Then she added: "I'm wearing boy-cut briefs."

He laughed. "That figures." They talked without looking at each other, eyes scanning both sides of the street, checking the parked cars, especially the illegal ones.

"How so?" she asked.

He waved a hand, talking while he smoked. "It's, you know, more asexual, right?"

She had to laugh at that, shaking her head. "Not the way they look on me." Then she punched him in the arm. "You idiot, they're better for running. You try chasing down a perp in a thong. See what happens."

"How do you know I haven't," Fusco asked, arching his eyebrows devilishly. "I'll tell you all about my undercover work someday."

"Now that's something I'd like to see," Chang said, "or maybe not."

"Seriously though," Fusco asked now, in a more thoughtful mode, as they reached York Avenue and made a right, "I've decided to take your advice."

"Oh yeah?"

He tossed his smoldering butt. "I'll order the sausage and peppers hero. That has veggies."

Chang was about to explain the concept of fiber when they heard a car alarm sound. Unfortunately, it was a block to the north of them. Fusco hit the siren and lights while Chang got on the radio.

"Go, go," he told her as she opened the door and bailed, taking off on foot while he threw the car in reverse, thinking his best chance was to get around and cut the guy off. He stomped the gas and shot backward down the block, and he was pretty good at driving that way, wobble-free, but at the corner a taxi appeared, that was planning to make a turn. Fusco slammed on the brakes, but it was too late. He plowed right into it, crumpling the front right quarter panel and denting his own rear fender, thereby adding a unique footnote to his checkered career: He "front-ended" someone.

Chang found the car, but even in running shoes and boy-cut briefs, the Avenger was long gone. The black BMW had diplomat plates, busted passenger side windows, a slashed front tire, and scratched in the paint job on the hood was the helpful four-line note:

NO
PARKING
ASS
HOLE

The patrol units reported in, but alas, they, too, saw nothing.

40

Yolanda and Gladys won big. Sticking to the slots with her pal and staying away from poker, which she considered work not play, Gladys ended up about a hundred bucks ahead. But Yolanda hit a five-hundred-dollar jackpot. The group trip they took to Atlantic City included travel and buffet, so they hadn't really celebrated until they returned to New York and bought a pint of bourbon and a pint of butter pecan ice cream on Yolanda's corner before going back up to her place. Yolanda paid off the babysitter—a teenage neighbor—and checked on her granddaughter, who was fast asleep, before grabbing two glasses, two bowls, and two spoons and settling on the couch with Gladys. Donna was working late, again, protecting that mystery man who, Yolanda suspected, was more than just a client . . . if that was the right word.

"She used to tell me everything," she told Gladys, who surprised her by scooping ice cream into the glasses. "But now it's what she doesn't say that tells me more."

Gladys laughed. "Try raising a boy. Joe hasn't told me anything since he came home with a black eye in the second grade." She poured the bourbon over the ice cream. "Here you go. Fit for a queen."

Yolanda tried it. It was sweet and creamy, but the alcohol burned through the cold. "Wow," she said and coughed. Gladys laughed.

"Careful, it's got a kick," she said.

"But it's good though." Yolanda took another spoonful but ate it a little slower. "You know what I think?" She licked the spoon and took more.

"What?" Gladys asked, consuming her own at a good pace, adding a little more booze.

"I think your grandson and my daughter are actually very alike."

Gladys laughed. "You might be right." She added more ice cream to Yolanda's glass and poured more liquor. "Have some more."

Yolanda took another, larger spoonful. "It's delicious. It gets better as the ice cream melts."

"Yeah, that's the secret," Gladys agreed, slurping another spoon.

"You know what else I think?" Yolanda asked.

"That we should have some more?" Gladys asked, scooping ice cream and pouring booze.

Yolanda giggled now. She was starting to get buzzed, but in a subtle way, the booze hidden in the ice cream and going down smoother. "Besides that."

"What do you think?"

"I think maybe we should get them together. Your Joe and my Donna."

Gladys smiled as she sipped melting ice cream like soup. "I'll tell you, the thought crossed my mind as soon as I met her."

"She definitely needs something," Yolanda said. "But it's tough to find a guy that could make her fall in love in spite of herself. She's dead set against it."

"Joe needs to settle down, but she has to be just as . . ." She hesitated, searching for the right word.

"Difficult?" Yolanda suggested. "Hardheaded?"

"Exactly. Just as hardheaded and difficult as he is."

Yolanda laughed. "Last time I set up Donna it didn't work out so good. She ended up having to shoot him. Though she did get a medal for it."

Gladys laughed too. "There's definitely a chance of that with Joe. To be honest, they don't even get along. There's always tension between them."

Yolanda pointed her spoon. "Exactly. Sexual tension. Because they both met their match."

"They're both too stubborn to know what's good for them," Gladys said, scraping the last of the ice cream into their cups. She poured the last of the bourbon over it. "That's why we have to do the thinking for them. For their own good." She held up her glass.

Nodding, Yolanda toasted her, clinking their glasses together. "But without them knowing."

◆

When Donna got home, unlocking the door slowly and pushing it open carefully so as not to wake anyone, she was amazed to find her mom and Gladys both passed out on her couch, sort of slumped together, with her mom's head on Gladys's shoulder and Gladys snoring loudly. It was a shocking sight, but the empty pint of bourbon and the crumpled ice cream container on the table quickly explained it. She tiptoed past and checked on Larissa, who was dreaming away like an angel. Donna considered waking the two women and getting them back to Yolanda's, but she was a bit high herself, on the wine, the food, the flirting, and she didn't want to ruin her mood, so she just went to the bathroom to brush her teeth and wash off her makeup and then crept by to her own room, shutting out the light. She got under the covers, and only then did she get out her laptop, sign into her secure work email account, and open the report that Carol, her CIA contact, had sent her about Evon.

"Classified. Do not circulate. Do not copy. Your eyes only. Colonel Evon Kozco former head of special security unit of national police. Organized paramilitary death squad responsible for at least sixty con-firmed executions of political rivals, dissidents, journalists. Evidence of extensive torture. Unconfirmed deaths are in the hundreds, with many 'disappeared' including civilians, women, children. Accused of corruption in opposition newspaper—journalist and editor both found with throats slashed . . ."

Under the covers, in her dark room, while her mom slept, just like when she was kid, Donna read on and on.

41

Fusco and Chang consoled themselves with heroes. Chang even got sausage and peppers too, figuring she needed it, and, in a gesture of solidarity, Fusco ordered fiber-rich broccoli rabe on the side.

"Blech," he said, sampling it, as they sat in their double-parked car, an irony that neither of them even registered. "It's so bitter. It tastes like tonic water or something."

"You're supposed to eat it with the sandwich," Chang told him. "That way the bitterness of the broccoli rabe cuts the spice and greasiness of the sausage and balances out the sweetness of the peppers and onions."

"What are you, the Galloping Gourmet?" he asked with a mouth full of sausage.

"I don't even know what that means."

"It means," Fusco said, a jet of grease shooting from the hero onto his sleeve. He smeared it with a napkin. "That I'm not the fancy type.

So you'll have to excuse me. I'm not used to dining with the Queen of England."

"I never would have guessed," Chang said.

"But one thing I will say, Mademoiselle Chang," he added, lifting his bottle of Manhattan Special coffee soda. "Your taste in beverages is superb."

"Thank you, Sir Francis." She clinked her own bottle against his and they drank. Fusco belched.

"Okay," he said. "Brutal truth time. What the hell went wrong tonight?"

Chang wiped her mouth. "Who knows? He was in our blind spot, right? The one weak spot in our plan. If he hit a block we just did, no way can we get back fast enough."

"But how?" Fusco wondered. "He saw us go by? We're in an unmarked car."

"Lots of people know what unmarked cop cars look like. We're not in deep cover."

"So then what? He just decides to wait by the car he wants to trash until an unmarked cop car happens to pass?"

"Well," she finished her food and sat back. "Either it's a coincidence . . ."

"No such animal."

"Or he knew." Fusco raised a greasy finger, and she added, with a sigh, "He's monitoring the police radio."

Fusco tapped the finger against his nose. "At the very least." He finished his soda and leaned in, "So here's what we're going to do."

42

Joe decided to sleep with Yelena.

Not that she had offered, or that anything particularly romantic had occurred that evening so far. It had been all business as usual, at least for them. And while the erotic energy between them had been there from the beginning and was quick to flame up during their first adventure, it had also faded into friendship without drama or hurt feelings—something mutual friends, like Juno and Cash, attributed to neither of them having any normal human feelings to hurt. But that wasn't quite true. While their similarities made them unlikely to ever be anything like an average couple—with an average couple's joys and sorrows, big dates, romantic vacations, operatic breakups—it also gave them a mutual sympathy, a deep connection that did not fade: their romance, if that was even the word, their sexual alliance, had cooled, but within their hard hearts—like two furnaces of tempered steel—the banked embers glowed on.

Anyway, that's what Joe thought as they drove to Brighton Beach, sitting side by side in the back of the Mercedes, passing the vodka bottle back and forth. Wild Balkan music, the sort Joe knew you weren't supposed to call gypsy anymore but didn't know how else to describe, was blasting from the front seat. A storm of brass charging over a driving, marching beat, with a high wailing cry from the horns. Delirious music, joyful and miserable at once. The city flashed by, with that dreamy cinematic feeling it always has seen through a car window at night, unless you were stuck in traffic. The vodka was coursing through his veins. It all combined to make him, if not exactly romantic, then reckless. Ready to take chances and make mistakes.

Joe took another swig and handed the bottle to Yelena, then laid his hand over hers where it rested on the seat, glancing over with a devilish gleam in his eye. She squeezed his hand back, with real feeling, but the look in her eyes was different. More curious and concerned than lustful.

"Do you feel sick?" she asked him. "We're almost there."

◆

"Take off your shoes," she told him as they entered the apartment. To say her place was cold or bare would be going too far, but it was big and starkly minimalist, with dark wood floors, bright white walls, expensive, sparse modernist furniture in black, white, and glass, and a panoramic view of the ocean, all, of course, scrupulously clean. Like a design exhibit not yet open to the public.

"Right," Joe said, dropping his bag and standing on one foot to untie his sneaker. He lost his balance and stumbled, grabbing Yelena's shoulder for support. He laughed as she clutched him, and they found themselves embracing. They looked into each other's eyes for a meaningful moment.

"Are you sure you're feeling okay?" she asked.

"What?" Joe pulled back. "Yeah, fine." He sat on a kitchen stool and removed the other sneaker, then tossed it by the door. "I mean, it's been a busy few days."

She got another bottle of vodka from the freezer.

"No, I mean besides all the people trying to kill you," she said, opening it and pouring shots into two glasses. "I feel like something else must be bothering you."

Joe did his shot, making a bitter face. "Nope," he said, and swerved toward the couch. "Everything else is just dandy."

"How are things with your cop girlfriend?" Yelena asked. "You know, the Fed?"

"Oh, her," Joe said, waving a hand as he reclined on the couch. "That's all over." He didn't realize that the couch, a severe black leather model, didn't have armrests, and when he drunkenly leaned against the pillow on the side he nearly rolled off. "She's with some rich guy now," he continued.

"Really?" Yelena said, carrying the bottle and glasses over to sit beside him. "I'm surprised. She seemed like a serious woman."

Joe shrugged. "You know how it is. She's from a different world. Cats and dogs." He grinned. "Cats like us have to stick together."

Laughing, she poured them two more shots and handed him one. "Meow," she said as a toast. They drank.

"Time for bed," she said, standing.

"Right," Joe said. "Good idea." He tried to get up, and Yelena extended a hand, hoisting him to his feet. She led him to the guest room, then gave him a little push. He dropped onto the bed and started to undress, then lay back as the room spun. "Just give me a minute," he said.

"Take your time," Yelena told him, and left as he began to snore.

43

Joe opened his eyes. He felt as though no time had passed, but Yelena was standing over him in different clothes, holding a cup of black coffee.

"Is it morning?" he asked.

"Sort of," she told him. "I know where Vicky is."

While Vicky had paid off Pepe, Yelena had paid Charles even more, and had put out word that anyone who helped her find Vicky would be thanked, and anyone who did not would also be remembered. She'd been spotted by the door guy at the club in Bushwick, who knew Charles, and had also said something to the car service driver who picked her up. He in turn worked for some Albanians who knew who Yelena was. Now they'd reached out to her people to say Vicky was on the move again.

Joe sat up and immediately it hit him, like a wave, his first hangover in a long time. He sipped the black coffee and spoke slowly, holding his head very still. "Can I have a glass of water and some aspirin, please?" he asked.

Yelena snickered. "This not drinking and then drinking one night is no good. You have to commit to one or the other."

"I'll keep that in mind," Joe said as he moved to the bathroom in a crouch, as if his head were made of fragile papier-mâché. He began to fill the sink with cold water. It was getting light outside. "Where are we going anyway?"

"Central Park," she said. "To get some fresh air."

❖

A black Navigator took Joe and Yelena into the city and stopped near the Columbus Circle entrance to the park, where Vicky had entered. Two men got out with them, big Russians, different and yet seemingly interchangeable with the two from the night before, and the driver remained idling at the curb. It was still very early, and though runners, dog walkers, and a few commuters were out, the real rush was more than an hour away. It was cold but slowly warming as the sun climbed over the trees, backlighting the ridge of buildings that loomed in the distance.

"Fan out," Yelena told her men, and added to Joe, "Remember, this could be a trap. Be careful."

Joe nodded, scanning the trees and bushes, identifying likely hiding spots, but without much expectation. "I almost wish it were a trap," he said. "At least she'd have to show herself."

They moved through the park. Yelena's men wore track pants and warm-up jackets but still did not seem quite like the other early risers, who stretched and jogged in place and squirted water from bottles into their mouths. These were grim, tattooed men whose dead eyes were constantly searching the grounds.

Finally, when they had crossed the park and reached the edges of the pond, Yelena had to admit, Joe had been right. "Forget it," she told him. "We are looking for a syringe in the haystack." She called to her men in Russian. "Let's go," she said with a shrug. "I will buy you a Russian breakfast."

And that's when they heard a shot.

◆

Vicky set up before dawn. Dressed in leggings and a zip jacket printed with camo—both fashion and function—she slipped into the park and found a spot, a dense bit of brush under trees that was padded with fallen leaves and slightly elevated with a clear view of the space where she expected to see her target. She set up her tripod, assembled her rifle and scope, slipped on gloves to keep her fingers warm and limber, and waited. Despite the many antisocial behaviors that ruled her personality, including poor impulse control and compulsive thrill-seeking, not to mention plain old ADHD, she was able to wait now for more than an hour, almost perfectly still. She was, after all, a supreme professional. But also, this intense focus on a target was one of the only activities that calmed her, stilled her inner chaos, by concentrating all her other drives and urges into one sharpened point, aimed fatally at someone else. The other activity, of course, was inflicting pain, which she found equally relaxing. Therapeutic really.

It was lovely too, if a bit cold, watching the light grow over the park, as trees, benches, and rocks emerged from darkness, taking on form and color and then slowly growing their own shadows. Finally, he arrived, the man she was there to meet, though of course their connection would be anonymous and distant. Like blowing a kiss a couple hundred meters away. She removed her gloves. She pressed an eye to the scope and placed a finger on the trigger. She found her target and placed him in the crosshairs. She was beginning to squeeze, slow and steady, when she heard a bullet whistle past and strike the ground, kicking up the dirt behind her. The sound sent a tiny tremor through her nerve endings, barely a flicker, but at that distance it was enough, and as she fired, the slight deviation, a few degrees, sent her bullet wide, missing its mark, and drilling into a tree. There was no time for a second shot. She rolled hard to the right and came up fast, ready to face trouble.

◆

The sicarios were cold. Rico was on watch, trying to stay awake in the dead hours before dawn, while the others slept in back, huddled under their coats. They were not used to this northern chill. Something else to hate about New York. He crept out of the car, in the dark, and went around to stand between the parked cars to relieve himself. They had a new rule about using empty bottles. That was another thing about this city: no public toilets. And the bars and shops wouldn't even let you in without buying something. A cruel, inhuman place. His cousin was right. The sooner they left the better. It was time to go home.

And then, just as he was musing on the feast they would have to celebrate his homecoming, there was action on the deserted street. A black Navigator pulled up in front of the building they'd been watching all night. Rico zipped up quickly and ducked down behind the car. A minute later, there was their target, Joe, coming out with the blonde woman and climbing into the SUV.

Subtle as possible, he slid back into the driver's seat and cranked the engine on. Without hitting the headlights, he put the car in gear and slipped out, trailing after the Navigator. With no traffic this time of night, or early morning, he lay back, following the taillights, then flicked on his own lights as well as the heat. The men in back stirred.

"What's going on?" Jaime asked.

"We're moving, cabrón," Rico said. "Let's finish this thing now. One way or the other."

They followed Joe back into Manhattan, and, when Joe, his companion, and two tough-looking men got out, they left their own car parked in a bus stop. They weren't worried about tickets. They'd torch them with the car when they dumped it. Weapons concealed under coats, they followed into the park, focusing on Joe as his companions fanned out.

"What the hell are they doing?" Rico asked the others. They were walking along a path that curved through trees, circling around Joe while keeping a discreet distance.

"How should I know?" Flaco said. "Maybe they're looking for a lost dog. Let's just kill this bastard and get out of here."

"Wait . . ." Jaime said, peering into the trees that gathered above a pond. "Ay cabrón."

"What?" Rico asked him and he pointed.

It was a sniper, lying prone, with a rifle ready, pointed just at the area into which their target was headed.

"Fuck that," Flaco said, drawing his gun and holding it against his leg to hide it slightly. They'd come too far to let this bastard, whoever he was, snatch their prize. In his mind the bounty already belonged to them. They'd earned it. "I'll handle this. You take the gringo down. Now. It's enough."

And without waiting for an answer, he took off, running low, in the direction of the sniper, while the others moved on Joe. More concerned with preserving their primary target then taking out this new one, he didn't worry about the perfect shot. There was no time. As soon as he was close enough to take a reasonable shot, he fired. The sniper flinched, firing off across the pond toward some figures on the far shore, and hitting a tree, then rolling away, vanishing from his sight for a moment and then popping back up. Flaco had just enough time to think "Cabrón! It's a woman!" before Vicky shot him through the heart.

◆

Donna was pissed off. To start with, she was not thrilled to be getting up at dawn just because Evon, whom she'd gone back to calling Colonel Kozco in her head, wanted to take an early morning run. But that was the job, and the truth was she hadn't slept much anyway. Her sense of justice was outraged; the FBI had, in essence, been used to shield a criminal. And she felt personally humiliated too; she'd been duped by a charmer, and she did not intend to let that pass. She'd tossed and turned for hours. Then, too angry to sleep, she got up and conceived a plan. She sent out a flurry of early morning emails to contacts in various agencies, cc'ing her boss so that technically he was in the loop, meanwhile setting in motion events that, by the time everyone got to work and had their coffee, would be too late to reverse.

As a result, when she arrived at the hotel, rendezvousing with her team, who stood outside breathing fog in the early morning chill, waiting for Evon and his guards to emerge, she was in a different headspace—still pissed, but with a cool, calm demeanor and her professional edge intact. She even stopped to pick up coffee—for herself and the agents only, of course.

Evon came out in a brand-new tracksuit with brand-new running shoes. His guards were in running gear too, though wearing looser clothing to hide their weapons. Like her fellows, Donna was in her normal work clothes. She didn't intend to do any running.

"Good morning, Donna," he called out as he came out, already stretching and warming up. "It's a lovely day, isn't it? So good to be alive."

"Every day is good to be alive, Colonel," she said. "But it's early. We'll see how lovely it turns out to be."

"Quite true," he said, a bit sobered. "Well, it's always good to start with a run. Shall we?" They crossed Central Park South at the corner and entered the park across from the Plaza, an odd little group, with Evon in the lead, bopping and jogging, his guards keeping pace but scouting ahead as well, like trained dogs, and three Feds in suits and topcoats hustling along after, trying to stay close without breaking a sweat.

"I won't make you follow me around the loop today," Evon said, still avuncular, as if her coolness were merely a professional pretense, as if nothing had changed. "Just a quick run along the paths."

Donna nodded, doing her job, scanning the area, as Evon started to stretch, squatting low and extending each leg, working his calves, then folding each leg up, opening up his quads. She glanced over the pond, its surface like a liquid mirror now, a few ducks floating on the wavering image of trees and sky and the humpbacked storybook bridge. She took in the bunched trees themselves and the arch of the real bridge, which formed a graceful circle with its own reflection. This was one of her favorite spots in the park, quiet at this early hour with just a few other runners, some walkers, and scattered people sitting on benches. She was just noticing some movement, a tourist exploring perhaps, in the trees above when she heard a crack and jumped. A bullet had hit a tree. Everyone scrambled. The guards pushed Evon to the ground. Her own people drew their weapons and ducked down, searching for the source. Passersby, none of whom had noticed the shot, first approached curiously, then scattered as the agents shouted for them to get back. And then Donna had a kind of vision: she saw a woman rise up holding a rifle and shoot a man who was standing over her. As she stood, her long red hair came loose, and in that split second, Donna knew who it was.

"Get him out of here," she called to her partners, and took off running. "Call for backup. I'm in pursuit."

44

Joe dropped and rolled.

Though the shot had not been aimed at him, when he heard Flaco fire at Vicky, Joe reacted on reflex, his training and experience. Or maybe it was just the fact that there had been two attempts on his life that week. In any case, it inadvertently saved him. Yelena, too, when she heard gunfire, dove to the ground. They landed on the damp concrete and rolled under a bench along the walkway. Meanwhile, the remaining two sicarios, Jaime and Rico, who had been closing in on Joe, instead found themselves confronted with Evon's guards, who came charging down the path around the pond, seeking the assassin, guns drawn. They saw Jaime and Rico, guns out, and they fired. As in an old Western showdown, the sicarios fired back, bullets tearing through the air over Joe and Yelena. Passing citizens ran or cowered behind trees, some calling 911 while others tried to get a shot with their camera.

Jaime was killed immediately, but Rico managed to hit one of Evon's guards, shooting him in the gut. However, he was distracted by Yelena's men, who had heard the shots and come running to protect her. The first Russian on the scene shot Evon's other guard, wrongly assuming he was after Yelena and Joe, just as he was killing Rico, who had gunned down Yelena's guard, while Evon's dying guard, took down Yelena's other man as he bled out. The roar of the crossfire was overwhelming for Joe and Yelena, who simply froze, knowing any move, even toward better shelter, could be deadly, as bullets ricocheted off the benches and concrete. And then, just as suddenly, there was silence.

Joe popped his head up. He saw scattered bodies. Yelena, lying on her back, gun in both hands, glanced around too, and then at him.

"Now?" she asked.

"Now." They moved, rolling and rising, first onto one knee, back to back, guns drawn. There was nothing but dead men around them. Then, from a distance, they saw more men coming, yelling, "Hold it! FBI!"

Joe and Yelena ran.

◆

Donna chased Vicky, running full-out, but she knew there was no chance. She'd spotted her from a distance, and took off, trying to yell into her mic at the same time, getting out a description in gasps of breath. But what could she say? Redheaded young woman? She'd barely caught a glimpse. Sprinting to where she'd been, already breathing hard, she found her sniper's perch—the rifle and scope left behind. More evidence she knew would lead nowhere.

Vicky had fled, bailing immediately when she knew her target was lost, seeking only to escape and perhaps circle back for another attempt later. She ran full speed, dashing across paths, lawns, and benches, until she saw a young man in spandex and cleats, kneeling beside a racing bike, checking the tires, his helmet hanging on the handlebars. Without hesitating, Vicky ran up behind him and knocked him to his knees, kicking him hard in the guts. As he groaned, trying to figure out what had happened, she grabbed the helmet and cracked him hard across the head. He went down. She slipped the helmet on and rode off on his bike. One old fellow taking a constitutional noticed, and began to hurry over, but he had no cell phone on him. A delivery guy on a moped saw her too, but he was in a rush. He'd get fired if he stopped for this and people's breakfast burritos got cold.

Peddling hard, Vicky biked onto the main loop of paved road that wound through the park. In a few minutes she saw a line of bikers, all in tight spandex, all pumping hard with their heads down. She joined the end of their string, her own tight camo leggings and top blending in nicely. When they reached the north side of the park, she slipped away, and they raced on without her. After a few blocks, she ditched the bike—grabbed within minutes by a kid—and hailed herself a taxi.

◆

Joe and Yelena fled. When they saw more armed men approaching, they took off, running into the closest stand of trees for cover, but as soon as they realized it was law after them now, they ditched their guns, and emerged, on the other side of the trees, holding hands, joining the other passersby who had rushed away from danger. By now uniformed police had arrived on the scene. Cops spilled from cars and came chugging in, while more cars pulled up, sirens screaming. Even a mounted cop thundered by at a gallop. Joe and Yelena walked right toward them, looking happy and relieved.

"Hey, you two, hold up," a cop called out. "What are you doing here?"

Immediately Yelena began to shout in rapid Russian, babbling about men and guns, explaining more or less what really did happen, except for their own involvement. Joe contented himself with nodding, pointing and saying "Da! Da!" in the best Russian accent he could manage.

Frustrated, the cop just nodded and pushed past them. He had no time for panicky tourists now. "Okay, okay. Just wait off to the side."

"*Chto?*" she asked, then added in halting English. "What you say?"

"Wait! Outside! The park!" He explained, loud and clear, pointing at the street. Nodding, they turned to go, Joe reaching out to shake his hand.

"Yeah, yeah, you're welcome," said the cop, hurrying off to catch up with his friends before he missed all the fun.

◆

It was then, as they walked out holding hands, that Joe looked up the block and saw Donna. She was not holding hands exactly, but she was in close conversation with Evon, guiding him toward a black car, with a casual hand on his arm. She glanced up, scanning the area, and saw him too. Their eyes met. For a split second, it was as if something, a signal flare, jumped between them, but neither acknowledged it. Like the pros they were, they just moved on, unmoved, eyes blank. They gave nothing away.

Joe and Yelena strolled on in the other direction, toward Columbus Circle, careful to remain in character as dazed tourists, looking around, gawping at the buildings. "Well that was awkward," Yelena finally said as they turned a corner onto Sixth Avenue.

"Just a morning walk in the park," Joe said.

"I'm glad she kept her cool," Yelena said. She shrugged. "I like her. She's okay for a cop."

"Sure," Joe said. "Why not? We're both adults."

Yelena raised her eyebrows. "That's one way of putting it."

◆

Stunned by the perceived attempt on his life, and rattled by all the sudden action, Evon didn't really say much till Donna was guiding him toward the car, a black Impala with government plates. Two agents stood waiting.

"Donna, my God, thank you, you just saved my life."

"Just doing my job. You're safe now."

"Yeah, I admit I'm a bit shaken up. It's not the first time of course, but I guess I wanted to believe that was all in the past."

"The past has a way of catching up."

He nodded. "You're right. Even in New York." He smiled at her. "But that's all the more reason to keep living right? Growing. Learning. Loving." Getting his groove back, he leaned closer, a hand on her arm. "And it means even more, that it was you. It's a sign."

Donna frowned at his hand. He dropped it. "I'm not sure what you think it's a sign of, sir," she told him, flatly. "But you're going to have to go with these agents."

The agents stepped forward. "Good morning, sir. I'm Agent Margolis. We're here to take you into custody."

Evon looked confused, then concerned, as he took in these new faces. He turned back to Donna. "Sorry, but aren't you in charge of my protective detail?"

"I was, Colonel," Donna said, more edge creeping into her voice. "But this isn't protective custody. And they're not FBI."

"But . . ." Evon stepped back, as the agents moved closer. Now Margolis put a hand on his arm.

"We are from Homeland Security, sir. Some new evidence has come to light that has caused us to reevaluate your request for residency."

Still taking it in, he looked at Donna. She explained: "You're being deported, Colonel."

"But, but, wait, Donna . . ." He began to sputter now, resisting as the second agent grabbed an arm and they cuffed him. "You can't do this, Donna, please. If they send me back, I'm dead. I just bought an apartment for God's sakes." He lunged toward her in panic. "Donna, how can you let them do this to me?"

Donna didn't flinch. "As I said, sir. It's all just part of the job."

◆

Joe and Yelena walked in and out of a few shops and Joe bought two coffees from a fancy coffee place while Yelena called her driver. Finally, confident that no one was following, they turned a corner and climbed into the back of the sedan. Joe sat back and took a long sip.

"I needed that," he said. "Remind me never to drink vodka again."

Yelena shrugged. "It's true you were not as much fun as you used to be." She looked at her phone. "Juno is trying to reach you. He says he has found something important."

"Good," Joe said. "I have to talk to him too. And Cash."

Yelena spoke to the driver in Russian, telling him where to go. "You have a plan?" she asked Joe.

"Maybe. I have the first step."

"Which is?"

"To make sure the next time someone tries to kill me, they succeed."

PART V

PART V

45

The fourth attempt on Joe's life happened after he left work at Club Rendezvous.

It had been a busy day and night. After slipping away from the park, Yelena and Joe drove to Juno's basement. With the lead from Doni, Cash had also gone back to his Chinese connections, who had dug further, and Juno had tracked down the new website.

"Just when you thought the internet couldn't get any more fucked up," Juno told them as he brought it up on the big screen. "I mean, I thought Twitter was treacherous but check this shit out. Talk about getting canceled."

It was a simple website, set in black and white, with names and photos, or, lacking photos, silhouettes, with brief personal descriptions and, in red, a price, ranging from $1,000 to six figures. The header read: HIT LIST—International Bounty Exchange.

"Welcome to the future of murder," Juno said.

"Is that for real?" Yelena asked.

"Afraid so," Juno told her. "And look whose stock is rising." He expanded the image: JOE BRODY, it read, and listed a basic description as well his work and home addresses. The original price of $50,000 was crossed out, with increases to a hundred and one-fifty also crossed out. It now read $250,000. There was also a blurred, black-and-white security-camera image of a man in a cap and work clothes, which normally Joe would not even recognize as himself.

"It's from the Eleonora hallway," he said.

"Right," Juno said. "It matches the angles and background. It's a still from their security footage."

"Can't you take down his listing?" Yelena asked. "Hack in?"

"Not so simple," Juno said. "This is very heavy-duty dark web shit. I had to set up proxies and use TOR just to get in."

"Tor?" Joe asked. "Like the Norse god?"

"Yeah. Or from the MCU."

"Is that a memory unit or what?"

"MCU?" Juno frowned at him. "Marvel Comics Universe? Don't you go to movies?"

Yelena intervened. "You know he doesn't. Let's all try to stay in one universe. This Tor is for illegal transactions?"

"It's just software that lets you be anonymous on the internet. So it can be good or bad. It's outlawed in China for instance, because it would enable free speech. It's used by whistleblowers all over, exposing political corruption and stuff. But it can also be used for drug deals, porn, even weapons trading. And now this." He waved at the screen.

"Point is, this is top-notch hacker stuff here. I don't even know where it's coming from. Yet!" he added, holding a finger up to the ceiling. "I'll crack it eventually. But then it will probably be easier to just crash the whole site."

"Good," Yelena said, eyeing the site like a detested adversary.

"No. Don't," Joe said. "I think we can make it work for us." He looked at his watch. "Let's order lunch, and when Cash and the others get here, I'll explain."

"Good idea," Juno said. "I'm starved. How about the barbeque place around the corner?"

◆

Later, after a repast of fried chicken, barbecued ribs, collard greens, okra with tomatoes, potato salad, mac and cheese, and corn bread, Joe explained what he had in mind to his crew—Cash, Juno, Yelena, Liam, and Josh, who'd gotten a break from his parents—while they were sitting back, licking their fingers. Juno got a package of wipes and passed them around.

"Nobody better touch my keyboard or remotes or anything else without wiping their hands," he declared, spraying down the surface with alcohol.

"Hey, watch the soda," Cash said, covering his drink. "Your producing handle should be DJ OCD."

Yelena pulled out a packet of those small plastic dental picks and offered them around as well.

"Yes, that's exactly what I need," Josh said.

"God bless you," Liam added.

"Everybody ready?" Joe asked. "I'm just about to explain why my life's in jeopardy here."

"Go ahead, no one's stopping you," Yelena said, cleaning her teeth.

"Juno?" Joe asked, and Juno tapped some keys, pulling up a photo of the Eleonora.

"The Eleonora, which I snuck into trying to snatch Alonzo's pigeon back for him, is actually a gigantic laundry for dirty money, and a kind of safe house for international bad guys. Here's how it works. Let's say you're a Russian plutocrat, like this guy."

Juno opened a photo of Volkov.

"Or a corrupt African warlord. Or a cartel boss."

More faces popped up on the screen.

"One of the problems you're sure to face during your career is retirement planning, often on very short notice. And one of the safest places to park ten or fifteen million of that blood money is in high-end Manhattan real estate. So what do you do?"

Juno pulled up a picture of Jeremy Blake.

"You have a shady lawyer set up a dummy corporation and use one of your offshore accounts to buy a luxury apartment from this guy, who can smooth everything over and make sure the board approves you, no questions asked. It's a cash transaction between private parties. So there's not the same scrutiny from banks or the government."

"Fair enough," Liam said. "But that's a large part of all the luxury apartments in New York now. That's who they're built for: super-rich foreigners."

"Everyone knows those towers are half empty," Josh said. "They're like giant safe deposit boxes. But they keep the construction going, and the money flows, so who cares."

"Exactly," Joe said. "But our friend Blake here is a real innovator . . ."

"Disruptor, they call it now," Juno said.

"He added another level to the scam. You see, owning a big piece of Manhattan skyline is nice, but you can't spend it. But by running the management company that handles all transactions at the Eleonora, Blake was able to have his clients set up another LLC, and sell the empty apartment back to themselves, at a profit."

"So," Yelena said, trying it out, "you mean I buy the place for ten million, let's say, then sell it to myself for twenty million? How do I make money?"

"You don't," Joe said. "You lose some, to taxes, and a few percent no doubt to Blake in commission, but what's left is clean. Now you have maybe eight or nine million sitting in a US bank with a totally legit source. And, when your government collapses back home, or police close in, or your cartel rivals get too powerful, you've got a safe, comfy apartment with excellent security and neighbors who know just how you feel."

Cash nodded sagely. "You've got to admit, this guy's clever. I'd give him ten or twenty mil to invest, if I had it."

"How did you figure it out?" Yelena asked.

"The lawyers," Juno piped in, happily. "And the banks. Like Joe said, you can keep making new LLCs under new names but the bank will be the same and usually you will use the same lawyer again and again."

"When you find a crooked lawyer you can trust, you stick with them," Joe said. He gestured at the faces on the screen. "Then, using the apartment details and security footage, Juno was able to work back and tie names and faces to corporations and apartments. It's a real who's who of international scumbags."

"So when you broke in," Liam said now, sitting forward and pointing, "Mr. Blake there must of shat himself, figuring you'd rumbled him."

"And he put the hit on you," Josh said, finishing his sentence, as couples do.

"Right," Joe said. "Even if I told him it was just to steal a pigeon, he never would have believed me."

"I almost pity him," Yelena said, staring at the smiling, polished photo Juno had found on LinkedIn.

"Why?" Cash asked.

"He picked such an expensive and painful way to commit suicide."

Joe laughed. "His turn will come. But first we need to buy some time and some breathing room. Now here's what I have in mind."

◆

As soon as she got the chance, Donna called Fusco.

As always when there is an incident involving gunfire or violent death, the aftermath took many hours. There was forensics and the coroner, all complicated by the multiple agencies involved, both city and federal—everyone from the Parks Department to the Bureau, with the CIA and Interpol keeping a curious eye on proceedings. Not to mention the various dead bodies that would eventually be identified as a notorious Mexican hit squad and a couple Russian Mafia enforcers as well as Kozco's guards, who were ex-military. What they all had to do with the assassination attempt was anybody's guess, and they were all making guesses. Donna herself was debriefed and rebriefed multiple times. It was during her lunch break that she finally called Fusco. Actually, she was in the restroom at the local precinct house, though she would never tell him that.

"This better not be about another rich douchebag's car, or I might just torch it myself," he said as a greeting when he came on the line.

"Nice to speak to you too, you grumpy old bastard," she told him, leaning on a sink. "At least you weren't shot at this morning."

"What?" He snapped into focus. "What happened?"

"It's a long story, and I'm not sure anyone even understands it yet . . ." From one of the stalls came the sound of a toilet flush. A uniformed officer came out and started washing her hands.

"Wait," Fusco said, overhearing. "Zamora, are you on the can?"

"You wish, you creep."

"Just don't forget to wipe."

"Shut up and listen before I report you for harassment. Again. Because this news is going to make your day."

"Please. Make it."

"Guess who's back in town?"

46

"I still don't like it," Yelena was saying to Joe when Juno's call came through. They were back at her place. Joe had hoped to rest and read, but instead they argued about Joe's plan. Yelena didn't like it. "You will be just a sitting pigeon."

"Duck," Joe corrected her. "It's sitting duck and stool pigeon."

"Why is a pigeon sitting on a stool?" she asked, dismissively.

"Enough," Joe said, when his phone beeped. "I don't want to hear any more about pigeons. Juno and Cash are downstairs."

◆

"Holy shit," Joe said, when they found them grinning in front of Yelena's building with the car they'd spent all day customizing in Cash's shop, Reliable Scrap, deep in the heart of Queens' junkyard empire.

"You said bright and flashy," Cash explained.

"I didn't mean literally aflame."

Yelena smiled. "Even in Moscow this would be over the top."

It was a Chevy Camaro SS 1LE, a low, sleek, nimble, and very powerful beast. It was also painted electric blue with orange and yellow flames that licked along the sides, bursting into a sun storm over the hindquarters.

Cash laughed, lowering his voice. "One of my guys happened to, you know, harvest it last night. Barely any mileage, practically brand new, and it's perfect for what you need. It's got the power and the handling."

Juno held up a laptop. "And I was able to get right into the onboard computer."

"It was a nice tasteful gray originally," Cash said. "But you said make it very easy to follow so . . ."

"So you went for it," Joe said.

Cash shrugged. "It was my big chance." Normally, when fitting a car out for a job, the idea was to blend in, drive powerful but ordinary-seeming cars that no one bothered to notice. "Besides," he added, "not even the owner would recognize it now."

"It's clean?" Joe asked.

"Clean enough. The plates are legit, swapped out with some old ones off a wreck, but not on any lists with the law. We ground off the VIN. Nobody will bother you. Unless you want them too."

While Joe looked the car over, a van pulled up behind them, and Liam stuck his head out.

"If it isn't every teenage boy's wet dream," he called out. "Sorry, I don't mean you, Yelena."

Grinning, she gave him the finger. Cash had provided Liam's ride too, but it was a few years old and painted dark green with a plumber's faded name on the door—no one would give that a second glance. All he'd done was tune it up and add new tires and old, legal plates, plus a high-powered, police-style whip antenna concealed along the line of the roof, per Juno.

"Should we take a spin," Cash asked, dangling keys he'd clipped to a ring shaped like a lightning bolt. It read *Hot Stuff.*

"Okay, wise guy," Joe said, grabbing them. "Let's see how hot your stuff really is."

"Have fun, boys," Yelena said, crossing her arms. "And be careful. I still don't think I like this."

Joe got behind the wheel of the Camaro, starting the engine, which seemed to clear its throat, while Cash and Juno climbed into the van, Cash in front, next to Liam, Juno in back. They took a test drive, Joe leading them first into Rockaway and along the wide, emptier roads along the waterfront, trying out the special modifications he'd asked them to make, then taking it through more crowded streets. Satisfied, he drove back to Jackson Heights, cruising around the neighborhood until he finally found a spot, at which point he locked the car and went into his own building. A few minutes later, Liam and the others, who'd been tracking him remotely, arrived to station themselves nearby.

Joe showered, shaved, and changed into clean clothes. He watered Gladys's plants. He wasn't hungry after such a big lunch but to kill time he made tea and ate a couple clementines, and a peanut butter and jelly sandwich. Finally, Liam called.

"Looks like you've got guests," he said. "Either that or lost tourists. Two guys in a rent-a-car circling the block."

"I'll be right down." Joe rinsed off his dishes and checked his gun one more time. Then he went downstairs. He considered it unlikely they would attempt anything now, on a busy block before a hundred windows, but he was still counting on Liam and the others to watch his back while he made a point of looking as casual as possible, strolling along and absent-mindedly tossing the keys as he made his way to the Camaro. He hopped in and revved the engine loudly, then pulled out, signaling of course. He turned on to the avenue, happy to see, in his rear view, that a tan rental Camry with two dark-haired men inside soon followed. He didn't see Liam, but that was as it should be; they were following from a discreet distance.

Then he drove to the club. His shift was about to start.

◆

Donna and Fusco started with the rifle.

It was the only piece of hard evidence and their only real lead. Everything else was supposition, instinct, and personal vengeance, which, for the bosses, were all red flags—whether the kind that warned off the cautious or the red-colored capes that drove on furious bulls. So Donna didn't mention any of that when talking to Tom. She merely informed him that she, along with her NYPD counterpart, needed to follow up immediately on this attempt on Kozco's life, a life for which the FBI had been responsible. Never mind that he had turned out to be a war criminal whom she herself had just sent home to almost certain death. It was official bureau business now. Not to mention, Donna had conveniently cleared her desk.

"Fine, fine, just keep me in the loop," Tom said, a phone in one hand, standing at his desk like the captain of a ship in a storm, holding the wheel steady. "And have what's his name loop in his superiors too. CC everything to everybody."

"Right." She saluted. "Will do."

◆

Fusco, however, did no such thing. He knew that, unless it resolved quickly, a dramatic multi-victim incident like this, in a public place, might very well end up with his unit, Major Crimes. But as long as he was working this damned parking thing, his captain would assign someone else. So for now, his best bet was to try to wrap this Avenger business up quickly while he moonlighted with Donna.

That's where Chang came in.

"You can handle it," Fusco told her, out in the narrow alley where cops went to smoke, standing beside a rank bucket filled with rainwater and butts. "I know you're just a rookie, but I have confidence in you."

"I know I can handle it," she told him, waving off the smoke. "And I'm not a rookie, I'm just new in this unit, as I keep telling you. And you can shove your confidence. I've got my own."

Fusco laughed. "See, that's what I mean."

"The point is . . ." She poked his belly with a painted nail. "This is your idea, your hunch we're supposed to be following tonight. And it's a two-person plan."

"Exactly. That's why I know it will work. Because I thought of it. And you'll have uniform backup on hand. And if you run into him, which might not even happen tonight, or tomorrow, then you just send up a flare, and I'll come running like . . ."

He hesitated, searching for a suitable phrase.

"A caped crusader?" Chang suggested.

"That's why this is such a beautiful partnership. You already know how I think."

"Oh I know how you think all right," Chang said, taking his butt and tossing it in the bucket with a sizzle. "Now you're thinking about how you're going to buy me lunch while we plot this out. And you feel like soup dumplings. Come on."

"See," Fusco said, following amiably. "You just read my mind."

◆

Janet hid her vape pen. As one of the FBI's top forensic scientists, Janet Kim was pretty much left to run her lab as she saw fit, and the trip from her basement den up through security and back hardly seemed an efficient use of her time, considering how important her work was to the cause of justice. Anyway, that's what she told herself to justify the occasional hit of nicotine she took and blew into the vent that cleaned the air in her lab. Donna was a pal as well as a colleague and a fellow basement dweller, but she kept her secret vice in her pocket when she saw the suspicious character in the visitor's badge she had along with her.

"Janet, this is Lieutenant Fusco, NYPD detective. He's okay for a big fat old white cop." Unruffled, Fusco nodded amicably. "Fusco, meet Janet Kim, she is a genius."

"Great," Janet said, pulling her pen back out of her lab jacket. "Then I guess that means you're okay with this?"

"Sure," Fusco said, pulling out a crumpled pack of Winstons. "If you're okay with me having one of these."

"No," both Janet and Donna said together. Fusco scowled and replaced his cigarettes while Janet took a hit and blew a discreet plume of vapor into the vent.

"That's better. Now let's get to business." She led them to the rifle that had been left behind in the park, now laid out like a patient on a table with a bright light over it. "Scientifically speaking, I can't tell you anything you don't already know. Yes, it was fired recently. And yes, the slug you pulled from that tree matches. No prints or trace DNA, but then I don't think you expected any."

"Some genius," Fusco muttered. Donna elbowed him. Janet laughed.

"But what I will tell you, O surly one, is that this is one very specialized, very high-end piece of custom equipment. The kind of thing SEALs use to take out bad guys long distance. No way did anybody just pick this up at Walmart or even underground. It's just too rare. Plus, with the scope and the tripod, it's very pricey too."

Donna thought about that. "So if the redhead," that's what she and Fusco called her, their nemesis, "flew in to do this job, then she had to get the hardware here."

Janet nodded. "And even in a town like New York that has the best of everything, there can't be that many people selling a piece like this."

"Does that give you any ideas?" Donna asked Fusco.

"It does," he said and winked at Janet. "You're not the only genius in the room."

◆

In his heart of hearts, Fusco knew what he was: a crooked cop. He was also a good cop—smart, dependable, tough, brave—and a top-notch detective, with the arrest records and medals to prove it. But among his numerous bad habits, perhaps the most damaging to his life (so far) was compulsive gambling. He racked up enormous debts, which, even when he won, were never reduced, since his addiction only drove him to gamble the winnings. Since the debts were illegal, his career would be over if the truth came out, which only led him to try and settle them by extra-legal means. Not to mention the havoc it played with his financial life, particularly his multiple divorce settlements and child support payments. And looming over it all, like a very suave and charming Grim Reaper, Giovanni Caprisi. But paying down his debt by doing Gio favors only dug him deeper—now he was not just a crooked cop who gambled illegally, he was a crooked cop in the pocket of a mobster.

That being said, it had its advantages. For one thing, having had, for years now, one foot on either side of the line, his connections were wider and deeper than the majority of cops', and in this case, he thought immediately of Pepe and Charles.

Several years before, he had arrested the hyper-muscular pair for dealing Molly at the club where they worked, and which was owned, in turn, by one Adonis Torrentello, whose real line, Fusco learned when he squeezed it out of Charles and Pepe, was arms dealer to the underworld stars. He'd turned them loose, and they'd been a useful source ever since, feeding him information about their boss's clients and the other villains who came and went from the club, information that Fusco might act on as a cop, or pass to Gio, depending. Of course, in New York, there were many ways to get a gun, and many weapons circulating at all levels of society. But Doni, as he was known, filled a special niche. He provided top quality, high-end weapons exclusively to professionals, often out-of-towners who wanted to travel clean and pick up what they needed for a job. He also rented weapons: let's say you were robbing an armored car and needed a rocket launcher. You'd rent it from Doni, leaving a hefty deposit of course, then return it afterward. In certain circles, therefore, he was well-known, but since both his clients and the people they killed with his weapons were generally pros, he had never been arrested or even become known to law enforcement. Except for Fusco, of course, who was content to leave him be, as long as no civilians were involved.

He and Donna drove over to Pepe and Charles's place, a studio in the West Village, arriving just as they were waking up for the evening. Dressed in matching pajamas and T-shirts, they reluctantly let them in.

"Morning fellas," Fusco said, taking a seat. The place was expensively furnished, but like a frat house, with laundry everywhere, an unmade bed, a weight bench, and a video game playing silently on a huge TV.

"Hi," they both said, shyly, checking out Donna.

"This is my friend Agent Zamora," Fusco explained. "She's FBI."

Pepe's eyes widened. *"¿Si? Que chevere."*

Donna smiled. *"Gracias."*

Charles nodded. "That *is* cool. You've got flair too. I like your long coat."

"Thanks," Donna said. "Cute pajamas."

"Great," Fusco said. "Now that we're all pals, why don't you tell us about the redhead? The one who bought the sniper rifle from Doni."

Pepe groaned, "*Ay Dios mio*," and crossed himself.

Charles shook his head. "Not Vicky again. Listen Detective, no offense, but I'm more scared of that crazy bitch than either you or Doni. So I ain't saying nothing. With respect."

Fusco raised his eyebrows at Donna.

Pepe agreed. "Yeah, we got a right to remain silent. I mean, she shot two guys right in front of us at Doni's just like that," he snapped his fingers. "Didn't even blink."

"Pepe!" Charles groaned.

"Oops." Pepe frowned. "Can I take that back? Like, you know, strike it from the record?"

By the time they left, Donna and Fusco had gleaned a fair bit of useful information. Pepe and Charles's descriptions of the dead guys with the English accents made it pretty clear who they were, which would please the police by at least giving them someone to hang two murders on. They also had, finally, a name of sorts for their redhead, "Vicky," and knew that she had an English accent too, but "fancier" than the dead dudes, "you know, kinda royal, like a Downtown Abby." They also learned that she was going, or maybe gone, and they might be too late.

"She said her job was like canceled, and she was leaving town," Pepe said.

But when did she say this? Surely not when she picked up the weapons, which had to be before the job? Cornered, Pepe admitted his side arrangement with Vicky. And how did he contact her? Reluctantly, he turned over a cell number, and Donna and Fusco left satisfied. Charles's own side deal, informing for Yelena, went unmentioned.

From the car, they called in the additional details on Vicky's description and added it to the alerts already out. They also added special alerts for the airport, particularly UK flights, and even for the trains at Penn Station and Grand Central, but they were not optimistic.

"You know she could easily be on a plane by now, heading home?" Donna said.

"Probably first class too," Fusco muttered.

And then, just to be thorough, they went back to the FBI office and had Mario, the tech wiz, look into the phone number.

47

At Club Rendezvous, Joe had been on a leave of absence since those two hicks got killed in the men's room. But tonight he was back, sort of. He walked around, sat in the back booth or at the bar, and stood near the door, as if playing the part of bouncer, while the other bouncer, Sunny, a very tall, very wide, very good-natured African man with gold front teeth, actually worked the door, checking IDs and cooling the overheated. It was amazing how calming it was to look up at that giant, looming figure and see that smile blazing down at you. It was a crowded night, and a boisterous crowd, but nothing out of the ordinary, until the two Sicilians came in.

"They're coming your way." Liam spoke over the tiny earpiece Joe was wearing. He'd trailed the two men in the Camry, who were in turn following Joe as he parked the Camaro in the club's lot. They too had found a space and, after a long wait in the car, had apparently decided to enter. They were dark, with black hair and eyes and dressed in dark clothing, but it was Nero, who was drinking at the bar, who heard them speaking Italian to each other.

"They're what, in a less enlightened time, they used to call zips," Nero said, when he sat next to Joe at the bar, keeping his voice low, both staring straight ahead, eyes on the girls. "Anyway that's what my grandfather used to say, even though he was the one from Naples." He shrugged and sipped his cognac. "But they've got Sicilian accents, these two. I remember from when we went down there on vacation. Hard to understand sometimes, but my God, the bakeries. You never had a cannoli like this. I know, I know, Veniero's, but believe me. And the best olive oil in the world, like you just dip the bread . . ."

"I got it, thanks, Nero," Joe said, sipping his coffee. "But I don't think they're here to deliver a care package."

"No. And Gio says they're definitely not sent by any friends of ours. This is strictly on spec." He shrugged. "I guess the high bounty is bringing out the top guys. One of those problems of success."

Cash meanwhile took a discreet look in the visitors' car, and confirmed there was heavy fire power, an AR-15 with a pistol grip and a shotgun under a blanket in the back, as well as two handguns in the glove compartment. No luggage. They were planning to be back on the plane home soon. Cash also planted a small tracking device for Juno.

After that, there was nothing to do but wait. Joe watched the crowd. The Sicilians watched Joe. And from outside, Juno, Cash, and Liam watched and waited for the Sicilians. Other than that, it was a very ordinary night.

◆

When Joe left the club, he walked slow, calling out good night to Sunny at the door, and sauntering to where the Camaro was parked under a light. He knew that the Sicilians had left the club a couple hours before and were waiting, no doubt bored and restless by now, ready to make mistakes. Signaling, as per the law, Joe exited the lot, and turned onto the road with the rental following behind.

Although the highway and main access roads to and from the airport might be jammed at any hour, for the most part this area was dead at night, closed businesses and big box stores, workshops and warehouses, with the residential streets full of private homes or commuter condo complexes and residential health care facilities that looked like they belonged in the suburbs, low-rise brick buildings with lots of parking, and few people on the street. It was the perfect setting for what the Sicilians had in mind, which was just what Joe wanted.

Arriving at an empty crossroads, Joe stopped at the red light. That's when the Sicilians made their move. Crossing the double yellow into the oncoming lane, the rental Camry pulled up on Joe's left, passenger window down, and the AR opened fire, spraying the Camaro with bullets. That's when Joe made his move and took off.

He had actually been pretty nervous. Although idling and staring ahead like a clueless driver waiting for the light, he'd left the car in drive, with one foot on the brake and the other revving the accelerator, and when he saw the rental pull up, he'd crouched low and released the brake. The car jumped forward, slightly but decisively ruining the angle of their shot. Still, a couple bullets hit the rear side and back windows and more struck the body of the car. But to Joe's immense relief, the thick bullet-proof plexi Cash had installed, which looked like custom tinted windows, and the steel plating he'd added to the side panels, held up just fine. It was impossible to roll the windows down now, of course, but Joe didn't mind. He'd trade fresh air to keep breathing, and he took a big breath now, exhaling in relief, as he shot forward through the light, with the rental in close pursuit. They were committed now. This was their chance.

Joe led the Sicilians on a tour of backwoods Queens, racing down side streets and past empty buildings, careful not to lose them and maintaining contact with the van, driven by Liam, who trailed them, sometimes out of sight, but never out of radio contact. The Sicilians kept shooting, and now and then a bullet smacked the plexi. You never got used to it, Joe noticed. He flinched every time.

Joe increased his speed, using the Camaro's powerful engine to pull ahead of the Camry as he tightened and checked his safety belt. He took a deep breath, preparing to place his life in Cash's hands for the second time that night. As he raced down the empty two-way road, passing industrial parks and storage facilities, he spoke over his mic.

"Okay it's all yours, Cash."

Cash replied. "I got you, bro."

"I hope so," Joe said. And then he let go of the wheel.

◆

Watching Sarah, the champion gamer girl, play at the Eleonora and then seeing Cash and company playing while they partied had given Joe an idea. Today's brand-new cars, especially a high-performance model like the Camaro, had sophisticated onboard computers monitoring, or even running and correcting, everything from temperature and location tracking to steering on ice and backing into a parking spot. Joe had asked Cash and Juno to take it a step further, to its logical conclusion, and set the Camaro up to be driven by remote control. When Joe let go, Cash took over, using the dash cam as well as the tracking software installed by Juno to steer and work the gas and brakes, while Liam kept them running a short distance behind. Joe was just along for the ride.

Joe sat back, bracing himself and fighting the urge to grab the wheel, or even more instinctively to stomp the foot pedals. They'd practiced all this extensively, racing up and down the beachfront in Rockaway and turning donuts in a parking lot, but it was jarring nonetheless, and Cash still took a couple minutes to get the hang of it, overcorrecting and swerving as Joe's stomach did triple flips.

"Easy, Cash, easy," he called over the mic. "The whole idea here is to keep me alive."

"Don't worry," Cash said, as his driving smoothed. "I'm going to drive like there's a baby on board."

"Here we go," Joe said, glancing into the rear view. The Camry was falling behind, as they passed a vacant lot full of head-high weeds. "Next left."

"I got it, Joe," Cash told him. "Hang on."

Joe hung on. He grabbed the seat, sitting back and trying to hold his neck still while Cash hit the brakes and spun the wheel. The car stuck and spun, the rear end skidding out, tires smoking and then, while Joe lurched sickeningly, Cash released the brake and they made the left, shooting into a narrow, broken strip of blacktop that ran through the weeds. Joe knew it ended in a flimsy locked gate that led into the rear parking lot of a gigantic Home Depot, closed for the night.

The Camry's driver cut the wheel, brakes screeching as he executed the turn. During that instant, when the Camaro was hidden in the weeds, Cash hit the brakes again and the car stopped hard, bouncing Joe in his seat.

"Thanks for the lift," Joe said, as he released his safety belt and opened the door. He bailed, slamming the door behind him and diving for the weeds.

"See you later, boss," Cash said, as the Camaro took off, rumbling down the narrow path with the Camry after it. While Joe watched from his cover, the Camaro smashed through the gate with the rental in hot pursuit. Joe waited till he was sure they couldn't see him, and then he followed on foot, jogging down the path. He didn't want to miss the show. It isn't often you get to witness your own death.

◆

While Cash was driving the Camaro, Liam had done some nifty driving of his own, with Juno's assistance. As soon as the Camaro had turned, he stepped on the gas, and the van sped around the corner and into the regular, front entrance of the Home Depot lot. He parked inconspicuously, close to some other sleeping delivery vehicles, and cut the engine and lights. Cash was beside him, running the Camaro with a gaming console and screen while Juno ran the tech from the back.

Now the Camaro sped around the parking lot, doing loops, as Cash pretended to be seeking an exit, with the rental right behind it. Then Cash steered toward the garbage dumpsters, which were gathered near a loading ramp at the rear of the building, as though he were heading for the narrow alley behind it. The Sicilians, seeing this, sped up.

Then, as Joe watched from the weeds, and the others from the van, Cash pulled his final trick. As if misjudging the angles, the Camaro missed the alley entrance and hit a dumpster, sending it flying. Swerving out of control, it ran up the ramp on two wheels, full speed, and flipped, skidding on its side and ending upside down as it banged into a concrete wall.

The boys in the van cheered. Joe grinned, hearing it over his earpiece. "Well done, Cash. You stuck the landing."

The Camry stopped and the Sicilians jumped out, leaving their doors open, and raced over, armed with the AR-15 and the shotgun. They began to fire wildly into the badly damaged car. Now even the plexi was smashed and they filled the Camaro with bullets as they moved in. Juno pressed a button, and the charge Cash had planted by the gas tank blew. The Camaro exploded in a fireball that knocked both the Sicilians back onto their asses.

The boys cheered again. Equally thrilled, the Sicilians jumped up and high fived each other. Then one took some video with his phone.

They hurried back to their own car and took off, leaving the lot from the front.

Joe stepped out of the weeds. A moment later Liam started up the van and they swung by to pick up Joe. Everyone was laughing and shaking hands. The others wanted to celebrate, get food or drinks, but Joe needed to stay hidden, just in case. Plus, tomorrow was another big day. Maybe tonight, now that he was dead, he could finally get some sleep.

48

B y the time Donna got home, she was exhausted and depressed.
Vicky's trail had gone cold. None of their alerts at the airports
or train stations had kicked up anything, and with the head start she'd
had, Donna guessed she was long gone. Even if she wasn't home in
London—if that was even home—she could be on a beach in Florida
by now or sitting by a fire in a remote ski lodge in Colorado, to name
just two places where Donna herself would rather be. The one loose
end was the phone number.

Mario was a young tech specialist, who was even nerdier than
Donna or Janet and buried even deeper in the FBI's basement. He
clearly crushed on Donna, and his combination of awed and awkward
made conversation a bit odd, but he knew his stuff.

"I'm so sorry Agent Zamora," he said, when Donna and Andy went
down there, sounding truly aggrieved. "But it's just a burner phone and

it's turned off. I've been pinging it, but there's no way to track it unless she turns it back on."

And why would she? Donna asked herself. *She's done here. Thanks to me!*

"I can still apply for a warrant to get the call records," Andy said. "A political assassination in Central Park. Even if it's just a foreigner, from a place no one heard of, that's got enough of a Homeland Security vibe on it to get fast action from a judge. But by the time it all goes through and Mario here's up and running . . ."

"How long?" Donna asked.

Mario shrugged, sighing plaintively. "Thirty-six hours? Forty-eight?"

"What the hell, try it," she said. "Thanks Mario. And keep on pinging for me, huh?"

"For you? I will always keep pinging," Mario said, which produced an awkward dead space.

"Okay then," Andy said, raising his eyebrows. "Moving on."

After that there was nothing to do but update Tom and go home. And it was on the way uptown that the delayed depression kicked in about the whole deal with Evon, or Colonel Kozco, as she had forced herself to think of him. Of course, in the big picture it was nothing, a minor flirtation, but the sudden deflation of that princess fantasy, like a shiny pink balloon brutally burst by the reality that princes were just dictators after all, left her back in her own real life: she was a thirty-something single mom, with one catastrophic marriage already behind her, and a passionate and tender but ambiguous and deeply frustrating relationship with a career criminal, if she still even had that. Or wanted it. She sighed. Of course she wanted it. She wanted to call and ask him to come over right now and take a bath with her, or just hold her. But she couldn't and he couldn't and that was the point. So why even call?

That's when she opened the door and found Gladys and her mom and her daughter all eating cookies and milk, watching some kind of cartoon princess on TV.

"Mommy!" Larissa jumped up and ran over for a hug, the best possible cheering up Donna could get.

"Hello sweetheart," she said. "Are you having milk and cookies?"

Larissa nodded, licking the crumbs from her lips. "And Aunt Gladys made zana."

"She means lasagna," Yolanda put in. "It's still warm. Sit down and I'll get you some."

Donna frowned at hearing *Aunt Gladys* but it did smell good, and she was hungry. She sat at the table and took off her shoes.

"Don't forget the sauce," Gladys called as Yolanda shuffled into the kitchen. She beamed at Donna. "And I brought the real Italian bread. Semolina. It's my thank you to your Mom for putting me up. Joey called and said it's safe to go home tomorrow."

"Oh yeah?" Donna asked, her romantic yearning shifting back to suspicion. "That gas problem of yours all fixed?"

"You got a gas problem?" Larissa asked Gladys. "Like when Mommy eats sauerkraut?"

"Kind of," Gladys said, and winked at Donna. "Now he's got to take care of some business for a day or two. But after that, your mom and I were thinking we should plan a dinner."

Donna just stared at her. She had no idea what to say. Or even what expression to make. She smiled, weakly.

Yolanda came in with a heaped plate and set it in front of Donna. "You know," she added, "just the four of us." Then she grinned at Larissa. "I mean five."

While she went back for silverware and a napkin, Gladys leaned in, grinning. "Don't worry, we won't order sauerkraut."

Yolanda came back and set down a fork and knife. She patted Donna, who was still staring, blankly, on the back, "Come on honey, eat," and smiled knowingly at Gladys. "She gets like this when she's tired."

◆

Vicky was bored. And she was frustrated, since she couldn't do any of the things she did to relieve boredom. She had not, as Donna and Fusco assumed, fled the city. She was actually just a couple miles from the scene of the shooting, in the random apartment she had rented online through a fake name, on a nondescript strip of the lower middle Upper East Side, in a soulless tower where no one knew their neighbors anyway. She'd picked up the keys from the doorman, who didn't even look up from his phone.

As a true pro, when her job went south, she did not panic and run, she retreated and lay low, waiting for things to cool off. She knew they'd be looking for her everywhere now, and it was too risky to travel, but she also knew that in a city like New York, the window during which cops would be urgently on the lookout for a redheaded woman in camo would close fast. And she was no longer a redhead. That was one of the things she did to relieve the boredom—she dyed her hair brown. And burned the camo clothes in the sink. And then she ordered Thai food and invited the sweet Thai boy who delivered it in for a cup of tea. At least that kept her amused for an hour. Then she took a long hot shower and got a good night's rest. It's true this trip had turned out to be a disappointment so far, but she was an optimist. New York was a city of opportunity, after all, and tomorrow was another day.

◆

"Oh thanks to bloody Christ!" Blake said when he heard that Joe was dead. He'd barely slept a wink. He had snapped at his kids, and had even been a bit gruff with his wife, who didn't appreciate the attitude since she was down with a migraine. She was in bed in a black silk nightgown with a wet cloth over her eyes, instructing the housekeeper on what the kids should eat for breakfast, when Blake, mumbling an apology, finished dressing and hurried out, pulling his tie so tight he almost choked.

He had to get ahold of himself. He was already stress sweating through his fresh shirt. His hands shook pressing the elevator button. He ran the gauntlet of complaining residents in the hall, smiling like a robot and muttering about emergency calls and fled into his office, where Blythe awaited, a gigantic grin on her face.

"Look," she said, holding out her laptop. "No, lock the door first."

He did and ran back over, and she showed him where on the website it listed Joe Brody as a confirmed kill, complete with video of a burning car. They hugged each other. They jumped for joy. And that was when, even though he'd never been religious, Blake uttered his spontaneous but heartfelt prayer of thanks. Maybe there really was a God!

"Now just go ahead and transfer the payment and this bloody nightmare will be over," he told Blythe, arm tight around her waist as she sat typing on the couch beside him. "And then, a day off, or at least an hour, to celebrate up in your apartment."

"Champagne?" she asked, nails clicking away.

"Yes. And hot roast beef heroes for lunch with cheese. No. One salami, one roast beef, which we will share." He sat back, relaxing, and loosened his tie.

"Both with cheese?" she asked.

"Indubitably, my love." They kissed deeply and he thought, I really am in love. For the first and only time in my life. But then her body went stiff and cold. She tensed up and moved away. He opened his eyes. "What?"

"There's no money. No money to pay."

"What do you mean?"

She pointed at the screen. It was their bank. "Colonel Kozco. The deposit from his purchase. It never came through."

They scrambled, both getting on phones, and soon found out that the deal was off since the Colonel, unfortunately, had to return home immediately for urgent personal reasons. Blake and Blythe were stunned. They sat back on the couch and hugged each other again, but not in joy. They clung to each other desperately.

"What will we do?" Blythe asked. "Maybe we can ask for more time? They might be understanding."

"I don't think they're understanding types. I mean, they just murdered a stranger last night. Burned him up alive in a car. What will they do if they're actually pissed off?"

"So then what? I'm scared, honey. I know I said my dad dealt with gangsters but all they ever did was break a few fingers once, and he was fine after that. They even came to the company Christmas party."

"There's no choice," Blake said, squeezing her hand. "We'll have to borrow from the resident's accounts."

"But if they find out . . ."

"They won't," Blake said, determined, then: "They can't." He sighed, sitting up straight and tightening his tie again, as if for battle. "We'll just have to pray they don't."

49

B ut it was too late for praying. Although they spent the day plundering the residents' accounts to pay their bill, and redoubled security, the fate they feared was already finding its way into the Eleonora, like a vengeful ghost or a New York roach. It arrived with the garbage pickup, while they slept uneasily that night.

After a call from Nero on behalf of Gio, the garbage contractor for the Eleonora happily let Liam and Josh drive the truck that night. Liam backed in at an angle that blocked the external security camera and the view of the guard on the corner, and while he and Josh were hauling and emptying the containers, Juno, Yelena, and Joe slipped into the basement. They'd come prepared this time, armed and with gear in small backpacks, dressed in dark clothes. Juno went to the electronics room, where the guts of the building's systems were stored, and made some quick adjustments, connecting the system to the van where Cash waited nearby. Joe went to the employee changing room, the old coal room, swiped a security officer's jacket from a hook and stuffed it in his bag.

"All set," Juno told Yelena and Joe.

When Liam and Josh left to return the truck, and the gate closed, Joe asked Juno to override the camera in the service elevator, patching in footage he'd taken from his files of the empty elevator. Then Joe and Yelena left him in the basement while they rode up to the ninth floor. The building was asleep. At the service door to 9D, Yelena easily slipped the lock, and Joe used the floor plan to guide them to the office, on the other side of the apartment from the bedrooms. Padding over the thick carpets, they passed silently through the dark rooms where he had run before, the furniture now in shadows, the masks looming shapes lit only by the moonlight that slid in the windows. He showed her the safe. Then he held the pin light for her while she got to work. He considered the stuffed trophy animals around them, the zebra, lioness, and antelope, and imagined them watching now with approval.

When she popped it open, it was better than he'd remembered: four sacks of gold Krugerrands, small velvet pouches of uncut diamonds and emeralds, no doubt smuggled from African conflict zones. They loaded it all into their backpacks—the gold was heavy—and left, taking care to erase all signs of their presence, but leaving the safe just one click from open, and the rear service door latched but unlocked. Then they crept upstairs, pausing at the service door for 10D.

"All clear?" Joe asked over his mic.

Juno, who was watching the building's security cameras from his laptop, had been keeping an eye on the lobby. It was dead, except for a doorman snoozing at the desk. "Free and clear. No sign of the Volkovs." The Russian couple had headed out hours earlier, accompanied by their guards. Yelena slipped the lock, and they went in, taking the same precautions as before, moving carefully by moonlight, but this time they searched drawers and peeked in closets, looking for a likely spot. Then, in the bottom drawer of an ornate antique desk, Yelena found something that made her chuckle.

"Look here," she said. "Treasure."

"More gold?" Joe asked.

"If you want to make a Russian man crazy, this is better than gold."

Yelena pulled out a handful of moodily erotic black and white photos of Mrs. Volkov, posed in lingerie, or nude under a sable coat.

"Interesting," Joe said. "Take them."

She slipped the envelope of photos into her bag while Joe hefted the sacks of gold coins from his backpack into the empty drawer. He kept one sack in reserve. Then, referring to the floor plan in his pocket and using a small laser-ruler that projected a tiny beam, Joe located a spot on the room's wood-paneled wall. Removing a small drill from his pack, he bored a tiny hole, wiping away the dust. Wire-thin and set in the groove of the panel, it was essentially invisible from more than a few inches away.

They made their way out, moving in silent single file, though Yelena paused in the kitchen to peek in the fridge and grab an armful of things, including a bottle of vodka and a tin of caviar. She shrugged. "He will never notice. And the servants will think he ate it."

Joe frowned but took a bottle of mineral water as well. "Let's go."

They left, locking the service door behind them. While Yelena checked in with Juno—the building still snoozed innocently—Joe took out his drill and pulled the screws on the dumbwaiter. He opened the bag of gold and took out a few coins, then sent the rest of the loot down to the basement before closing the shaft.

"Coming at you," Joe said over his mic to Juno, who would retrieve it at the other end. They walked down to eight. Joe got a pen out and addressed the envelope with the photos of Mrs. Volkov to Fernando Lopez, writing PRIVATE in big letters and underlining it. Meanwhile Juno had unloaded the dumbwaiter in the basement.

"Juno," Joe whispered into his mic. "The door guy still snoring?"

"Oh yeah, he's sawing logs."

"Okay. Switch the hall cams for me and you're out."

"Hang on. Okay, done," Juno said from the basement. Once again, old footage of the empty halls played for the sleeping doorman.

While Juno slipped out via the employee side entrance, Joe tiptoed out into the main hallway and left the envelope by Lopez's door. Then he and Yelena placed devices in the potted plants and wastebaskets in the halls of ten, nine, eight, six, and four. Finally they climbed back upstairs and Yelena let them into the Dunwoody place, which was now comfortably familiar to Joe. By then Juno had reached the van and, connecting remotely, he turned the cameras back on.

Joe slipped off his pack and sat on the couch, as if coming into a friendly inn where he had stayed before. While Yelena nosed around, like a cat exploring a new territory, Joe called Juno, speaking in a regular tone now.

"Listen, can you write up a text, send it to Mrs. Volkov's cell when I tell you to?"

"Sure. Saying what?"

Joe told him and he chuckled. "Man, you are stirring up some shit."

"That's the idea."

Yelena came in with plates and cutlery from the kitchen. She spread two Zabar's bagels with cream cheese and then scooped out caviar, smearing on a thick layer of the precious little black eggs as if it were jam. "I've always wanted to try this," she told him. Joe took his plate but waited, watching curiously as Yelena took a big bite. She moaned slightly, eyes closing, as she chewed thoroughly and then swallowed. "Oh my god," she said. "That is orgasmic."

Joe laughed. He tried it. It was indeed a unique and rarified experience, but he preferred the sturgeon and lox that she'd set out, and which, these days, seemed almost as expensive. She washed it down with vodka. He drank his seltzer and found some coffee still in a sealed bag in the freezer. He boiled water and made some. Yelena stretched and yawned.

"Might as well take a nap," she said, curling up on the couch. "I remember when we had more fun ways of passing the time."

"Yeah," Joe said, uncomfortable, staring at his coffee. "About that. I was pretty drunk. Sorry if I acted like a fool."

Yelena laughed. "I was teasing you." She waved it off. "All men are fools. Most are assholes too. At least you're not. Most of the time."

"Thanks. I guess."

That's when they heard the door lock turn. Joe leapt up and hit the light. Yelena drew her gun. They both held their breath. The door opened slow and closed carefully, but the steps were casual, careless. Joe pressed himself against the wall, ready to take down whoever came around the corner. A hand reached for the switch and flipped it on. It was Sarah. With Joe behind her, she saw Yelena aiming a pistol and gasped.

Joe put a hand over her mouth. "Sarah, it's me Joe," he told her. "You're safe. Please just don't scream, okay?"

She nodded, eyes still wide. And he let go. Yelena put the gun away.

"Sorry," he said as she caught her breath. "We didn't mean to scare you. This is my friend Yelena." Joe turned to her. "This is Sarah, the friendly neighbor who helped me last time."

Yelena smiled and waved. "Howdy neighbor."

Sarah waved weakly. "Hi?"

"What are you doing here so late?" Joe asked.

"I couldn't sleep. I come here to play games sometimes."

Joe looked at Yelena. She shrugged. "Go ahead," he said and told Yelena, "She's famous actually. A champion."

Sarah smiled, blushing. "Well not like famous famous. Internet gamer famous."

Yelena nodded, serious. "That's even cooler." She made room for Sarah on the couch, and while the teenager got her game going, she spread more caviar on Joe's untouched half of a bagel. "Here," she said, "try this. You'll never get another chance."

Curious but wary, Sarah sniffed the offered treat. Then took a tiny nibble. Then smiled. "Yum," she said, munching as she began to play.

"I'd give you some vodka to wash it down," Yelena added. "But I don't think Joe would approve."

Joe laughed. "Let's take it easy. Some of us have to work."

"Work?" Sarah asked.

"Don't worry," Joe said. "Just some unfinished business from last time."

"The pigeon?" she asked.

"Yeah," Joe said. "Time to take the pigeon home."

◆

"The Volkovs just pulled up out front."

When he got the word from Juno, Joe stood and nodded at Yelena, who quickly slipped into her gear. They had already cleared the table and the dishwasher was running. Sarah stopped her game, looking at them expectantly.

"Go ahead and send the text in a minute," Joe told Juno over his mic. "We're moving now." He turned to Sarah. "I think you should go home now," he told her. "And you and your mom stay put till this is all over."

"How will I know it's over?" she asked.

"There will be silence," Yelena said. "Or sirens."

Sarah gulped. "Wow."

"Don't worry. It'll be fine. And here, thanks for being a pal." He pulled a golden coin from his pocket and flipped it to her, spinning as it arced. She caught it, brightening as she realized what it was.

"Thanks!"

"That's for the future. Hide it good."

"I will," she said and scampered off. Yelena looked at Joe, eyebrow arched.

"Best way to keep a witness quiet," he explained. "Make them an accessory."

"Sure, sure," she said. Then, handing Joe a ski mask, she said, "let's go."

50

J oe and Yelena came in fast.

Wearing ski masks and gloves, they entered through the unlocked service door, made their way swiftly to the office, and re-opened the safe, which now contained only documents, passports, and some cash. But this time, Yelena tossed a small charge into the interior, while Joe turned on the lights, then stood to the side of the door, holding a blackjack—a lead sap covered in leather. Yelena aimed her AR-15 pistol at the door.

The charge blew, setting off a loud bang that shattered the early morning silence, and the explosion sent shreds of paper blasting into the room. Instantly, there was commotion from inside the apartment. A guard rushed in, clothed in gray sweatpants and a white T-shirt, holding a pistol, followed immediately by a second, in purple briefs and a white tank, holding a bat. Joe tripped the first guard and sapped him hard. He pitched forward, gun clattering across the floor.

"*Derneshsya I ya ub'yu tebya!*" Yelena yelled, brandishing her weapon. Whether he spoke Russian or not, the guard understood. He froze, dropping his bat, as Yelena rushed him and cracked him across the forehead with the butt of her gun. He went down.

"*Poydem!*" Joe shouted, which meant *Let's go*, and which he had just learned an hour before. "*Poydem!*"

They ran back through the apartment, making as much noise as possible. More people emerged—a young woman in a silk robe, an old woman in a thick cotton robe and a hairnet, a middle-aged man Joe recognized as the General, looking outraged and still somehow commanding—even his robe and slippers were hung with epaulets and tassels. "No one move!" Yelena yelled and then in Russian again: "*Nikomu ne dvigatsya!*" She fired off a burst of ammo, shattering a chandelier and reslaughtering a giraffe and a lion, blasting the stuffing out of them. Everyone cowered and hid.

They ran through the kitchen and out the door, rushing up one flight. Joe left a gold coin on the steps and another at the door to the Volkov's. But they did not go in. Instead, moving quietly now, they slipped into a janitor's closet, containing a sink, mops, and buckets, and locked the door behind them. Yelena turned on her pin light. Joe took out his hand-drill. According to the original blueprints, an old servant's passage ran along this line on each floor. It had been sealed off when the closet was created. Joe found the screws and pulled them. Only a plywood panel, painted white and covered in decades of dust, stood in their way, and Joe soon had it loose. With the pin light, they made their way quietly down the narrow passage, single file, until they had paced out the distance to the office. Joe found the tiny hole he'd drilled, and Yelena handed him an equally tiny camera, like a pinhead on a long flexible wire. As he fed the camera just a few millimeters into the interior room, Yelena attached the other end to a handheld viewer, and saw the Russian's office, in a fish-eyed but surprisingly clear view.

"Got it," Yelena said. "We lit the fuse. Now we stand by for the fireworks."

◆

General Mtume was beside himself. At first, assuming this was an assassination attempt by his enemies back home, he'd mainly been alarmed and frightened for his safety. But when he and his other guards came into the office to find the safe blown, his gold and jewels missing, and two men groaning on the floor, he switched immediately from fear to rage.

"Arm up!" he commanded his men, pulling out the gold-plated Kalashnikov he had received as a gift. Then, realizing he and the others were all still in pajamas or less, he added. "And get dressed!"

"They were Russian," the man in the purple briefs said, rubbing the lump on his head. "A very mean Russian woman."

"How many?" The general demanded. His son, who was twenty, came in, holding a machine pistol.

"At least half a dozen," purple briefs said. Sweatpants agreed.

"I only saw two run by," the General said.

"Maybe I was seeing double?" Purple briefs offered. "They hit my head hard."

While the rest of the family carried on, fretting and arguing among themselves, the general, his son, and his guards, four in all, dressed, geared up, and quickly formed an expeditionary force, following the path of the marauders. They went through the kitchen into the service hall, trying doors.

"Look, sir, up here," a guard yelled. He was pointing to a gold coin on the steps.

"Don't touch it," another cautioned him. "It's evidence."

"What are we, CSI?" The general's son, General Jr., asked, grabbing the coin. "They went upstairs, Pop." Leading the way, he slipped the coin in his pocket. The guards frowned and followed.

On the tenth floor, General Jr. saw another coin, this time on the mat outside the rear door to 10D. "Shhh . . ." he told the others, a finger to his lips. "Pop, look . . ." As the team of heavily armed men crowded the hall, the general examined the coin.

"Russians, huh? This is the Volkov's place. I should have known. That bastard. Remember when he got those new flower boxes and the water dripped down onto our balcony?"

Purple Briefs, who now wore jeans and a purple sweatshirt over his underwear, carefully tried the door. "Locked," he whispered.

Sweatpants, who was still in his sweatpants but with sneakers and a sweater, stepped up. He had a small charge. "I can blow it," he offered, sotto voce.

The General nodded, signaling his men. "On my command . . ."

◆

When the safe blew, Mikael Volkov and his wife, Alina, were just about to get out of their car. They were in the back of a Bentley, with a driver and guard upfront and four more men in a black SUV behind them, and had just pulled up in front of the building. They did not hear the sound. Although it thundered through the building, echoing down the halls, the old walls were thick and solid, and nothing much came into the street. Not to mention the loud techno that was pulsating in the car. But what Volkov did hear was his wife's phone beeping as a text came through.

"Who would text you at this hour?" he demanded.

Alina shrugged. "My mother, she forgets the time difference?"

But Volkov, who was extremely jealous, grabbed her purse and looked at her phone. *I can't wait to see the pictures. Your naked body will drive me mad till I can have you for real.*

"What the hell is this?" he demanded, showing her the text.

Alina was horrified. "I don't know. It must be a mistake."

The sender's number was unfamiliar to him, but the text said *Love Fernando*.

"I knew it. It's that Colombian bastard from downstairs."

"You're wrong," Alina pleaded. "I have no idea what this is about." She was telling the truth. Sarah had been right. Alina was in fact having an affair with Fernando and had given him several naked pictures of herself, but she did not understand this particular message at all and that was the honest truth.

But her husband did not believe her. "We'll see. Let's go," he ordered, and everyone piled out.

"You two," he told his driver and bodyguard. "Take her upstairs. The rest come with me."

"What about the cars, sir?" the Bentley driver asked, while his comrades armed themselves from the trunk and the back of the SUV. "This spot is street cleaning tomorrow."

"Leave them," Volkov said with an irritated wave. "Who cares?"

Then he led his entourage into the building lobby.

51

In the lobby of The Eleonora, the doorman on night duty had heard the explosion. It woke him up. Jarred into consciousness, he had no idea what was happening, and when he glanced at his monitors, he saw that they were out. But he had been trained never, under any circumstances, to call 911, so he hit the button for security (which was pointless since they'd heard the explosion as well) and ran to see what had happened, leaving the lobby empty when the Volkov group came in.

The security men on duty had likewise headed up to see what was going on, after alerting Mickey, who was asleep on the couch in his office. He sat up immediately and alerted the Ex-Men. Though the initial report was of an attempted break-in on ten, and his team, as they scrambled, felt confident of their overwhelming force and firepower, Mickey also knew, in his gut, this had something to do with Joe, and that it would not end well. He'd been on edge since the first break-in, and when Blake assured him, yesterday, that it was resolved, that only made him more uneasy. Tucking his shirt in, pulling on his jacket, he barked orders as he strode through the lobby, dispatching one team to take the elevator and another the stairs. The men were ready, cocky even; after months of swaggering around, chasing the occasional graffiti writer and rousting homeless people, they were eager to be fully armed and heading to face intruders. As they rushed off to battle, Blake emerged from the elevator, suit jacket over his pajamas, looking dazed. Blythe arrived too, dressed in sweats, looking younger and more innocent without makeup.

"There's an intruder on ten, sir," Mickey told them. "We don't know who yet. My men have them isolated though."

"Good work," Blake said, then, "No cops!"

"Of course not. We can handle it. But you better wait in your office, sir, just to be careful. And tell your family to stay put."

"Right. Right," Blake said. "Come on," he added to Blythe, who seemed stunned.

"And sir . . ." Mickey asked, as they turned. "About the other thing, with you know who? You're sure that's taken care of?"

"What? Of course, I told you." Now Blake, flustered, assumed a more commanding tone. "Just take care of this disturbance. Quickly." And he went, with Blythe in his train.

"Yes sir!" Mickey called after them. His walkie was squawking. His men were ready, and he told them to move in. Then, as soon as Blake's office door was shut, Mickey turned off his own walkie and walked. He left through the front door, got in his car, and went home. He'd tried.

He'd warned them. Now they were on their own. He didn't know how this connected with Joe exactly, but he knew that it would somehow come back to bite them in the ass. It was like a curse. So that was it. He quit. Better yet, he retired. He would drive home to Staten Island and stay there. If it were up to him, he would have rolled up the Verrazano behind him, like an old-time drawbridge over a moat.

❖

When the general and his men blew the Volkov's kitchen door open and rushed in, fanning out to clear the rooms with military precision, they were happily surprised to find the place empty.

"Dad, look, in here," General Jr. shouted, and the others hurried in. It was the Russian's office, right above the General's own. As the General entered, his son pointed at an open drawer. And there was the gold, just as they suspected.

"See? I knew it," the General trumpeted. "Make sure it's all there. Search the whole room." He waved his Kalashnikov, giving orders and, feeling victorious, reached into his pocket for a cigar. That's when Volkov's men came in. Curious about the noise, they sent Mrs. V to her room and went to investigate, surprising the Africans and themselves. Startled, everyone raised and pointed their weapons, including the general, who scrambled to aim his gold rifle, cigar falling from his mouth. Gunfire erupted. Mrs. V, hearing it, dove under her bed.

❖

Volkov came out of the elevator on eight and strode down the hall, flanked by his men. And there, right on the mat before that damned Colombian's door, he saw it, a manila envelope. He ripped it open and saw the photos of his wife. A strange mixture of feelings surged through his body, murderous rage and desecrated pride tinged with a weird satisfaction in proving that he had been right all along. His jealousy was finally vindicated. He pounded on the door, and when one of Lopez's men answered, he smashed him across the nose with the butt of his gun and stormed in followed by his men, who were like a pack of dogs catching the scent of blood. Meanwhile, hearing the explosions, Lopez and his men had already sent the women and children to hide in a back room as they armed up and prepared to investigate. They were locking and loading in the living room when the Russians poured in. Everyone opened fire.

◆

At the same time that Joe and Yelena saw the firefight break out in the Russian's office, watching on her small phone screen, they heard it from the beyond the wall, like a thunderstorm next door. Luckily this old building had solid walls, built to retain heat and block sound, but also handy for stopping bullets. As the bodies crumpled around the room, and the survivors took cover, Joe spoke to Juno over the mic.

"Blow those charges," he said, and Juno did. The flash bombs that they'd set around the building went off, with deafening explosions and thick clouds of smoke, injuring no one, but igniting even more panic and chaos. Residents ran into the hall. Even Mr. Van der Pots, the South African, ran out dressed in his blue pajamas and fired his pellet gun at an armed man who was passing by. As it happened, he was a security guard, but he wasn't wearing his jacket. He hadn't been able to find it.

In their secret hall, Joe and Yelena removed the pin camera from the hole. Then they changed, peeling off their ski caps and dark hooded sweatshirts. Yelena zipped on a pink hoodie and shook out her hair. Joe put on the security guard jacket. They moved back down the passageway to the janitor's closet, less worried now about noise, and left much of their gear in the passage when Joe screwed the panel back. Then, listening and peeking cautiously, they stepped out into the service hall.

"Coming down," Joe said into his mic. Then he and Yelena split up. She ran out into the hallway, which was now full of panicked residents, some dressed and hauling suitcases, some in pajamas and slippers.

"Wait, please, help," she called and jumped onto the packed elevator. She rode down with the others but when they got off, she remained and went to the basement. She had one pistol still hidden in her waistband, but she tossed that in the garbage now, in case the law had begun to arrive. Then she walked out of the building and around the corner to the van.

◆

Joe went upstairs to ten. He came out into the hall and made his way through the crowd of worried residents. "No reason to panic folks," he intoned, loud but calm. "Just proceed downstairs in an orderly fashion." Then he held a hanky over his face and banged on the door to 10E. It opened immediately and a young Chinese man he hadn't seen before, in a untucked shirt, jeans and slippers greeted him.

"Security, sir," Joe said. "We need to evacuate immediately."

"Yes, we heard all the noise," he said, in polished if accented English. "What is the problem?"

"There was an attack on a resident. Security has it under control, but everyone has to go down to the lobby right now while we check the building and let the smoke clear."

The man nodded and rushed back inside. Joe stepped into the entrance hall and heard excited voices talking and then arguing in Chinese. Then the young man returned with two women, one older, one young, both in pajamas and robes. The older woman held a baby, the younger led a child by the hand.

"Please hurry," Joe said.

Then another woman in her forties came out, dressed, leading the old man, Wing Chow, who was still in pajamas, arguing. She was trying to drape a robe over his shoulders as he resisted. "He is worried about a pet," she told Joe. "A bird."

"It will be fine, I promise. You will back very soon. But right now you have to go."

Arguing with him in Chinese, and with the young man now helping, they moved the old man out and down the hall to the elevator. Joe shut the door. Pulling a cloth bag from his pocket, he hurried back to the office and there it was, right where he'd left it, sitting on its perch in its cage, the damned pigeon.

"Hello Ramses," Joe said, speaking low, as he would to a cat or dog. "Time for you to go home." And Ramses, true to his royal nature, didn't make a fuss. He fluttered a bit but didn't resist as Joe gently but firmly took hold of him and slid him in the bag. He retained his dignity. Joe pulled the bag tight and hung it over his shoulder. And he left. Rejoining the flow of residents, he helped herd a group onto the elevator and rode down. Then, as they joined the crowd milling in the lobby and spilling out onto the front steps, he found the door that said Jeremy Blake Management. He knocked.

◆

When the knock came on the door, Blake jumped. Blythe, who'd been sitting beside him on the couch, looked up at him, wide-eyed.

"Who is it?" he called out, his real accent breaking through. This shocked Blythe even more.

"Security, sir, please open up."

He cleared his throat. "Just a moment please," he said, in his usual, posh tones, and opened the door. As soon as the man walked in, wearing a security jacket but pointing a gun, Blake knew he had to be Joe.

"Good morning," Joe said. "I thought I should stop by and introduce myself, though I feel like we know each other already."

Blake actually smiled in a sickly sort of way, but Blythe's eyes grew even wider. She was, after all, seeing a ghost.

"But, but, but . . ." she stammered.

"But I'm dead?" Joe finished her thought. "I'm afraid that report was a little premature." He shrugged. "Good luck getting a refund."

"That wasn't me," Blake blurted. "It was . . ." He searched for something to cling to.

"It was a mistake," Blythe said.

"You got that right," Joe said. "But don't worry." He waved the gun. "I'm not here to kill you. I just want you to know that all I ever came for was this." He held the bag up. "A stolen pigeon that needs to go home."

Blake and Blythe both stared, as if they were trying to believe him.

"You're going to let us go?" Blythe asked finally.

Joe nodded. "Exile, that's your punishment," he said. "You leave New York now, this second, with nothing, and you never, ever come back. Understood?"

They nodded.

"Understood," Blake said. "And thank you."

Joe put his gun away. "Now I've got to get this pigeon back where he belongs," he said, and walked out. The sun was just coming up.

52

When Vicky turned her phone on, right before dawn, it was just for a last check before tossing it. She didn't expect a job offer. She'd already cleared out of her Airbnb, after erasing all signs of her presence, and picked up the car that she had similarly rented with an app, linked to a fake credit card, on this phone that she was about to dump. Her plan, quite simple really, was now to drive away. She planned to head north, stopping at a quaint B&B, and then ditch the car and cross into Canada like a Niagara Falls tourist with a fake passport. From Montreal she would fly home. But then she checked her messages, and found one from her contact, the one who'd booked her on this job to start with.

As long as you're in NY, it said, *want to earn a fee? Something has come up.*

Why not, she answered, thinking to herself, might as well make the trip worthwhile. She made a turn and drove across town.

◆

When Donna's phone buzzed, she was deep asleep. It had been a stressful few days at work, with long hours, and stressful at home too. So when she realized there was nothing more to be done about hunting the woman they now knew as Vicky, Donna was bitterly disappointed, but it was also like she was finally off duty, and all the exhaustion caught up to her at once. She was wiped. So she went home, reheated some leftover lasagna—she had to admit it was terrific—and after a bedtime story session with Larissa, basically staggered into her own room and put herself to bed too. She slept deeply and was having a vivid dream when the phone rang. In the dream, Joe was with her, in her bed in the dark. She'd snuck him in like always, but this time both her mother and Gladys were outside in the living room, playing a kid's card game with Larissa and betting big stakes with a pile of chips between them. The sense of danger was exciting but fretful too. Then her mom knocked on the door and they had to run. In the dream her closet led to a secret passage and they fled, holding hands, but they quickly became lost as in a maze, and then, running in the dark, she realized she was no longer holding Joe's hand. She was alone.

When she woke up and grabbed her buzzing phone in the dark, just barely remembering to mumble, "Agent Zamora . . ." she could almost feel Joe's presence in her bed, smell his scent on the sheets, as if he had really been there.

"Hello? Agent Zamora? This is Mario. Am I waking you?"

"Um, uh, yeah, it's . . . Jesus, five A.M. Aren't you asleep too?"

"Oh God I'm so sorry. I shouldn't have called. It's just that you said to if, you know, it pinged."

"If what?"

"The cell you gave me? The one you've been tracking? I set the system to keep pinging that number and then alert me if it found anything, and it did. And you had told me to call you if that happened so . . . Was that wrong? God I'm so stupid."

"No you're not," Donna said. She was fully awake now and already getting dressed, pulling on the same clothes, looking for her bag, her badge, her gun. "You're a genius. Now just text me the location of that ping."

Thinking it would be faster than waking and then explaining to her mom, Donna went to her daughter's room, and lifted her up, along with her blanket and the stuffed bear she was clutching, and carried her, mumbling, across to her mom's place, letting herself in and setting her right next to her in bed. Her mom stirred, but Donna said, "Everything's fine. Larissa's here. Go back to sleep," and she did, immediately, while Larissa cuddled right up. Donna locked up and headed out, calling Fusco on the way.

◆

When Fusco got the call from Donna, he was asleep. He and Chang had spent the night on Parking Patrol, as he thought of it, even though now at least they had a plan, setting and baiting a trap with the three patrol cars that had been detailed to them, though no one was told what they had in mind, nor was it written down or recorded anywhere in the system. Everyone just assumed this was because Fusco was too lazy. But he and Chang had another idea.

Just like last time, they had a patrol car cruise through the target area, cutting back and forth through the one-way streets and reporting each block as clear over the radio. But this time, instead of leading the way, Fusco and Chang hung back, trailing by several blocks, entering each stretch of street, and passing each illegally parked car with diplomatic plates, each illegally set up private loading zone, after it had supposedly been checked. Meanwhile the other units loitered on the avenues, lurking on the perimeter of the zone.

But cruising silently through the dark streets, hour after hour, was also dull. And the car was warm. And after switching off with Chang after a few hours, and letting her drive, Fusco found himself drifting off to sleep. Chang noticed but said nothing. True, he snored like a chainsaw and drooled too, but it was still more pleasant than listening to him philosophize. When Donna's call came through, he was deep in a dream about football. He'd actually won big but was scurrying around like a squirrel with a nut, worrying about where to hide the money from his ex-wives and his creditors, running in circles like a rat in a maze. The ring jerked him awake.

"Phone's ringing," Chang told him as he sat up, blinking.

He nodded, rubbing his face, and realized he had drool on his chin. He wiped it with his tie. "Yeah, Fusco," he said into the phone, then listened. Then said, "Right. See you soon," and hung up. He found his cold coffee and guzzled. "So listen, Chang," he began. "That personal business I've been handling?"

"The chick who killed your old partner?" Chang asked, turning a corner.

"Yeah. Her phone was just tracked. She's on the other side of the park."

"Then go get that bitch. I got this."

"You sure?"

"No problem. If someone killed you, I'd want my new partner to do the same."

Fusco laughed. "Thanks Chang. You're a true friend."

Chang reached the corner of Fifth Avenue and stopped at a light. "Um, across the park huh?" she asked. "You want me to drop you?"

Fusco sighed, unhooking his safety belt, pulling on his coat. "No. Better stick to the plan. I'll run across."

"Run?"

"Fuck you, Chang," Fusco said and opened the door.

◆

It was about thirty minutes later that their quarry took the bait. The patrol had reported a block between Madison and Park as clear. And right smack in the middle, right in a tow-away zone marked for street cleaning, there was a shiny new black Mercedes with diplomatic plates. And ten minutes after the all clear, as Chang was easing along the block, she saw a white male, thirties, in jeans, sneakers, and a hoodie, scamper up to the car, pull out a hammer, and smash in the driver's side window.

"All units, the suspect is in view," she called into the radio, breaking her silence as she accelerated. She pulled up beside him, but before she could jump out, like a rabbit, he was off.

But now the net was tightening, and when he reached the corner, a patrol car was there, with two officers leaping out to grab him. Like a running back, he dodged and darted through, running full tilt for Fifth Avenue. Another car raced around and stopped him from turning north, the fourth patrol car was blocking the south, and Chang was now right on his ass, so he just sprinted through, across the deserted street, heading right for the wall.

"He's going into the park," she called out over the radio. "All units, he's heading into the park."

53

When Joe came out of the Eleonora, he was pleased. He'd eliminated the threat to his own life, and to Gladys and his friends, making them all a nice payday in the bargain. And, finally, he'd retrieved Alonzo's damn bird. He blended easily into the crowd that was now gathering out front, residents mingling with some early passersby, joggers, and door men from a nearby building. He heard sirens, but the first vehicle he saw approaching was a fire truck. It was the smoke and noise that got reported. As the sun rose and light began clearing the remainders of night, Joe felt a pleasant calmness, a freedom he had not felt in days, as he headed to the meeting place, a block down and around the corner, where the van would be waiting.

Then he saw a black Impala with government plates come screeching to a stop, and he ducked into a doorway out of sight. That was law. And then, to his amazement and dismay, the driver's side door flew open, and Agent Donna Zamora jumped out, running right into the building. He had no idea what she was there for, or if she knew what she was running into, but a moment later, after she entered, he heard fresh gunfire crackling within.

"God damn it," he muttered, under his breath, to himself, then spoke into the mic: "You all head out. I've got to circle back."

"Why? What's up?" Juno asked. "We can come get you."

"Negative. I'll meet you later." Joe said. "And Juno?" he added, "Better call the law."

"What?"

"You heard me. Put in an anonymous 911."

Then he opened the bag and let the pigeon out. At first, Ramses didn't seem to care much about being free. He stepped out of the bag and just stood there, looking around. "Go! Fly, dummy!" Joe said, stomping his foot. The bird rose, magically, on flapping wings, and in a moment was gone, soaring out over the park and into the sun.

◆

When Joe left the office, declining to kill them, Blake and Blythe were stunned. Their fortunes had flipped so many times they didn't even know how to feel or what to think. They were ruined. Their operation was clearly in meltdown. They were penniless. And the residents whom they'd robbed to pay the hit men would be coming for them soon. But they were alive, spared. And if they left now, like refugees fleeing a disaster, they would have a new life, a new start, together.

"Let's go back to Florida," Blake said suddenly. "We can take a bus."

Blythe brightened. "That's a good idea."

He grabbed her hand. "From there we can get new ID, go to South America or Europe."

And despite everything, Blythe smiled. "That sounds wonderful."

"Let's go," Blake said, leading her out. He opened the door. An attractive brunette stood there, smiling. She spoke in an English accent, which Blake immediately recognized as much higher class and more genuine than his own.

"Sorry, but I wonder," she asked, smoothly, her eyes calm. "Are you by any chance Jeremy Blake?"

"Yes," he said. "That's me. What is it?"

"Special delivery," she said, drawing a pistol, and shot him right through the heart. Blythe jumped, gasping, as he fell before her. She was about to kneel over him, but the brunette calmly leaned forward, put the gun between Blake's lips and fired again, blowing out his brains. Blythe froze, trembling like a rabbit.

"Take care," the brunette said. And she left. She had only been paid for one target.

◆

Yelena heard Joe over her earpiece, instructing Juno and the others to call the police and then leave. She stopped. Something was up, obviously, but she knew there was no time, and no point, in debating with Joe. She waited till he signed off, then called Juno over her own mic: "I'm going to hang back. Better get the van out of here." Then she crossed to Central Park West, walking along the side by the park, her sneakers on the cobblestones, and when she saw the ruckus outside the Eleonora, with residents gathering on the steps and people stopping to watch, she slipped into the shadows of the trees to wait and see.

◆

As Donna entered the Eleonora, she was careful. She was tracking a highly dangerous armed suspect after all, and Mario had just sent through coordinates indicating that Vicky's phone was at this address or had been before being shut off. The people standing outside in pajamas made her even more careful. She had her weapon out, if lowered, and opened the door slowly, coming in low as she entered. She was ready.

But the one thing she did not expect was that a uniformed building employee, a doorman for Chrissakes, would look up from his desk and, when she identified herself, flashing a badge and saying "FBI," would take a random shot at her. With what looked like an AR-15, no less. He sprayed in her direction, killing a potted tree and shattering the inner door, then ducked behind his desk. But not low enough. Donna fired back, one handed, and took off his cap, which was impressive shooting, but not that helpful in the moment. She dropped and crawled behind a couch, still trading shots with the doorman, who blasted the guts out of the couch cushions. Then a few more building employees, security guys in uniform blazers, came out of the stairway and began exchanging fire with what looked like some residents. What the hell was going on here? It had seemed like such a nice building, full of rich, boring people. And where the hell was Vicky?

◆

Vicky left the Eleonora. She dropped her gun in a planter in the lobby, just walking out, blending easily into the background, a young woman in exercise clothes and sneakers, while people stood there confused, or ran around, yelling about bombs and smoke and fires. She simply walked away, texting—*Done*—to her contact before turning the phone off and dropping it in the gutter. Then she crossed the street to the park. She was just about to cut through and circle to her car, when she heard someone call out her name. "Vicky!"

◆

At first, when Yelena saw Vicky, she couldn't believe her eyes. She had only glimpsed her after all, and she constantly altered her appearance, but when she saw her exit the Eleonora and move away, looking calm and natural—*too* calm, *too* natural—she instantly thought, *That's her.* So she began to move calmly and naturally herself, circling around to intercept her, cursing herself for having ditched all her weapons. And when Vicky passed by, on a gentle slope under the trees, heading down to a path across the park, Yelena took a chance and, in a bright, friendly tone, called out: "Vicky!" The brunette stopped and looked. And smiled. It was her.

"Yelena," she said. "How lovely to meet you here."

54

When Joe got back to the Eleonora there was chaos. Chaos had already been raging, of course, engineered by himself, but it had been contained largely on the upper floors and, when he left, many of the residents still thought that maybe this was a kitchen fire or electrical problem. But now open warfare had reached the lobby, and the small crowd gathered outside had fled, screaming, only to regather, like scared pigeons, to watch from a bit farther away. There was no point in running in there and catching a bullet.

So he ran to the side of the building and back into the basement, which was open now as more residents used it as an alternative exit. Some were clearly just confused and frightened, dressed in sweats or bathrobes, clutching their kids. Others had larger fears in mind and seemed to be making a run for it. A mustachioed, red-faced white fellow with an expensive Burberry overcoat over his blue pajamas hailed a cab. An Asian couple each dragged a huge suitcase, tied closed with bungee cords. Joe could see silver plates and bowls bursting from one.

Joe moved quickly through the throng, still in his security blazer, telling people to stay calm, with his hand on his gun in his coat pocket. He ran through the corridor and found the service stairs, going up one turn. He could hear gunfire now, right above him, and knew it was not safe to proceed. He'd be stepping out into a crossfire. Instead, he went back to the employees changing room in the old coal chute. Climbing onto a stack of cartons, he crawled up into the guts of the building, then moved along in the darkness, judging where he was by the dull roar of guns. He knew that, as on every floor, this sealed passage would end at the janitor's closet, and he found that spot, once his eyes adjusted, by the faint trace of light where a piece of plywood had been nailed in. He kicked it down, no longer worried about subtlety. And there he was, in another janitor's closet, with mops, brooms, and a slop sink. Drawing his gun, he knelt low and eased the door open an inch.

What he saw was a pitched battle, with one group of gunmen, mainly security, firing from near the service entrance and another, who looked like the Colombian's crew, firing from the main stairs, while a couple of Russians were camped behind a turned-over table, their backs to Joe. Also with his back to Joe was the doorman, who was behind his desk, AR-15 braced on top. And pinned down, behind a couch, sneaking out the occasional shot, was Donna.

Joe took a deep breath. Then he plunged out, flinging the closet door open, and as they turned, he shot down both Russians. He yelled out, "Now, Donna!" firing across the lobby to give her cover, raking the walls and pillars and mirrors, as he ran for their table. The doorman, distracted, turned to look, and at that moment, Donna jumped up and shot him. She then began firing across the room herself, charging forward, hiding behind his desk. Joe ducked behind the table, tossing his empty pistol, and took up the Russian's discarded Kalashnikov. As the sound of sirens grew outside, Donna called, "Joe!" and tossed the dead doorman's hat, spinning into the air. Once of the Colombians, acting on instinct, shot it, and Joe, seizing the moment, popped up and shot him through the chest. He kept it up, laying down a field of fire that forced the others back, as Donna jumped up and ran, firing too, across the lobby to the elevator. Joe backed on beside her, still shooting until the door closed. He hit the button marked B.

As the elevator descended, they looked at each other. Donna's hair had fallen loose, and she pushed it back from her face.

"So how have you been?" Joe asked.

She shrugged and nodded. "Good, you know." Then she touched his arm. "Look, I'm sorry, I meant to call. I mean, I should have . . ."

Joe nodded. The door opened, and they both tensed, drawing their weapons and hiding on opposite sides of the car. Cops were standing outside, weapons drawn.

"FBI," she yelled, raising her hand, letting the gun hang from a finger. Joe dropped his weapon and put his hands up too.

"Building security," he said.

◆

Yelena and Vicky circled each other, like dancing partners, looking for weaknesses and strengths, each seeking an opening that would let the other in.

"I've been looking forward to this for a long time," Yelena said.

"I'm flattered," Vicky said. "Your reputation is well known, Yelena Noylaskaya."

"You know my name," Yelena said. "That's good. You should know the person who will take your life and why. You killed Vova."

Vicky frowned, thinking, then smiled. "Ah yes, the old Russian. I forgot. Was he your grandpa or something?"

"My friend."

"Aw, sorry." Vicky made a little flourish with her hand. "As long as we are sharing here, I will tell you too. My name is Victoria Dahlia Amalia St. Smythe. A mouthful, I know. But you won't have to remember it long. Just till I break your neck."

With that, they ran at each other, two furies bent on destruction, and they were about to engage, when they heard a booming male voice call out, "Excuse me, ladies!" They looked up and saw two mounted police officers approaching, staring down from their horses. They paused.

Vicky spoke. "Yes, officer?"

"What are you doing?"

They hesitated. They were unarmed after all, and the cops were not. And no way could they outrun a horse. Finally, Yelena piped up, in a chipper tone. "It's Muay Thai. You know, kickboxing."

Vicky nodded enthusiastically, and added, in an American accent: "You should totally try it. Keeps your bod super tight."

"Oh yeah, I heard of that," the second cop said, sounding interested, but the first one waved his gloved hand.

"Well, I'm sorry but there's a major police action in the park right now. They're pursuing a suspect. And something's going on over there too." He peered toward Central Park West. "So I'm going to have to ask you to cancel this workout or whatever."

"No problemo," Vicky chirped, and looked at her watch. "Oh my God, I'm late for Pilates anyway. See you soon," she called to Yelena, waving as she sprinted off.

"Definitely," Yelena called out in agreement. She smiled at the cops. "Guess I will go for a run. Stay safe!" She ran off, in the same direction as Vicky, but she was gone.

◆

By the time Fusco got there, huffing and puffing and sweating through his suit, the main action was over. Several cop cars were now parked in front of the Eleonora, with police in position behind them. Further back, a fire truck and two ambulances waited their chance, and back from them, a bigger crowd was now watching. SWAT was on the way, but by the time they arrived it was done with. The suspects inside, realizing that they were trapped, and seeing no further advantage to killing each other, had begun to surrender, and now all were loudly claiming self-defense, though they had a hard time saying against whom or what.

While Fusco made his way through the chaos, waving his badge, Chang called. He'd missed that too. With the help of the uniformed patrols, they had run the Avenger down and cornered him. He was now in custody.

"Good work, Chang. I knew you could do it."

"And here's the kicker," she added. "Guess what?"

"He's a cop. Traffic, I'm guessing."

"Bingo. How did you know?"

"I think we all knew, but didn't want to know, if you know what I mean?"

"He could have been a citizen with a scanner. And a deep knowledge of the parking laws," Chang said.

"Yeah, but it was the anger that really tipped me. The righteous indignation at seeing scofflaws go free. That sounds like a cop to me."

"How did your other date turn out?"

"I think I'm being stood up," Fusco said. He had worked his way around to the side of the building and was at the basement entrance. And then he saw Donna coming out. And standing beside her was Gio's guy, the bouncer, Joe. "Gotta go," he said, and hung up.

"Fusco," Donna said, breaking the odd silence. "Great. As you can see, it's a shit show here. I don't think that other suspect showed." Fusco nodded at that. She gestured to Joe. "He's building security. Really stepped up and helped."

Joe waved politely. "Hi."

Fusco nodded again.

"I wonder," Donna asked, pulling her car keys out. "Do you mind taking him downtown, getting a statement while I deal with all this? I think it's going to be a long one."

"Um, sure, right," Fusco said. "Glad to."

And so, they walked, Joe and Fusco, to where Donna had parked, in an illegal spot by a bus stop down the block. While Fusco unlocked the door, Joe looked back at the Eleonora, taking in the beautiful ornate facade. High in one of the towers, on a little cuplike balcony, he saw two figures, one tall and shaggy, one smaller and with long dark hair. It was Sarah and Lucifer. They waved. Joe waved back. Then he got in the car beside Fusco and shut the door. Neither of them had spoken yet, but as he was pulling out, Fusco asked, "So, where do want me to drop you this time?"

Joe shrugged. "The same train as last time is fine."

55

The pigeon came home later that morning. Terry headed up to the roof to do his normal feeding and cleaning and there was Ramses, as if nothing had happened. He called Alonzo to tell him, and then he got his stick out and flew the flock in the morning light, like a conductor stirring winds and strings and voices, or a wizard waving a wand, summoning a cloud of winged spirits over Brooklyn.

◆

"Figures. The guy was a cop." Nero tapped the paper that Pete was reading while they waited in the car. PARKING AVENGER UNMASKED, the headline blared. Little Eddie sat in back. "That's what happens when people start taking the law into their own hands."

"At least he stood up for what he believed in," Pete said. "Justice. Equality under the law. Every man should have the same chance at a parking spot. That's America."

"My ma told me they said on TV he's gonna write a book," Little Eddie put in. "She says only the little guy has to obey the rules these days."

"Little guys like you?" Pete asked. "You take up the whole back seat."

"Since when did either of you obey a rule?" Nero asked.

It was true though. The outpouring of public support and media interest had turned the so-called Parking Avenger, a disgruntled traffic cop, into a city celebrity and minor folk hero. According to his lawyer, who'd done the morning news shows, he already had a book deal in the works. The legal case against him was proceeding, but he would eventually be given a suspended sentence as well. The fact that he was a cop was embarrassing enough. The government did not want to risk the circus of a trial; the jury might give him a medal.

Little Eddie's stomach growled. "I'm starving," he complained. "Didn't have time for breakfast today."

Nero looked at his watch. They were parked in front of the construction zone for the new apartment building that had been stalled due to a labor dispute between Gio and Alonzo. Now the two men were in there, resolving it. Nero made an executive decision. "Here." He peeled off a couple twenties and handed them to Little Eddie. "Run over to that deli across the street and get us three bacon-egg-and-cheeses on a roll. And three regular coffees."

"Make mine light and sweet," Pete added.

"Right," Little Eddie said.

"No wait," Nero said. "Better make it four." That way if Gio came back while they were waiting, or eating, he wouldn't be as pissed.

"Right," Little Eddie said again and went.

Nero sighed, philosophically. "When the cops are criminals, and the big shots break the law, who's left?"

Pete grinned. "Us."

◆

Upstairs, on the top floor of the half-built building, Gio and Alonzo were surveying their domain. The luxury, loft-style apartments, which dwarfed the rows of four-story houses around them, would mostly go to wealthy transplants and foreign investors, staring down at the neighborhood folks whose light they now hid.

"So the king is back in his castle," Gio said. "Or pharaoh, I guess."

"No worse for wear either," Alonzo said. "I got to admit, your boy Joe came through in the end." He shifted his big hands as if weighing out his words. "Caused considerable mayhem in the process though. They carried a lot of bodies out of that joint. Lot of people in hand-cuffs too."

Gio laughed and patted Alonzo's broad back. "That, my friend, is what happens when you send a lion to fetch a pigeon."

Alonzo laughed. "True. Guess I should be happy he didn't come back licking his chops and just give me a few feathers." He turned from the landscape to consider the raw interior of the building, or the shell of a future building. "I told my guy in the union they can start up tomorrow. So let your truckers know."

Gio nodded, and raised a hand, like a pharaoh raising a pyramid. "All's well in the kingdom. Let the concrete flow."

◆

The bounty on Ramses was duly paid, and what everyone had taken to calling The Case of the Maltese Pigeon was closed. The extra plunder Joe had held back was also sold, to Princess the Fence, and added to the pot, which Joe split six ways, after expenses. Joe returned to the apartment in Jackson Heights, to his job at the club, and to the bookshop as well. He even attended the monthly Proust Club that Alexis hosted. They discussed the famous obsession that the character of Swann had for Odette, the beautiful courtesan he would eventually marry.

"You see," Margaret, the retired schoolteacher, was saying, "Proust suggests that we should be grateful for romantic trouble, because it forces us to become seekers after truth, explorers with a passion for knowledge."

"He's being ironic, no?" Theo asked. Theo was a butcher whose shop was around the block. "It's not like Swann becomes a scientist or arctic explorer. He's just sneaking around, snooping in her stuff, trying to find out who Odette is sleeping with. His concerns are petty."

"It's the truth of the human heart, my friend," Alexis said, drawing and exhaling smoke. "To Proust there is nothing more petty or more profound."

"Right," Margaret added. "It's like jealousy, this sordid motive, finally turns Swann the dilettante into an artist or, I don't know . . ."

"A detective?" Joe, who'd been listening silently, suggested.

"Or a crook," Theo added. Everyone laughed.

◆

It was two weeks after the return of the pigeon, and, with it, normal life, that Gladys announced she was taking Joe to dinner in the city.

"Why the city?" he asked. They lived in Queens after all, the center of the food world.

"I feel like French," she said. "Steak frites and maybe escargot. My treat."

So they took a cab to Soho, where Gladys had booked a table at Raoul's, one of the last old-school French places around. And who was standing by the bar when they walked in? Agent Donna Zamora and her mother, Yolanda. Joe could tell, from the stricken look on Donna's face, that she was as shocked as he was. Not Yolanda. She smiled and waved and gave Gladys a hug and kiss.

"Hi, hon," Gladys said, pecking Donna on the cheek. "You remember my grandson, Joe."

"Hi, Joe," Donna said.

◆

They settled in a booth, Gladys and Joe across from Donna and Yolanda. The waiter passed out menus and, when he tried to hand Joe the wine list, Gladys took it instead.

"Joe doesn't really drink," she announced, then turned to the waiter. "But we will have red." He smiled and nodded and backed away. She went on: "Now everyone get whatever you want. My treat. I'm ordering us chocolate soufflés, too. It's my way of saying thanks for putting me up."

"But it's not necessary," Yolanda said. "After all, you cooked. And babysat." She grinned at Joe. "My granddaughter loves her."

Joe smiled awkwardly.

"But," Yolanda went on, "we did think it was time for you two to get to know each other better, you know, socially. You really have a lot in common."

"Like what?" Donna asked, innocently.

"Well," Yolanda said, turning to Joe. "Gladys told me you were in the military. And you know Donna is a big hero at the FBI. She just saved a royal visitor from assassins. A prince practically."

"A prince?" Joe asked, smiling mildly at Donna. "That really is impressive. I'd love to hear all about him."

Donna buttered some bread. "Not much to tell really. He was more of a frog in the end. Or a poisonous toad." She took a bite. "I had him deported."

"What about you, Joe?" Yolanda asked. "Have you ever considered a career in law enforcement?"

Gladys broke in. "Maybe not law enforcement per se, but Joe's in a similar field. Security. And, you know, helping people."

"Is that so?" Donna asked, looking him in the eye now, slyly. "How interesting." Her toe touched his under the table. "Tell us more."

Joe smiled. "Well, I wouldn't say law is my thing, so much, Donna, but I do a little bit of enforcement now and then."

ACKNOWLEDGMENTS

First thanks go to my old friend, co-conspirator, advisor, and hero Hampton Fancher for sending me an article about a million-euro pigeon with the note: "You can do something with this." He was right! I also want to express my heartfelt gratitude to Otto Penzler, who has sagely guided this series into being, Charles Perry, for his insightful editing and overall publishing wizardry, and to all the wonderful people at Mysterious Press. As always, I am deeply thankful for my agent, Doug Stewart, and everyone at Sterling Lord Literistic, most especially Maria Bell, Danielle Bukowski, and Silvia Molnar. Thanks to William Fitch for being an ideal friend and reader, and special thanks to Nivia Hernandez and Anastasia Lobanova for help with languages. And of course, as always, I would like to thank my friends for their continuous support and patience, and my family for their infinite love and faith.

THE WILD LIFE
by David Gordon

SOMEONE IS KILLING NEW YORK CITY'S
MOST DESIRABLE CALL GIRLS...
AND JOE THE BOUNCER IS ON THE CASE

Joe Brody, classics-reading ex-Special Forces operative with severe PTSD and a related drug habit, is getting his life back together. He now has a steady job as a strip club bouncer.

The only catch is that childhood friend Gio Caprisi, now head of New York's Italian Mafia, relies on Joe's extra-legal expertise when things get particularly nasty on the streets.

The criminal underworld has been shaken by the disappearance of its most successful call girls, with all the hallmarks of a serial kidnapper at work. When a woman turns up dead, the hunt for the predator becomes even more urgent.

To find the killer, Joe will have to plunge into the seediest fringes of New York City on another wild ride.

'Gordon brings an outstanding new voice
to the contemporary crime novel'
Robert Crais